TAKE A SAD SONG . . .

TAKE A SAD SONG . . .

The Emotional Currency of "Hey Jude"

JAMES CAMPION

Guilford, Connecticut

An imprint of Globe Pequot, the trade division of
The Rowman & Littlefield Publishing Group, Inc.
4501 Forbes Blvd., Ste. 200
Lanham, MD 20706
www.rowman.com

Distributed by NATIONAL BOOK NETWORK

British Library Cataloguing in Publication Information available

Library of Congress Cataloging-in-Publication Data

Names: Campion, James, 1962– author.
Title: Take a sad song : the emotional currency of "Hey Jude" / James Campion.
Description: Guilford, Connecticut : Backbeat Books, 2022. | Includes bibliographical references and index.
Identifiers: LCCN 2021044608 (print) | LCCN 2021044609 (ebook) | ISBN 9781493062379 (cloth) | ISBN 9781493062386 (ebook)
Subjects: LCSH: Lennon, John, 1940-1980. Hey Jude. | Beatles. | Rock music—1961–1970—History and criticism. | Nineteen sixty-eight, A.D.
Classification: LCC ML421.B4 C343 2022 (print) | LCC ML421.B4 (ebook) | DDC 782.4216609—dc23
LC record available at https://lccn.loc.gov/2021044608
LC ebook record available at https://lccn.loc.gov/2021044609

∞™ The paper used in this publication meets the minimum requirements of American National Standard for Information Sciences—Permanence of Paper for Printed Library Materials, ANSI/NISO Z39.48-1992

In memory of

JAMES V. CAMPION

1938–2019

Genius, all over the world, stands hand in hand, and one shock of recognition runs the whole circle round.

—Herman Melville

CONTENTS

"HEY JUDE"

It begins with two notes, formed as words, announcing its title.

Hey . . . Jude . . .

They are clear. Unadorned by echo or sheen. The singer is in your ear already, an airless tone pervades. Piano follows. Three chords. Played softly.

Don't make it bad
Take a sad song and make it better

The melody rides a seesaw, taking you down to *bad,* where you don't want to be, to an ascending discovery of a *sad song,* musically alerted in the chordal lift, making the mythical Jude aware of his current state while discovering the key to happiness is within his grasp . . .

Remember to let her into your heart
Then you can start to make it better

A slight shift in the melodic structure allows the vocal to hold onto the first word and conclude the epiphany beside a charming inner rhyme easing sweetly into the shifting notes back downward; a mysterious *her* that Jude should let into his heart, for only then can he *make it better.*

Hey . . . Jude . . .

Similarly begins the second verse, this time accompanied on the downbeats by a gently tapped tambourine and the placid strum of an acoustic guitar, which warms the singer to stress . . .

Don't be afraid . . .

Lifting ever so slightly, even excitedly . . .

You were made to go out and get her

Angelic, distended voices ring out to join the singer . . . *Ahhhhh . . .*

The minute you let her under your skin

The voices descend along with the piano's journey before arriving together at *better*, a harmonic exclamation point to its positivity.

Then you begin to make it better

A triumphant drumroll announces the arrival of the bridge following an unexpected piano flourish to usher in the acknowledgment of Jude's plight. The beat, accentuated by a pinging ride cymbal, drives the returning angelic *Ahhhhhs* that glides along with another descending chordal structure.

And anytime you feel the pain
Hey Jude, refrain
Don't carry the world upon your shoulders

The three insistent piano chords underlining the tension prelude the singer's advice, which is joyfully approved by background *Ohhhhh.*

For well you know that it's a fool
Who plays it cool
By making his world a little colder

The acoustic guitar, now distinctly strumming along, heralds the ascension of the piano once more, accompanied tenderly by a nuanced vocal line that sneaks a peak of what is to come . . .

Na-na-na, na, na
Na-na-na, na

A slight ritard, a breath, a moment of Zen, a reflection in exhale . . .

Then . . .

Hey Jude, don't let me down
You have found her, now go and get her

The extension of the note on the first *her* is anxious, denoting how little the window of opportunity stays open to welcome happiness. The second relieving vocal melisma on the second *her* completes the journey from discovery to action. A lone, distant voice calls out; *Let it out and let it in* . . . followed by another calling out *Hey Jude,* as if snapping fingers to keep the subject of this sermon aligned with the groove the band is laying down. The singer is now attesting to lend a helping hand to a lost soul. Landing firmly on . . .

Remember to let her into your heart

A supportive harmony beneath *Remember* and on into *let her into your heart* boldly underlines the lyric introduced in isolation in the first verse. It is subtly jarring to hear a second voice, as this has been thus far a singular expression, especially on the word *heart,* punched onto the note set against the wispier lead vocal.

Then you can start to make it better

On *start* the second voice takes flight. It is rawer, even more passionate, raising the melodic stakes. Both singers incline into the smooth landing of *better*; the second voice blissfully completes the line in unison, presaging the ascension of *better* to come.

The piano again riffs into the bridge, coyly imploring the drums to follow, as Jude must follow, tumbling into his destiny, adding greater purpose to . . .

So let it out and let it in
Hey Jude, begin
You're waiting for someone to perform with

The choral of *Ahhhhh* returns with a stronger resolve, extending once more with a knowing *Ooohhhhh* that is bolstered by the drums—first a proclamation, then riding gleefully along. The lead vocal slowly breaks free of balladry and into a soulful blues phrasing . . .

And don't you know that it's just you
Hey Jude, you'll do

And then a telling, enigmatic line . . .

The movement you need is on your shoulder

Again, a slight ritard, a moment of contemplation, if not release . . .

Na-na-na, na
Na-na-na, na, yeah

A third verse, just like the first verse . . . but not really. After holding a gratifying *yeah* at the denouement of the bridge, recalling a time of youth, frenzy, hormonal explosions, the vocal arrives as if a parachute landing—the thrill of cheating death and a resolved connection once more with Mother Earth. The note driving *Jude* is filled with intense liberation. It is the last *Jude*, the final shout-out, and it is made to count. The second voice finishing the line, completing the proposal . . .

Hey Jude, don't make it bad

It all coalesces now—the voices, the drums, the piano, the guitars, the band . . .

Take a sad song and make it better
Remember to let her under your skin

An echo of a far-off prescient *Oh!* cuts through it all . . .

Then you'll begin to make it better

One splash on the drummer's hi-hat and a final roll as prelude to the episodic arousing explosion of voices . . .

Better better better better . . . Oh, make it . . . better, ahhhhh! Yeah, Yeah Yeah Yeah . . .

Then they begin . . .

Na . . . na . . . na . . . na na na na . . . Na na na na . . . Hey Jude

And on . . . and on . . .

Into infinity . . .

INTRODUCTION

> *[The Beatles] are confident and cheerful and the human condition will be thrilled by the coming results of their willing and enduring Beatle bondage . . . they will give all of us new wonders to soothe our pain.*
>
> —Derek Taylor, "Hey Jude" press release, August 1968

Na . . . na . . . na . . . na na na na.

Seven notes comprising a single musical phrase. Everyone knows it. Consider that for a moment. Everyone. All over the planet. Anthemic. A mantra. For over a half century it has been a communal celebration of song with no language barrier. Infectious. Commanding. Unforgettable in its simplicity. *Na . . . na . . . na . . . na na na na.*

When I was a young boy, around six years old, I would sing it to help me sleep whenever I awoke from a nightmare. It soothed me, made me feel less alone, as if I were included in its rousing chorale. I am sure I had no idea who sang it, its title, or where I first heard it. Still, *Na . . . na . . . na . . . na na na na* comforted me in the foreboding darkness of what always seemed to be endless night. In more ways than one, it performed a similar task for its time. *Na . . . na . . . na . . . na na na na* is what everyone needed to sing at that precise moment. The Beatles provided it—of course they did.

Released on August 26, 1968—the eighteenth single by a musical quartet from Liverpool, England, whose astoundingly proficient and magically eclectic career of pop culture dominance would span a decade—"Hey Jude" provided consolation in a year of violence, upheaval, assassination, and war. It also offered solace to the band, a respite from its personal, creative, and professional fractions that began to emerge in the shadow of unprecedented fame, adulation, riches, and the ensuing isolation all that engenders. The Beatles, by the summer of 1968, were more than a rock band. They had been a phenomenon, become a movement, transitioned smoothly into an enterprise, and were fast approaching living god status; every move, haircut, fashion choice, and ancillary interest to personal obsession was diagnosed, parsed, discussed, and then followed as if a roadmap to salvation.

In this way, "Hey Jude" was a statement. As such, it would surpass the Beatles' already record number of chart successes, reaching #1 in eighteen countries and remaining there on the US *Billboard* charts for an unfathomable nine weeks. Simultaneously, it acted as a glimmer of hope to the wayward boomer generation, reflecting the light of change, evolution, and youthful solidarity that had once shone brightly in the wake of "Beatlemania," a culture-altering spectacle that defined its times. A single song and its creators standing together at the epicenter of the zeitgeist and providing its soundtrack; *Na . . . na . . . na . . . na na na na* arrived as a universal elixir.

"There were plenty of other songs (in the band's canon) that equaled 'Hey Jude' in melody and inventiveness," writes Bob Spitz in his extensive 2006 Beatles biography, "but nothing was as ravishing or instantly accessible as 'Hey Jude' . . . it enchanted listeners."

However much "Hey Jude" echoes that steamy and combative summer of 1968, *Na . . . na . . . na . . . na na na na* seems to find its way into any and all times. "When you hear 'Hey Jude,' and you *need* it, you're so grateful for it," says my friend, Kiley Lotz, an intimate and engaging singer/songwriter working under the name Petal. "It comes on and props you up." When I was working on this book, the 2020 global pandemic gripped us all, followed later in the spring and into summer by protests across America against police brutality and systemic racism. By year's end, as I was wrapping things up, domestic terrorists stormed and sacked the US Capitol building, leaving five dead. Many pointed to the furor of 1968 for comparison. As I plunged into those times searching for the echoes of "Hey Jude," it seemed so had the present.

But, for me, the social impact of "Hey Jude" pales in comparison to its emotional impression, woven deeply into its musical fabric.

I was first inspired to write this book after watching the song's composer, Paul McCartney, on a 2018 segment of James Corden's *Late, Late Show* called "Carpool Karaoke." Aptly named, the multitalented host joins a signature performer to sing their songs while riding around in a car. This particular episode features the two men touring McCartney's childhood neighborhood in the British port town of Liverpool, from which all four Beatles hailed and which first came to prominence in the early 1960s. It is a wonderful sojourn into the personal history of one of the most famous musicians in Western culture. McCartney pleasantly interacts with his fellow Liverpudlians until the nearly twenty-five-minute segment ends with a surprise concert for a few patrons at a local pub, concluding with "Hey Jude." At this finale, more people rush into the packed pub to sing: *Na . . . na . . . na . . . na na na na.* Amid the sudden euphoria is a young woman crying tears of abject joy. I look over at my wife. She is crying. Right then I get the chill of stark recognition, returning to that dark bedroom over fifty years earlier, being six, in bed, frightened, and singing quietly, *Na . . . na . . . na . . . na na na na,* then just a little louder to shoo the demons away, *Na . . . na . . . na . . . na na na na,* until I softly and contentedly drift off to sleep.

Na . . . na . . . na . . . na na na na.

Why did the Beatles sing this refrain for the final four minutes and two seconds of what would be the longest #1 pop single released at seven minutes and eleven seconds? McCartney would later say: "It wasn't intended to go on that long, but I was having such fun ad-libbing." From the first, it appears *Na . . . na . . . na . . . na na na na* was too much for its composer to tame. It certainly seems so by the unhinged vocal descants and improvised abrasions he adds to the final chorale—*Jude . . . Jude . . . a-Judey . . . a-Judey . . . a-Judey . . . ahhh . . . wha-dow!*—as if he cannot contain the excitement within him. This is especially prevalent at the 6:08 mark of the final fade-out when McCartney completely loses all sense of structured singing and wails with the primal intensity of an infant. When considering the understated, soulful rendering of the rest of the song, these voice-shredding outbursts are both alarming and ecstatic, as if channeling something deeper. McCartney recalled that when he wrote the famous ballad "Yesterday," one of the most recorded-songs in popular music history, it was as if it came from somewhere else. He went around for weeks asking anyone if they had heard it before. Someone *must* have already written it. That is what *Na . . . na . . . na . . . na na na na* did, I think, to the then twenty-six-year-old Paul McCartney. It happened *to him* and he could not stop it.

Music Webzine *Stereogum* blogger, and one of my favorite pop culture commentators, Tom Breihan, pens a column called "The Number Ones" which, at the time of this writing, covers every #1 *Billboard* song in its history. About "Hey Jude," which he readily admits is not a personal favorite, he cites, "It's a song that instantly conjures massive singalongs, one that echoes down through history" and that *Na . . . na . . . na . . . na na na na* is "a refrain that we can basically sing the moment we're born, one that's imprinted on us."

To wit: I caught McCartney's 1989 *Flowers in the Dirt* tour at Madison Square Garden in New York City, the first time in thirteen years he would cross the world with a band and the first wherein he would revisit the Beatles' vast catalog. During the coda to "Hey Jude," I combed the packed venue from my upper-deck seat along stage left and was overwhelmed by the unadulterated pandemonium; *Na . . . na . . . na . . . na na na na*—song fusing with audience. I vividly recall McCartney shouting, "I can't stop it! I can't stop it!" You can hear a stirring example of this on the 1990 live album, *Tripping the Live Fantastic,* in which he shrieks uncontrollably, "I can feel it! Can *you* feel it?"

In July of 2005, McCartney headlined a series of ten free concerts featuring 150 acts engineered by Live Aid founder Bob Geldof to implore world leaders to "Make Poverty History" before the annual G8 summit meeting in Auchterarder, Scotland. Over a million people worldwide on four continents joined on television and radio, and another three billion on the internet. It concluded in London with an all-star rendition of "Hey Jude," including among others Sting, U2, Coldplay, and Elton John. The world beseeching its leaders to feed the hungry with a chorale of *Na . . . na . . . na . . . na na na na.* Not a single global leader would dare stop it.

Longtime musical analyst, author, and composer Tim Riley touches upon this effect in his *Tell Me Why—The Beatles: Album by Album, Song by Song, The Sixties and After*: "'Hey Jude' reflects a larger realm of experience and conveys a richer vision of how good life can get."

The following year, McCartney had twenty thousand Russians of all ages singing *Na . . . na . . . na . . . na na na na* in Red Square. Framed by the Kremlin and Lenin's Tomb, the emotional release of oppressed generations poured out in the song's finale for all its worth. To them, perhaps it represented the sound of unchecked freedom. A camera captured Russian president Vladimir Putin's expression, caught between awe and bemusement. The former KGB intelligence officer, and a despot for whom arresting artists is a light afternoon, suddenly looked small and insignificant, dwarfed by the multitudes as these nonsense words reigned down upon him. *Na . . . na . . . na . . . na na na na.* A tyrannical reign fifteen years after the fall of the Soviet Union could not stop it.

John Robertson and Patrick Humphries note in their book, *The Beatles: The Complete Guide to Their Music*, that "'Hey Jude' sounded like a community anthem, from the open-armed welcome of its lyrics to its instant singalong chorus."

In 2010, upon receiving the Gershwin Prize for Popular Song in the East Room of the White House, McCartney led the august gathering in a rendition of "Hey Jude." During its "imprinted refrain" the evening's multigenerational superstar performers wandered up to sing along. These included Stevie Wonder, the Jonas Brothers, Faith Hill, Emmylou Harris, Lang Lang, Herbie Hancock, Elvis Costello, Jack White, Corinne Bailey Rae, Dave Grohl, and comedian Jerry Seinfeld. McCartney looked over at President Barack Obama and First Lady Michelle leaving their seats and figured it was protocol for them to exit before the finale. But they were not leaving. Instead, they crammed onto the small stage with their two daughters, Malia and Sasha, singing *Na . . . na . . . na . . . na na na na.* Paul leaped from his piano seat to join them. It went on for another six refrains. Not even the most powerful person in the world could stop it.

The late Ian MacDonald in his seminal work, *Revolution in the Head,* writes "Their [the Beatles] instinct for what worked was rarely sharper, the huge chords suggesting both Jude's personal revelation and, along with the accompanying chorale, a vast communality in which artists and audience joined in swaying to a single rhythm all around the world."

Walter Everett, professor of music theory at the University of Michigan and author of the musicologist series, *The Beatles as Musicians,* noted to me during the course of several emails, "The fact that it's always an audience singalong, no matter who the artist, attests to its universal appeal."

Some fantastic lunatic on the internet even took the time to count 216 *nas* in the song, including the eighteen that complete its two bridges, but "Hey Jude" is more than *Na . . . na . . . na . . . na na na na.* Far more. Although McCartney wanted those *nas* to matter as a general proclamation by the Beatles to drive home the very idea of togetherness, a tribal call, a mighty yawp to new beginnings—as long as there is life, there is indeed hope. Yet, it is within McCartney's country/soul/singsong ballad that the underlying theme of taking a sad song and making it better materializes. Its uplifting message with a singular focus on both an embrace of community and its lyrical nod to self-realization has given "Hey Jude" over to the ages.

The song begins quietly—no music—just words; *Hey Jude . . .* It is conversational yet understated. Coming out of late-sixties Top 40 radio with all its gory sound effects, manic DJ chatter, and advertising cacophony, it demanded attention, as if a monologue to nudge procrastination into action. In a way, "Hey Jude" is a microcosm of its composer; Paul McCartney started out with the intimate need to express himself in song, and then, as a Beatle, developed a larger-than-life persona and became part of an all-encompassing cultural detonation. The song's cleverly devised arrangement is as much a marriage of natural inclination as it is formula.

My dear friend, Eric Hutchinson, whose prolific output as a composer and performer for nearly two decades has earned him accolades and awards, smiles when he notes of "Hey Jude": "You end up getting two songs for the price of one."

"Hey Jude" is a song birthed in a vacuum *and* a reflection of its times. It reveals the empathy and insight that a true songwriting genius must possess to make the personal universal and vice versa. "Hey Jude" comes when the world needed it—whether by one person or in greater numbers. It is a pep talk, a self-examination, and, as stated above, a song of hope. There is a purpose to each of its notes, every stanza and syllable, and its overarching leitmotif of a band in flux and of society on the brink of racial, gender, and generational divides; a world-weary ode to stepping out of the darkness and into the possibility of light. Together.

However, nothing is guaranteed here; it is not an *absolute* proclamation like the Beatles' other famous anthem, "All You Need Is Love" from the Summer of Love—an allegory of flower-power and psychedelic idealism, free love, and hippie transcendence. "Hey Jude" comes from a less lofty perch, a humbler suggestion that a sad song *could* be better, but only if that first step to realization occurs. It is there for the taking, if you choose to take it.

This book will examine "Hey Jude" because it is a song that begs to be examined. It came out of the gate as the most popular song by the most popular band in the world, when it seemed as if the entire planet was in utter chaos. It has remained a beloved tune for over half a century because it still speaks to us, but also because its composer is still alive. Two of the four Beatles are gone. McCartney's songwriting partner and cultural icon John Lennon was gunned down in front of his New York City luxury apartment building in 1980 at the age of forty, and George Harrison, his childhood friend and Beatles' lead guitarist, succumbed to lung cancer in 2001 at fifty-eight. Drummer Ringo Starr is still with us, and remains one of the most beloved figures of the era, as indeed the Beatles remain pop music's benchmark for popularity, innovation, and manic devotion.

It has taken some time for Paul McCartney to get there. At first, he was dismissed as the cute, emotionally slight Beatle who gave us wonderfully melodic songs that didn't mean as much as the dark and witty Lennon or the spiritually polemic Harrison. It didn't help that he was the first to announce to the world that the Beatles were no more, although all three of his fellow bandmates had already quit and returned by the time he did. He was also the one who sued the others to get out of what he believed was an untenable contractual stranglehold. His solo career with his late wife Linda and his band Wings was mostly derided by critics and prompted underwhelming response from fans, despite selling millions of records. But time has healed those wounds. As the "Carpool Karaoke" segment illustrates, Paul is a survivor, not only of his looming legend but as a man whose songs, and one in particular, still make it (excuse the corniness) *better... better... better... aahhhhhhh...*

My dear friend, singer/songwriter, author, painter, poet, and lifelong Beatlemaniac, Dan Bern recalls: "My dominant, emotional memory of the song is quite recent, last summer, when we surprised our daughter Lulu with a Paul McCartney concert at Dodger Stadium. I had never seen Paul, and it was like going to see the Beatles. It's an incredible experience, and when 'Hey Jude' came along, and he came to the extended vocal jam, fifty-six thousand people stood up and sang. There wasn't a dry eye in the place. Maybe it has something to do with the familiarity of it, the fact that it's not really words at that point, so it has a universal feel; everybody singing along to the same thing at the same time. It continues to resonate in that way."

And so "Hey Jude" lives on, passed from generation to generation, like all the special songs do, with a powerful message of love that begins modestly with an endearing story of inspiration, while also telling the tale of the Beatles' final years and the promise of their entire oeuvre. It is also a song that reveals its songwriter, where he comes from and where he's going, while providing succor to a deeply divided world confronted daily in 1968 by horrible news of war, assassination, and riots. All of this continues to provoke thousands of moistened eyes.

To best cover these topics, I've reached out to learned professors and experts in the fields of musicology, philosophy, sociology, psychology, history, pop culture, pop music, and 1960s politics. Also included are the voices of songwriters, whose creative experiences will help us to better understand all that is going on inside and outside of "Hey Jude." With their assistance, and the inclusion of insights and commentary from Beatles historians over the years who've preceded this endeavor with volumes of perspective, I will attempt to place "Hey Jude" in the context of the Beatles' career and the tumultuous year it was released, discover its thematic origins and inspiration, deconstruct why it is widely considered among the finest songs of the period, and demonstrate how its emotional currency has transcended time to become a modern classic.

CHAPTER ONE

Don't Let Me Down . . .

Factoids & Such

Released—August 26 (in US) and August 30, 1968 (in UK)
Format—7-inch record
B-side—"Revolution"
Length—7:11
Label—Apple
Songwriters—Lennon/McCartney
Recorded—July 31 and August 1, 1968
Studio—Trident, London
Producer—George Martin
Engineers—Ken Scott, Barry Sheffield
Mixing—George Martin, Ken Scott, Geoff Emerick (Malcolm Toft mixed at Trident Studios)

Let's begin with perspective.

As noted, "Hey Jude" was the longest-running #1 US hit the Beatles released in an epic ten-year career. This is especially impressive when considering the band spent eight of those years producing colossally popular singles—a staggering twenty went to #1 in the United States (seventeen in the United Kingdom), and "Hey Jude" spent nine weeks at the top of the seminal *Billboard* Hot 100 chart. It also logged the longest run of any Beatles' release on that chart at nineteen weeks.

Author and essayist, Devin McKinney, whose *Magic Circles: The Beatles in Dream and History* is a brilliantly devised study of the band in its times, noted to me: "'Hey Jude' was a moment where people decided once they heard this on the radio that this is something I need to *feel*, and it connected them with others who felt the same way, so they could all sing *together*. Maybe it was on top for nine weeks because people just wanted to live in a dream that lasted nine weeks."

I bet when you think of Beatles songs that define their incredible run of success, "She Loves You" or "I Want to Hold Your Hand" immediately come to mind. Especially in the United States, as these songs represent the first wave of Beatlemania when four lads from Liverpool were seemingly the only thing that mattered. Both songs were certainly smash hits, remaining on the charts for fifteen solid weeks but, again, four weeks shy of "Hey Jude." It should be pointed out, because Beatles fanatics sure as hell will tell you, that "She Loves You" remained on the UK charts for thirty-one consecutive weeks in 1963. Yes, but it remained at #1 for four weeks, and then again later for another two, not nine. "I Want to Hold Your Hand" is close, holding the top spot there for seven weeks in February 1964, but still, not nine. The US run of one of the band's last releases, the double A-side single "Come Together"/ "Something" enjoyed a sixteen-week stay on *Billboard* but was only at the top of the charts for one week in late November 1969, not . . . all together now . . . *nine*. And in case you were wondering, and I am sure that you were, "Yesterday"—generally considered "the most popular Beatles song"—spent a month at #1 in early October of 1965 in America. It wasn't even released as a single in the UK.

Not surprisingly, "Hey Jude" ended up as the biggest-selling song of 1968. It moved six million units worldwide in three months, reaching #1 in eighteen countries, and garnering the Ivor Novello Award (named for the Welsh composer who dominated the UK music scene for the first half of the twentieth century) for the highest certified record sales in Britain. It also stood alone atop the Hot 100 US *Billboard* year-end charts. It was nominated for three 1969 Grammy Awards—Record Of The Year, Song Of The Year, and Best Pop Performance By A Duo Or Group With Vocal—but surprisingly failed to win any of them. Still, losing to Simon and Garfunkel's brilliant "Mrs. Robinson" from the finest film of the year, *The Graduate,* for Record Of The Year and Best Pop Performance By A Duo Or Group should cause no shame. Songwriter Bobby Russell's "Little Green Apples" winning Song Of The Year over "Hey Jude" raises eyebrows now but is less egregious when considering it was recorded by not one or two but *three* different artists in 1968: Roger Miller, Patti Page, and O. C. Smith. It was Smith's version that has stood the test of time due, in part, to the fact that it reached #2—kept out of the top spot by, you guessed it, "Hey Jude." Meanwhile, across the pond in Britain's most noteworthy music periodical, the *New Musical Express,* the annual Readers' Poll overwhelmingly voted "Hey Jude" as the Best Single of 1968.

None of this is to compare "Hey Jude" in quality to any other Beatles song, each one a spectacular example of the range and span of the band's musical scope and immense popularity from its explosion as a cultural phenomenon in 1963 to its demise in 1970. That stuff is subjective. We all have our favorite Beatles song. However, it does raise the question: Why does the immediate and lasting popularity of "Hey Jude" reign when set against some of the most groundbreaking pop music ever made?

Eric Hutchinson, whose work has not only invaded the pop charts but adorned television soundtracks and marketing campaigns, wonders if, given its historical imprint, we can efficiently answer this question: "It's difficult to talk about 'Hey Jude' as a songwriter because it's just so influential. It's just one of those songs it's hard to believe it didn't ever exist, it just feels like it's been around *forever*. I always assume that's how Paul McCartney felt when he wrote it, like it just fell out of him and the melody wrote itself."

Emotive and introspective singer/songwriter Kiley Lotz, a.k.a. Petal, concurs: "That's the dream, right? To be able to write a song that has *that* kind of effect on people. My friend and I were talking about it today while we listened to 'Hey Jude' in the car. He said, 'If I had never heard this song before and you just brought it to me my mind would be blown.' It's a song you've heard your *whole* life, so sometimes you forget how wonderful it is."

Then there is the song's length.

"Hey Jude" was the longest run-time pop single ever to top the charts—later eclipsed by Don McLean's two-sided 1972 hit "American Pie" (8:42) and, most recently, Taylor Swift's ten-minute and twelve second 2021 epic "All Too Well." It was a grand anomaly merely to release a single longer than three minutes before, during, and even after 1968, but a single over seven minutes in length was plain nuts. Notably, Bob Dylan's folk-rock burner "Like a Rolling Stone" timed in at just over six minutes and made it to #2 on the *Billboard* charts in 1965, proving once again his immense influence on the Beatles. However, it was another lengthy number that year that got closer: At seven minutes and twenty-one seconds, "MacArthur Park," a rather bizarre reading of prolific songwriter Jimmy Webb's melodramatic opus by British actor Richard Harris, managed to reach #2 on *Billboard* and #4 in the United Kingdom a couple of weeks before "Hey Jude" was released in the summer of 1968.

In grand Fab Four fashion, by dominating the charts once again, another pop totem was trampled. Radio stations, the driving force of popular music since early in the twentieth century, stringently contained the length of singles to two to three minutes—the shorter the songs, the more time for the money-generating ads. Even the band's legendary producer, George Martin, whose musical influence on the band had no peer, bristled at the elongated outro. He recalls in the Beatles-sanctioned *Anthology* book: "I actually said, 'You can't make a single that long.' I was shouted down by the boys—not for the first time in my life—and John asked: 'Why not?' I couldn't think of a good answer, really—except the pathetic one that disc jockeys wouldn't play it. He said, 'They will if it's us.' And, of course, he was absolutely right."

"It must have been so incredibly bold then," says Hutchinson. "I would assume that there were very few bands, if any, that had the sort of cachet to pull *that* off. Even now I think if you were to try and make a song pushing seven minutes, the record company would say *no way*."

"A seven-minute pop song is even more outrageous *now*," cites Aaron Keane, a professor in the North Carolina State University Department of Music. Prior to teaching, Keane worked for two decades as a composer, producer, and engineer on album, television, and advertising projects, including assisting popular artists from singer/songwriter

Shawn Colvin to rapper Mos Def. He told me; "Everything seems to be about three minutes or so now. I think the pressure to have it shorter is even *stronger* today. I'll play songs from the 1960s era to my classes and I've heard this comment a couple of times, 'Boy, it sure is repetitive.' The youth market wants you to give it to them right away and get out. Even for the Beatles, a seven-minute hit song is beyond comprehension."

Celebrated singer/songwriter, front man for Counting Crows, and my podcast partner on *Underwater Sunshine,* Adam Duritz marvels: "When I look over two volumes of *Past Masters* (one of the collections where the song resides), there's only one song that even has a four in front of it, which is 'You Know My Name (Look Up the Number).' Other than that, there's nothing that goes above three minutes. 'Hey Jude' is seven-ten! It's not just a little past, where pop singles were, it's a *fucking* mile past it! And what's really astonishing is that it's not a weird album track or a prog rock, FM thing, it's a huge AM radio hit."

Frank Samarotto, Indiana University's associate professor of music theory, adds: "While the Beatles at that point were really at the height of their popularity and could nearly have done anything and the record company would have said, 'Okay fine,' it *still* should have been Top 40 death. I grew up in New York and they played 'Hey Jude' on the radio all day long, but they didn't do it with *any* other song."

Author Rob Sheffield, whose *Dreaming the Beatles: The Love Story of One Band and the Whole World* may be my favorite book on the subject, goes farther in his assessment of the song's length as a reflection of the Beatles' boldness for experimentation. "I firmly believe 'Hey Jude' is an extreme, avant-garde statement for merely releasing it as a single, but also the bait and switch to begin with a very programmable if not unconventional pop song, even before you get to the ending, but then for it to lead into that repetitive chant at the end? The fact that it became their biggest hit single around the world is an act of colossal arrogance in that really beautiful, benevolent Beatles way."

Singer/songwriter and activist Seán Barna, whose songs speak to both personal expression and cultural issues, notes the song's length as a transitory artistic statement from the Beatles to their audience: "It is devastatingly effective because it lets the listener paint their own picture, and its length is absolutely paramount to this. After a while, the Beatles fall away, as much as the Beatles *can* fall away, and the listener starts to use this blank canvass of *na na na* to move through their own experiences, emotions, and little nostalgias."

"The basic song, before you get to the long ending, is a nice, regular Beatles song," says Dan Bern, a prolific singer/songwriter, who also teaches the craft. "The extended vocal jam speaks to the confidence they had in their ability as writers and as a musical outfit that they could do anything and get to what would be the end of the song for anybody else and turn it into something the world is *still* singing."

Hutchinson concludes: "I think long, epic songs like this owe everything to the Beatles saying we're doing it and then people following up by saying, 'Well, the Beatles did it so it's okay to do it.' Pretty soon you have the Rolling Stones' 'You Can't Always Get What You Want.' The Beatles paved the way, giving permission to experimentation. You never get to Queen's 'Bohemian Rhapsody' without 'Hey Jude.'"

The enormous hubris displayed in arguing for a seven-minute pop single was an element of the Beatles' strength that was already baked in. During their initial recording sessions in 1962, George Martin directed the neophyte group to record "How Do You Do It," a song the producer believed was a hit, as it would be for another Liverpool act, Gerry and the Pacemakers, the following year. And although they deigned to record it, the band unanimously nixed its release and instead offered up their own songs for consideration. The proof was in the material, and the rest, as they say, is history. A year later, for what would be the somber black-and-white cover for their second album, *With the Beatles* (*Meet the Beatles,* US title, 1964 release), they again stood firm against suggestions for a cheerier image by management and the record company. Once again, the Beatles' instincts proved correct, as photographer Robert Freeman's indelible image of four faces suffused in equal light and darkness went on to arguably be the most influential album cover ever—repeated and parodied ad nauseum over the decades. "It always seemed an unsafe idea to try and be safe," McCartney recalled to Beatles author and archivist, Mark Lewisohn, in a late-eighties interview that appears in his pivotal work on the band's studio output, *The Complete Beatles Recording Sessions.* Paul later drives the point home by emphatically stating, "We did things every which way."

One interesting aspect of the Beatles' "every which way" edict is on display on "Hey Jude" with the inclusion of the mother of all expletives, *fuck.* More to the point, *Fuckin' hell!* Yup, in the song's final bridge section, at 2:58, as Paul sings, *The minute you let her under your skin / Oh, then you begin* . . . buried but clearly audible in the mix is the offending remark. And once you know this, it is impossible *not* to hear it.

Granted, background weirdness was a Beatles' trademark and witty playfulness part of their charm; as some will argue that Paul McCartney counts off, *One . . . two . . . three . . . fuck!* on the very first song on the very first Beatles album, *Please Please Me,* but McCartney has often denied this, and although it is fun to consider, you really have to *want* to hear it. The band did, however, admit to singing a background vocal comprised of *Tit, tit, tit, tit, tit* on the 1965 *Rubber Soul* track, "Girl," but nevertheless could also be construed as *dit dit dit dit dit.* Still, no one has denied the existence of *Fuckin' hell!* nor can one substitute it with anything else.

EMI engineer Geoff Emerick, who worked on many of the Beatles' most experimental pieces of the period, claims in his memoir *Here, There and Everywhere: My Life Recording the Music of the Beatles* the *Fuckin' hell!* came from Paul. In the same account, junior engineer John Smith vividly recalls John Lennon pointing out that "Paul hit a clunker on the piano and said a naughty word!" However, Malcolm Toft, the mixing engineer on the master recording, remembers Lennon overdubbing his harmony vocal when, in reaction to the volume being too loud in his headphones, shouting it in anger. The aforementioned Lewisohn concludes that it was indeed Lennon during his overdub session, but it was because he blew the line, *Let her under your skin* . . . by singing *Let her into your heart* . . . instead. This makes the most sense, timing-wise, as it comes right after that line.

The biggest mystery might be who decided to leave it on there in the first place? Emerick writes that he was about to erase it but, ever the prankster, Lennon intervened. Once again Emerick recalls Lennon "snickering with impish delight" and ordering him to "Leave it in, buried just low enough, so that it can barely be heard. Most people won't ever spot it . . . but we'll know it's there!" Emerick gleefully concludes: "It's amusing to think that millions of fans have heard the record millions of times without ever realizing that it contains a dreaded four-letter word that was strictly taboo back in 1968."

In his 2018 presentation "Weeps Happiness—The Dysfunctional Drama of the White Album" for *The Beatles'* White Album:

An International Symposium at New Jersey's Monmouth University, author Devin McKinney writes with some delight: "In our diegetic experience of 'Hey Jude,' *Fuckin' hell!* has no connection to anything, no meaning. It's a flaw, a flub, a thing to be regretted. But I suggest it adds something ineffably human, yet no less mysterious for that. Another layer of life, an aspect of the uncontrolled; a certain energy, anger, absurdity, humor, desire, surprise. It gives a sound to something hidden and betokens the weirdness that comes with experiment and exploration. It's merely one of the innumerable nuts and bolts that go into making music in the moment, pushing it to meet one's own very specific creative demands, yet crafting it such that it will live on in the imaginations of millions of strangers."

McKinney wrapped it up succinctly to me: "On a very simplistic level, I always found it amusing that you have this kind of religious experience of this chant, and you have John saying, *Fuckin' hell!* beneath it—it's a beautiful Beatlesque contradiction."

"Hey Jude" boasts less controversial firsts.

It was the initial release from Apple Records, the epicenter of the historic Apple Corps Ltd. enterprise, launched and run entirely by the Beatles. Although the whole Apple idea was ill-conceived and poorly run, Apple Records was an immediate and lasting success, mostly due to the weight and grandeur of its Beatles releases, but also as an outlet for many successful careers to come with post-Beatles solo efforts, including those of Paul McCartney with his hit-making band, Wings. James Taylor, Badfinger, Billy Preston, and Yoko Ono all debuted on Apple. Initially part of a larger campaign called "Our First Four"—which included "Sour Milk Sea," a George Harrison composition and production for British singer/songwriter Jackie Lomax; and the Paul

McCartney productions of the nostalgic "Those Were the Days" by Welsh folk singer Mary Hopkin, which eventually knocked "Hey Jude" out of the top spot on the UK charts; and a Northern brass ensemble, the Black Dyke Mills Band's "Thingumybob"—"Hey Jude" would become the biggest selling song dropped by a new label.

In its considerable wake, approximately 141 Apple singles were released between the summer of 1968 to May of 1996, in addition to eighty-one albums bookended by two George Harrison projects: his experimental *Wonderwall* in November of 1968 and the posthumous *Let It Roll: Songs by George Harrison* collection in June of 2009. Since then, new reissues of Beatles music have gone on to further fill Apple's coffers, joined by multimillion dollar "use" deals first with Apple Computers and eventually Apple Music.

In one fell swoop, "Hey Jude" underlined the power and promise of the Beatles after six years in the spotlight. Spearheading a larger business initiative and signifying the band's chart-topping pedigree, it would go on to sell an incredible eight million records, standing behind only "Yesterday" as a publishing windfall.

"Hey Jude" was also the first Beatles song to be recorded on eight-track equipment. Prior to this, the band, along with producer George Martin and several talented EMI engineers, had worked their magic first on a two-track machine and then, for the bulk of their early- to mid-sixties output, on the four-track of Studio Two at EMI (Abbey Road) Studios. Tracks allow musicians to record instruments separately, even when playing together—for the Beatles this would include drums, bass, and two guitars, along with the occasional piano/keyboard, which would be overdubbed on open tracks later—and then to "mix down" those tracks onto one or two tracks to free up more space to add their signature lead and background vocals, and perhaps strings, brass, and sound effects. The advent of eight-track machines started an upward trend that led to sixteen tracks becoming the standard in the 1970s, giving way in the 1980s to 24-track and then 48-track decks. In today's digital age, tracks are infinite. Not that expanded tracks alone can in any way create a song as good, popular, or lasting as "Hey Jude" but, as Eric Hutchinson, an accomplished producer, points out; "Choosing to use Trident and its eight-track capabilities is a clear indication that the Beatles were purposely trying to make a song that was bigger than anything they'd made before, in every way possible—it's length, its arrangement, *and* its recording. They challenged even their own norms and set out to make something epic."

Having traveled around America, where eight-track facilities were popping up, the band had first become intrigued at the prospect of having twice as much space in which to work. Harrison and McCartney had previously decamped to Trident Studios to record with Lomax and Hopkin and were duly impressed with its eight-track capabilities. Trident, which was located in a nondescript alley in the Soho district of London, was indeed the first studio in England to claim such a deck. In fact, Trident, which would go on to be one of the premier studios in the United Kingdom, was in its infancy when the Beatles came calling. The studio's founder Norman Sheffield and his co-owner and brother Barry were paid twenty-five pounds an hour by EMI for the sessions. Barry, who would also engineer the historic "Hey Jude" recording, later claimed that the studio earned about a thousand pounds for the session but that having the Beatles record a massive single there made the value of the session incalculable. After "Hey Jude," a who's who of artists flocked to Trident, including the Rolling Stones, David Bowie,

T-Rex, Elton John, Queen, Carly Simon, Genesis, and more. In fact, the Bechstein grand piano that Paul plays on "Hey Jude" is the same one you hear on the 1971 recordings of Bowie's "Life on Mars?" and Elton's "Levon," Lou Reed's "Perfect Day" the next year, and Queen's "Bohemian Rhapsody" in 1975.

Beyond what it did for the Beatles as a band and a brand, its burgeoning label and company, and the reputation and legacy of Trident Studios, "Hey Jude" did tenfold for a generation and its times.

Thanks to The Paul McCartney Project, a website dedicated to all-things Sir Paul (McCartney was knighted in 1997 by Queen Elizabeth II), we know that "Hey Jude" has at the time of this writing been played in concert 631 times. But even if Paul wasn't around to lead the chorus of *Na . . . na . . . na . . . na na na na*, there have been hundreds of cover versions from around the world, most notably by Bing Crosby, Count Basie, Elvis Presley, Maynard Ferguson, Ella Fitzgerald, the Supremes, and the London Symphony Orchestra. Perhaps the finest is the late, great soul king, Wilson Pickett, who released his version within months of the original. Featuring twenty-one-year-old guitar phenom Duane Allman, soon to form the legendary Allman Brothers, and recorded in the celebrated Muscle Shoals Studio in Alabama, many rock historians point to this recording as the birth of Southern rock.

The song's legacy lives on in a myriad of countdowns, top lists, and accolades from every corner of the music world. Just a sample is its official induction into the National Academy of Recording Arts and Sciences Grammy Hall of Fame in 2001. Three years later, during its thirty-fifth anniversary celebration, America's premier rock magazine *Rolling Stone* ranked "Hey Jude" at number eight on the "500 Greatest Songs of All Time," the highest-placed Beatles song. Nostalgic rock magazine *Mojo* also placed it seventh on its "The 100 Greatest Singles of All Time." The Amusement & Music Operators Association ranks "Hey Jude" as the eleventh-best jukebox single of all time; again no Beatles song tops it. In 2018, "Hey Jude" peaked at #12 on *Billboard*'s "All Time Hot 100 Songs," still the highest-charting Beatles song. In 2015, the ITV program, *The Nation's Favourite Beatles Number One,* ranked "Hey Jude" at the very top of its countdown.

Again, absolutely none of this tells us why "Hey Jude" is the most popular and, as we can see, one of the most beloved and lasting Beatles songs. The time has come to try and dig deeper. To do this, it is probably best to start at the beginning: A twenty-six- year-old Paul McCartney tooling along the English countryside in his beloved green Aston Martin one steamy summer day in June of 1968 on his way to do something nice for a friend's son and his mom.

CHAPTER TWO

The Movement You Need Is on Your Shoulder

Inspiration

I just dive right in and hope for the best. And it seems to work.

—Paul McCartney, *Conversations with Paul McCartney*

June 1968, sometime around his twenty-sixth birthday, Paul McCartney is experiencing a rare convergence of invincibility, romanticism, and nostalgia. He's emerged as arguably *the* significant figure in the Beatles, the most influential band in the world. As such, he is a spokesman for his generation in rhetoric, comportment, and creativity. An accomplished, celebrated, and chart-topping songwriter for his band and others, he is immersed in London's art community, helping to finance and launch both the Indica Bookshop and Art Gallery as well as an underground newspaper, the *International Times*. The Beatles, having spent the past six years dramatically transforming the pop world, recently incorporated their brand into Apple Corps with hopes of launching an egalitarian mixture of music, fashion, film, and technology. Perhaps most important of all, having just returned from a trip to the United States to act as point man for Apple, one of the planet's most eligible bachelors consummates a tryst with a twenty-six-year-old American photographer named Linda Eastman, whom he had first met the previous year. Linda will become the great love of his life, and he seems to know it almost immediately.

You have found her . . . now go and get her . . .

After a winter with his band in India studying Transcendental Meditation with the Maharishi Mahesh Yogi, McCartney has reassessed his pursuit of fame as a false elixir to his search for truth in music, drugs, spirituality, and love. He's especially moved by the Maharishi's expression, "The heart always goes to the warmer place." This single maxim seems to underscore his need for the embrace of a loving woman—which leads him to Linda, whom he finds relatable and comforting, unlike his fiancée, the erudite and driven actress and model, Jane Asher.

Beatles biographer Philip Norman wrote in his 1981 *Shout!: The Beatles in Their Generation* that Linda "idolized and pampered him in precisely the way in which Jane had always refused to do. Gripping his arm, she would gaze at him with awe. She would say in his hearing what an honor it would be to bear his children."

The career-driven Asher, not yet ready to settle down into family life, prompts Paul to end their five-year relationship to marry Linda nine months later. The couple will have three children and be together for twenty-nine years until Linda succumbs to breast cancer in 1998 at age fifty-six.

McCartney is talented, famous, successful, and newly in love, a man completely in control of his destiny. Much of his success is due to his songwriting partnership with bandmate and friend of eleven years, John Lennon, who is coincidentally leaving his wife of six years, Cynthia, to pursue what will soon become a very public affair with thirty-five-year-old Japanese avant-garde artist, Yoko Ono. McCartney's relationship with Lennon has been simultaneously prolific and complicated since their early teens and is partly the impetus for the trip he'll take out to John's home in Weybridge this sunny summer day to visit the tattered remnants of his partner's personal life.

No one has endured Lennon's radical personality shifts between affection and derision more intensely than Paul and Cynthia. McCartney sees in Cynthia the fragility of his cherished rapport with John and, in turn, his band. Cynthia is an indelible link to their younger days in Liverpool when it was all out in front of them—the adorable, blonde art student who managed to quell his mate's outwardly rebellious fury while he and John were just beginning to unlock the secrets of the beloved music that had given them purpose and direction. When she became pregnant, John did what he felt was right and, just before her twenty-third birthday, when he was only twenty-one, he married her. Around the same time, Paul was engaged to a young woman who also became pregnant and, like John, he believed the honorable thing to do was to marry her, but fate intervened when she had a miscarriage.

Don't carry the world upon your shoulders . . .

McCartney had always felt a connection to Cynthia and John's son, whom he joyfully coddled as he did all the youngsters in his life, including Ruth, the eight-year-old stepsister from his father's second marriage, and Linda's five-year-old daughter Heather from a previous marriage. Thus, Paul thinks nothing of taking the hour's drive from his London home in St. John's Wood on Cavendish Street to visit Lennon's abandoned family to "try to cheer them up."

Ostracized from the impenetrable Beatles' inner circle for fear contact might upset the always volatile Lennon, Cynthia and Julian are holed up in their twenty-seven-room mock-Tudor mansion called the Kenwood Estate, the Lennons' place of residence since July of 1964. The sprawling acreage and suburban refinery exemplifies the spectacular largesse of the Beatles. During the band's halcyon days, Paul and John, as they did in their childhood homes in Liverpool, composed some of the most beloved and inventive music of the era in a tiny music room in the attic. Each trip to Weybridge held the seduction of creativity, as music always percolated inside McCartney, incessantly pondering a melody or clever lyrical aside to share with John when he arrived.

The movement you need is on your shoulder . . .

Paul had always known how to instinctively tap into the muse, whether dreaming his most popular song "Yesterday" or drawing from juvenile memories in the chart-topping "Penny Lane." During a previous chauffeured trip, Paul made small talk with the driver about his busy schedule, to which the gentleman sighed that he'd been working "eight days a week." It would become the title for the Beatles' seventh #1 hit. Other Beatles classics like "Help," "Day Tripper," "Drive My Car," "Norwegian Wood," "In My Life," "Paperback Writer," "Eleanor Rigby," and many others were begun or finished by the songwriting duo there.

During this particular drive out, Paul might well remember the time when Julian, then only four, had shown his dad a drawing he'd made for school—a fanciful rendering of his schoolmate Lucy floating in a sky filled with stars that a teacher had thought looked like diamonds and entitled, "Lucy in the Sky with Diamonds." John couldn't wait to show Paul. The two immediately took it as a song title and went to work.

However, while Kenwood housed many fond memories for McCartney, for the now-absent Lennon, the mansion had come to represent an upper-middle-class trap, the antithesis of his humble origins which had inspired his art. Subjugated by domesticity and the rigors of remaining at the top of the pop charts, he was mired in depression, gaining weight, and experimenting with mind-altering drugs, while Paul and Jane were the "it" couple of Swinging London, frequenting underground clubs, art galleries, and theater premieres. These contrary, personal lives are best expressed in one of the Beatles' sonic masterworks that closes their revolutionary *Sgt. Pepper's Lonely Hearts Club Band* album in the summer of 1967. "A Day in the Life" features Lennon's dreamy verses regurgitating newspaper headlines, war movies, and suburban mundanity in a drugged-out haze, briefly interrupted by McCartney's peppy ramble into town to be part of the bustle.

While George and Ringo ease into suburban life, John is envious of his songwriting partner, who has thrown himself into the international art aesthetic, expanding his innovative and intellectual pursuits throughout mid-sixties London. McCartney gorges on the electronic musical experiments of Italian composer Luciano Berio, also studying and later purchasing the surrealist paintings of French artist René Magritte. He seeks out political, social, and philosophical thinkers like Nobel laureate Bertrand Russell, accomplished composers like playwright Lionel Bart, and literary Beat heroes Allen Ginsberg and William Burroughs. He is the first of the Beatles to discover German composer Karlheinz Stockhausen, introducing his type of experimental electronic music into the band's scope.

But now, through his love for Yoko, John will soon gain his own entry into the realm of the avant-garde, with renewed creativity and a passion for the underground. Both men are leaving long-term relationships in the dust: Lennon's six-year marriage, which has spanned the struggle and rise of the most famous band in the world, and McCartney's five-year, extremely public, affair with Asher. And as Paul's car whirs toward Weybridge, he knows that as much as the two men move differently through life's changes, there is still an impenetrable, almost mystical bond between them that has created some of the most gripping, influential, and wildly popular music ever, much of it filled with themes of longing for true love in an infinite search for spiritual connection. That is precisely why Paul could see in Julian where he had once been: alone, frightened, and in need of a song.

CHAPTER THREE

Remember to Let Her into Your Heart

Paul McCartney—Man as Song

> *Music penetrates every pore of the body, moves the body and conscious where it will, and endows those who create it with an incredible power.*
>
> —Dr. Randall Auxier, *Metaphysical Graffiti*

On October 31, 1956, Mary Patricia McCartney died of an embolism after surgery for breast cancer. She was forty-seven years old. Paul McCartney was fourteen. He didn't even know his mother was ill until his father brought him to the hospital to see her as she lay weak and dying. She was here, then she was gone. Moreover, her death left a visceral and lasting void in the McCartney home, not the least of which was her place as the primary breadwinner. Her vocation as a nurse/midwife allowed the family to move from a postwar working-class neighborhood to a middle-class posh council house. Upon her death, a concerned Paul turned to his father and asked, "What are we going to do without her money?" While some observers parse this as a commentary on McCartney's cold, calculating demeanor, it may have better revealed his immediate sense of self-reliance and a preternatural tendency toward steely pragmatism even at a young age. "Over the years it became plain that Paul saw his world shattered that autumn night in 1956," writes Howard Sounes in *Fab: An Intimate Life of Paul McCartney*. "The premature death of his mother was a trauma he never forgot, nor wholly got over."

This tragedy drove young Paul like nothing else could, leading to a self-confidence and unflinching focus on his talent and purpose in life. "Paul is obviously a highly intelligent, level-headed, sensible, and grounded person, and, of course, he's also a bit of a genius, and that's a magic combination to rocket-power a career," Sounes told me. "Tragedy also gives an artist something to reflect upon and write about, and he writes about his mother very fondly. When he talks about her in interviews, he almost cries, *even now*, when he's an old man. Which shows how soft-hearted and sentimental he is."

Mary McCartney represented a strong, self-reliant, educated, and successful female figure to her first-born son and his younger brother Michael. Loving, affectionate, and attentive, she had been the spirit of the McCartney home, duly reflected in her well-adjusted and mostly cheerful sons. "If you ever grazed your knee or anything it was amazingly taken care of because she was a nurse," McCartney recalls in *Many Years from Now*. "She was very kind, very loving. There was a lot of sitting on laps and cuddling." Assertive in stressing proper diction and punctuality along with her acts of compassion for human suffering, she would be a template for Paul's most ardent love songs and a symbol of the women he chose to share his life. A family friend told Beatles biographer Philip Norman: "She was a beautiful person; it came from deep inside her." Crucially, it was her lasting influence that ultimately provided him the empathy and sentiment that would shape his meteoric musical journey.

Take a sad song and make it better

Music was the way Paul McCartney would assuage his sorrow, express his passions, and eventually color his dreams. It was there from the start, naturally, like his hazel-brown eyes and his impish smile. Paul's father, Jim (Paul, whose given name is James Paul, was named after him), had been a professional trumpet player in his own group, Jim Mac's Jazz Band. Fifty-four at the time of his wife Mary's death and struggling to make ends meet as a cotton salesman, Jim returned to his love of piano to relieve his heartache. Seeing his father, a broken man, resurrected through joyous piano playing sparked something in his son. "To this day, I have a deep love for the piano," McCartney said in the late 1990s. "Maybe from my dad: it must be in the genes. He played the piano from when I was born until I was well into the Beatles." McCartney also credits his father, whom he described as an "instinctive musician," with teaching him the intricacies of harmony, which he later used prodigiously in his work with the Beatles. But perhaps Jim McCartney's greatest contribution to the lore of Paul McCartney was a dictum he imparted to his son throughout his youth: "You should learn to play an instrument," his father told him. "Once you do, you'll be invited to the party." Soon, the young Paul was singing in the Anglican choir at St. Barnabas Church and later performed a duet for a talent contest with his brother. The comfort found in music sustained him, then fueled him, until eventually he *became* the party.

Let it out and let it in . . . Hey Jude, begin

Knowing songs was a prerequisite around the McCartney home, where music was everywhere—aunts, uncles, cousins, and friends came and went with tunes on their lips, huddled around the family piano during the holidays performing melodies of all types. Sounes told me, "One of the first things that comes to mind when you dig deep into Paul McCartney is that he is first and foremost a song-and-dance man, a hoofer, an entertainer, because he comes from a family of entertainers, and that's written all over *everything* he does. He just loves putting on a show, and when you speak to people who knew him as a kid, he and his family, his cousins and uncles and aunts, are all full of jokes and laughter, and even today they'll sit down and sing you song before they'll give you a cup of tea. That's part of the McCartney family thing."

Paul recalled to British TV personality David Frost in 2012: "And that's where I heard these old songs. And without realizing it, I was noting the structure of the songs that found their way into *my* songs, because they were already in my subconscious."

Musicologist, assistant department head, and associate teaching professor at North Carolina State University, Dr. Tom Koch described McCartney's unique connection to the music of his youth to me: "Through the relationship Paul had with his father, you get this sense that he just *absorbed* twentieth-century British popular tradition, and it gradually became a part his musical vocabulary, everything that he did with the Beatles and beyond. He *heard* it. And that's part of the trick of it; he was not taught, he could not read music, he relied from the very beginning on a tremendous *hearing* ability."

McCartney *discovered* music, he would say. And it was very much a discovery, as if a hidden gem. And what of these songs on everyone's lips? Might he conjure his own? Making songs for Paul McCartney was as if magic was conceivable. He would be its conduit—figure the songs, massage them, tame them, and share them. One of his first compositions, the auspiciously titled "I Lost My Little Girl," came to him soon after his mother's death. Years later, one of the last songs he would write for the Beatles, "Let It Be," reverentially evokes Mary's name, an echo of a dream in which she comes to him to allay his growing fears about the breakup of his beloved band. The healing of music for McCartney was immediate and absolute, and he developed a burning desire to express it. Years later, reflecting on choosing the themes and tones of his compositions, Paul told his friend Barry Miles: "I often try to get on to optimistic subjects in an effort to cheer myself up and realizing that other people are going to hear this, to cheer them up too."

Dr. Koch notes, "I think there is that kind of empathy that people feel with Paul. He invites them into a conversation that he has when he's performing, and you can't fake that. I think it was always a part of him."

And anytime you feel the pain . . . Hey Jude, refrain

The same year his mother died, McCartney glimpses a photo of the sleek and greasy twenty-one-year-old Elvis Presley and immediately trades in the trumpet his father had given him for a guitar. The echo-drenched moan of Presley's first RCA hit, "Heartbreak Hotel," seals the deal. The foundation beneath his feet shifts. His mind reels. Soon this alien music from the United States, magic in another form, raucous and exciting, begins to find its way onto Radio Luxembourg, as opposed to the stodgy BBC which pompously ignored its existence. He is specifically glued to a late-night music show hosted by Cleveland DJ, an early town crier for the cause, Alan Freed, which floods his fertile musical sensibilities with what Freed was calling rock and roll; featured musicians included the bespectacled Texas song-machine, Buddy Holly; the inimitable inventor of teen-poetry in sped-up blues, Chuck Berry; the sultry-voiced Everly Brothers; and, his favorite, Little Richard, whose shrieking vocal calisthenics he could pristinely mimic. Since he was left-handed, he had to restring his new right-handed instrument, demonstrating another level of his musical erudition. On it, he would learn Eddie Cochran's word-salad boogie, "Twenty Flight Rock," and then move onto the hiccup-ooze of Gene Vincent's "Be-Bop-a-Lula."

You're waiting for someone to perform with . . .

Less than a year after his mother's death on July 6, 1957, fifteen-year-old Paul McCartney's life is transformed when he meets the nearly seventeen-year-old John Lennon. A friend had prompted him to trek down to St. Peter's Church Hall fête in nearby Woolton to see a fellow rock-and-roll obsessive perform. Lennon's band, the Quarrymen, facetiously named after the Quarry Bank Grammar School they had attended, clumsily worked their way through some rowdy tunes on a makeshift stage. Paul is immediately taken by John's charisma—a little bit of that Elvis thing—and how he effortlessly concocts clever lyrics for popular songs on the spot. After the gig, Lennon asks McCartney to join the group simply because he can tune a guitar and flawlessly sing *all* the lyrics to his favorite songs. Once in the fold, McCartney's innate self-confidence greatly impresses the sharp-witted Lennon. They become inseparable.

The connection between the two young men strengthens when, one year later, Lennon's forty-four-year-old mother Julia is struck and killed by an off-duty constable in a drunk-driving accident. John is seventeen at the time and utterly devastated.

Later, in *Anthology,* McCartney recounted, "That became a very big bond between John and me. We both had this emotional turmoil which we had to deal with and, being teenagers, we had to deal with it very quickly. We'd be sitting around and we'd have a cry together; not often, but it was good."

Scott Freiman, lecturer and creator of the popular *Deconstructing the Beatles* series, made sure I understood the pertinence of the impenetrable connection Paul and John forged through tragedy: "I will say that one of the key factors, I believe, in the relationship between John and Paul was that shared experience of losing their mom when they were very young. It's such a horrible thing few people experience, and John and Paul had it within a few years of one another. When you talk about building a friendship with someone, what makes it deeper than all the others in your life is an experience, good or bad, that you share together that no one else has shared. I truly believe that we owe the John/Paul relationship, the one that changed the course of popular music, largely to the deaths of their moms."

Peter Ames Carlin—whose *Paul McCartney: A Life* covers, among other aspects of his subject, the Paul/John phenomenon—told me he believes while their shared trauma fused a creative union, it also expressed a productive dichotomy the young artists used to great effect: "The great contradictions between Paul and John is that John once said,

'Genius is pain,' which is both self-pitying and self-aggrandizing, but also very true in a lot of ways. Many of the books I've written, whether about Bruce Springsteen, Brian Wilson, or Paul Simon, to one extent or another become a study in emotional dysfunction. These are people who have had really tough, emotional lives and process it through their art. Lennon fits neatly into that category, whereas Paul's reflexive position is something closer to 'Genius is a breeze' because he can just sit down, put his hands on the keyboard, and it all just flows right through him. John's grief opened him up and Paul's grief tightened him up, but they both had the same release, which was music."

Don't carry the world upon your shoulders

Years later, Lennon reflected on how much this tragedy had subconsciously affected him and his art. "I never allowed myself to realize my mother was gone," Lennon is quoted in the Beatles *Anthology*. "We have the ability to block feelings and that's what we do most of the time. These feelings are now coming out of me, feelings that have been there all my life. I don't know if every time I pick up a guitar I'm going to sing about my mother, I presume it'll come out some other way now."

Music's impact on memory and emotions can be powerful, but its results can be inexact, as professor of psychology at Bucknell University Andrea Halpern shared with me: "Some of my colleagues have been studying what they call Music Evoked Autobiographical Memories (MEAMs), which are hard to study for accuracy because the only thing you can study in personal memories is self-reported vividness or self-reported emotionality, etc. People do describe some characteristics in their memories that are evoked by music. I'm a little bit of a skeptic that they're any different than any other cue to autobiographical memories, but certainly, like other things in our life, music can evoke autobiographical memories. And whether they're accurate or not, they may *feel* that way."

Serendipitously, as with McCartney's first attempt at musical expression, "I Lost My Little Girl," Lennon's first song, "Hello Little Girl," reflects his musical yearning. He shared in one of his final interviews how he based the song on something his mother sang: "It's all very Freudian, so, I made 'Hello Little Girl' out of it."

"One of the types of memory I study is auditory imagery," Professor Halpern continues. "I do research on what happens when you're 'replaying' memories. And at least for some people, considering their vast individual differences, they report *vivid* experiences when they're replaying. I have a scale to report how vividly you experience auditory imagery, and that correlates with some objective measures, like pitch-matching, and the ability to synchronize to expressive music. So, certain people likely reevoke memories of music more strongly than others."

The search for reconnection with female tenderness and maternal intimacy fired a burgeoning songwriting kinship, something McCartney has described through the years as a special, wordless communication that each understood implicitly. They helped to finish the other's artistic expressions, whether musical or lyrical, feeding off a kinetic energy forged from a shared trauma in youth. John and Paul would write about their mothers regularly, either directly or metaphorically, in their famous songs of love and longing—before, during, and after the Beatles. In one of their first colossal hits, "She Loves You," written in the front room of the McCartney home together, line for line, note for note, the two young men sang its title from the deepest reaches of their souls, *Yeah! Yeah! Yeah!* Reassuring the other through a clever second-person narrative—a device Paul would use when writing "Hey Jude" years later—the two young men offer counsel to a confused friend that the woman he wants does indeed love him and that couldn't be bad, and moreover he *needs* to appreciate this gift, all of it underlined by a pitch perfect *Oooohh!*

McCartney later concluded that the haunting bridge to his most famous song, "Yesterday," one he would play by himself on acoustic guitar with string quartet accompaniment in 1965 at age twenty-three, was a subconscious reference to Mary's illness. In one of the most beautiful melodies ever conceived for a two-minute pop song, he asks why she had to go and admits he finds no answers simply because she provided none. Mary ignored the symptoms to not alarm the family or trouble the doctors she worked with, and consequently the circumstances of her death were kept from him.

Other early examples of Paul's poignant subtexts dealing with loss and longing include "Things We Said Today" from 1964, with its confession of loneliness and fleeting memories expressed from a young man on top of the world, adored by millions, and the misty "Here, There and Everywhere," a 1966 song Lennon revered, with its unashamed need for an undying faith in everlasting love, wherein the narrator hopes for his reflection in a woman's eyes.

Professor of philosophy and communication studies at SIU Carbondale, and author of the delightfully engaging *Metaphysical Graffiti: Deep Cuts in the Philosophy of Rock*, Dr. Randall Auxier offers: "Consider Paul's sense of the finality of death in 'Eleanor Rigby.' As Father McKenzie wipes his hands and walks from the grave, Paul notes that *no one was saved.* There's an anti-Catholic despair that rejects the idea of a reward in the next world. His characters clearly do not believe it, and through them, he is definitely struggling with the idea of faith. Yet, I would still ask; who's telling the story? He is not the people in the song. Instead, he uses the narrator to capture their grief. He's letting us know, he sees it, he *understands* what these people are feeling."

Paul recognizes this connection to grief in the very first song Lennon and McCartney collaborated on, "I Call Your Name," which years later continues to intrigue him. "That was John's. When I look back on some of the lyrics, I think, 'Wait a minute—What did he mean? I call your name but you're not there? Is it his mother? His father?'"

A key difference in Lennon's childhood, compared to the happy McCartney home held together by the familial thread of music, is the absence of a loving and caring father. Years before Julia's death, when John was only five years old (nearly the same age as Julian in 1968), his mother became pregnant with another man's child, causing his father Alfred, a merchant seaman who was mostly absent in their lives, to leave her. Upon his exit, he asked his boy to choose between the two. Lennon chose Alfred, but as he saw his mother start to walk away, he ran to her. He would not see his father again until the Beatles were at their height of fame, and Lennon summarily rebuffed his attempts at reconciliation.

Julia, unable to handle the boy, necessitated her sister Mimi to raise him. Just the same, Julia adored her son, teaching him to play the banjo and supporting his artistic side. But just as John had come to truly know his mother as a person and a mentor, she was killed. "It absolutely made me *very* bitter," Lennon admitted right before his death in 1980. "The underlying chip on my shoulder that I had as a youth got *really* big then."

Unlike his partner, who depicted his mother in his art as a loving angel of mercy, Lennon would chase the ghostly image of Julia for the rest of his life, starkly revealed in his first solo effort, *Plastic Ono Band* from 1970, with emotionally reflective songs like "Mother," "I Found Out" and the gut-wrenching closer, "My Mummy's Dead." However, very much like Paul, his most emotionally fraught songs as a young man expressed his sense of loss—from "I'm a Loser" in 1964, with its telling lyric of having lost someone dear to him, to the following year's "Help!" featuring an opening line that not only forcefully beseeched the need for help from *somebody*, but a voice that would accept *anybody*. Lennon later told journalist David Sheff in an in-depth *Playboy* interview weeks before his murder that the girl with kaleidoscope eyes from his ethereal "Lucy in the Sky with Diamonds" cast an "image of the female who would someday come out of the sky and save me." On his 1966 song "Girl," Lennon remarked: "That's me writing about my *dream* girl again—the one that hadn't come yet. That's Yoko." Years before, arguably Lennon's finest ballad, "If I Fell," touches upon his wounded heart when looking for an elusive love he can trust. For John, Yoko Ono fulfilled the role taken from him as a boy. He would refer to her as "mother" in both private and public for the rest of their time together. Lennon's 1968 sleepy folk ballad, "Julia" evokes *ocean child,* the English translation of Yoko Ono.

"I think from studying John, he possessed more of a consciousness of Yoko as a mother figure than Paul would see in Linda," says Lennon biographer Tim Riley. "I find Yoko to be a combination of Aunt Mimi *and* Julia. She could be very stern like Aunt Mimi and then, like Julia, she could be wildly flirtatious and colorful."

This may explain why "Hey Jude," as surmised by Beatles biographer Philip Norman, had "moved John Lennon like no song of Paul's ever had before." The lines, *Remember to let her into your heart,* and for Lennon, specifically, *You have found her, now go and get her,* caused McCartney's songwriting partner to later remark, "I took it very personally." In an extraordinary turn of events, both men—who had been on a wide-ranging search for women with whom to connect on a profound level throughout their youth—would ultimately come to that very place within months of each other: McCartney ending a five-year relationship with Jane Asher to pursue his new love, Linda Eastman, while Lennon was swept up in a sudden and obsessive love for Yoko Ono.

Adam Duritz, whose stirring songs of romantic longing and loss have filled the Counting Crows canon, surmises: "When Paul sings, *Remember to let her into your heart* . . . and *Remember to let her under your skin* . . . he's not talking about what you get, he's not even talking about what you give. It's 'remember to let her in.' You rarely hear that said in that way in pop songs, it's just not in the format. And that difference is significant. Paul's singing about a fear of commitment and vulnerability, and when he sings *You have found her now go and get her,* the very next line is *Remember to let her into your heart,* only then can you *begin to make it better*. You have to be open to *receiving,* I guess, is the best word. And this takes vulnerability and risk. Vulnerability is *always* a risk. What 'Hey Jude' says is that without that risk it's nothing. It's a wildly insightful line that's easy to pass up, but John understood it implicitly."

"There is always this Beatle-layer of meaning in all their songs, but when you hear John's 'Don't Let Me Down' or 'If I Fell,' he's saying, 'I'm jumping off a cliff here, and I feel totally petrified,'" notes Riley. "Both songs are about the perilousness of falling in love, and how scary it is to fall in love, because it's very risky, and you're setting yourself up—you've been hurt before, and you understand that there are no guarantees here. It is one of the great things about love. You have to make that leap of faith. That's why John sees himself in 'Hey Jude,' which says, 'Let's take this giant leap together.'"

You have found her . . .

Although wildly different personalities in many ways, like their men, Yoko and Linda had eerily similar pasts. Both were the progeny of wealthy fathers—Yeisuke Ono, a successful banker, and Lee Eastman, a prominent lawyer. They both spent part of their childhoods in the same upscale Westchester, New York, town of Scarsdale and each dropped out of Sarah Lawrence College before escaping into the underground Manhattan bohemian scene. Before they met John and Paul, Yoko and Linda had each endured difficult marriages that produced a daughter and, after divorce, became single mothers while simultaneously trying to make their way in the high-pressure, male-dominated worlds of art and journalism. McCartney's biographer Howard Sounes writes: "Two men who had been like brothers since school days were falling for almost identical women."

The "Hey Jude" line *You're waiting for someone to perform with* may have harkened back to Paul's teenage meeting with John but was also quite prophetic, as each replaced the other with these special women creatively and professionally. John and Yoko would release albums in the late-sixties and make performance-art appearances throughout the 1970s, and Paul and Linda would form and play in the band Wings during the same period. "I've always felt that John and Paul bringing their wives on stage was an expression of how they saw a musical partnership as the most intimate union," says Riley. And to add to the uncanny similarities in timing for two kindred spirits, they would soon marry the women who had altered their worlds within ten days of each other in March of 1969. Both famous couples remained together until Lennon's murder in 1980 and Linda McCartney's death, sadly like Paul's mother, from breast cancer twenty-nine years later.

Upon Linda's death, Yoko Ono chose a line from "Hey Jude" to end her *Rolling Stone* tribute to her: "We communicated in deeds more than in words. When she was strong, I felt strong. She took a sad song and made it better."

All of these odd parallels were not lost on John Lennon, who observed to McCartney upon hearing "Hey Jude" for the first time that he was sure the song was about *him*. Twelve years later he called it "one of Paul's masterpieces" and expanded on this assumption in *Playboy*: "If you think about it . . . Yoko's just come into the picture. He's saying. 'Hey, Jude—Hey, John.' I know I'm sounding like one of those fans who reads things into it, but you can hear it as a song *to me*. The words 'Go out and get her'—subconsciously he was saying, 'Go ahead, leave me.' On a conscious level, he didn't want me to go ahead. The angel in him was saying, 'Bless you.' The Devil in him didn't like it at all, because he didn't want to lose his partner."

When McCartney argued that the song, like most songs, was subconsciously about its author, Lennon, realizing the incredible serendipity of both Yoko and Linda entering their lives at the same time, told him, "We're both going through the same bit!"

"These new relationships that they found that were keepers caused them to reaccess the childhood grief about their mothers that had never gone away and always been part of their connection," says Beatles author Rob Sheffield. "And I do think that's why, for John and Paul, 'Hey Jude' was a communication between them. It's one of the many mysteries in a song that everybody knows, yet none of us *really* know, or truly understand."

"Like 'We Can Work It Out' or 'Don't Let Me Down' or 'A Day in the Life,' we can hear 'Hey Jude' as a commentary on their partnership," adds Riley. "It's a song about how it feels to be in a really intimate partnership."

Then you can start to make it better

While filled with mythical affinity, the prolifically successful Lennon/McCartney connection had always been a study in contrast. John Lennon was an angry young man, tending to lash out and display emotion in fury. Paul McCartney aimed to please. Eternally optimistic and amiable, he tapped into the spices of life. Paul was open. John wary. Paul smiled. John grimaced. "When I used to talk to John about his childhood, I realized that mine was so much warmer," McCartney shared in *Anthology*. "I think that's why I grew up to be so open about sentimentality in particular. I don't really mind being sentimental. I know a lot of people look on it as uncool. I see it as a very valuable asset."

Both young men absorbed their shared obsession very differently. John saw music as vengeance, an outlet for his inner strife. To him, rock and roll was the sound of the working class rising up. Consequently, the teenage Paul viewed music as refuge, salvation, a blessed distraction. For him, rock and roll was an expression of youth and fun. They wrote songs apart, then together. Together turned out to be better. Dark rage mixed wonderfully with irrepressible bliss. Resonant chords meshed seamlessly with sweet melodies. And while these distinctions are found in their directly collaborative efforts, it was when they worked apart, using each other as a sounding board to complete a song or improve on it, that their distinctive personalities emerged.

"This was a songwriting partnership that, for them, was much more than even a brotherhood," says Riley. "It was a kind of a mystical union of their minds."

A prime example of this creative duality is found in the Beatles' 1965 #1 hit, "We Can Work It Out," with McCartney's combative yet hopeful calls to *work it out* set against Lennon's sternly phrased counterpoint about life being too short to muck up with petty disagreements. Two years later, in "Getting Better," McCartney's hopeful tone shrewdly comingles with Lennon's snarky reference to things having already hit rock bottom. This too can be found on the Apple single of "Hey Jude," an empathetic song of reassurance, backed by Lennon's raucous flip-side, "Revolution," filled with dubious rancor for the underground movements of 1968.

Author and professor Walter Everett told me, "I think the enigmatic balance between John and Paul is central to the Beatles; their different interests and approaches, and the way they were very much in competition—one writing a song that drew from a recent one by the other, for instance, kept them from sticking to formulas, kept them growing."

"The simplicity and earnestness of 'I Want to Hold Your Hand' is also there with 'Hey Jude,' but the songs offer two totally different things—a sense of yearning becomes pushing someone to keep going and offering comfort," notes singer/songwriter Kiley Lotz. "And I think these sentiments arrive with maturity, to be able to write it sincerely without sounding contrived comes with time for John and Paul as songwriters."

"I think Paul is the more original thinker of the two," says Professor Auxier. "This is because Paul doesn't work from the outside-in, he works from the inside-out. What you'll discover is that his thoughts are built around feelings. If you look at his earlier songs, like 'When I'm Sixty-Four,' it's mostly sentiment, whereas by about 1965 or '66, he's moving away from sentiment and into *feeling*—deep, interior feelings, and not just his own. Lennon had tremendous insight into how you felt, but he didn't care, at least not very much, because if he did, he wouldn't have been so cruel, so often, to so many. Whereas Paul never had the reputation for cruelty. He could feel what other people were feeling, and, of course, 'Hey Jude' is about just that."

Sheffield recalls: "Part of why I loved 'Hey Jude' as a little kid was it was surprising to hear one man singing to his male friend and having the kind of conversation that I would go on to find as an adult is very rare for two adult men to have."

The conflicting and ever-evolving John/Paul personality traits were not intractable. Oft times the roles were reversed; Lennon, the hopelessly naïve romantic, easily led astray by faint hope of passing fads, set beside McCartney's suspicious pragmatism and an uncanny proclivity to stand aloof from a subject with intrepid objectivity. Lennon's infinite search for a guru, a messianic figure to allay his insecurities forged in youth and exasperated by fame and drug abuse, would almost always be met by McCartney's respectively lukewarm shrug-and-nods. Whether considering John's obsessions with the band and its entourage living on a Greek island, embracing the notions of the weird con man Magic Alex's outlandish technological whimsies of building flying saucers and designing wallpaper with sound, or even the Beatles' famous trip to India to study Transcendental Meditation with the Maharishi Yogi, John's instincts eschewed evaluation while Paul clearly preferred measured strategy, even with regard to experimental sojourns into art and sound, especially his music and its messages.

Take the narrative of "Hey Jude," with its suggestion that Jude *can make it better* by taking that next step to happiness on his own and set it against Lennon's demonstrative philosophical specificity of "All You Need Is Love"—a step-by-step journey to realization versus giving yourself over to an axiom. The year before "Hey Jude" was released, the double A-side single "Strawberry Fields Forever" backed by "Penny Lane" played with themes of boyhood touchstones juxtaposed with sardonic psychedelic expressions. Both arrive at the same place, but from opposite viewpoints—McCartney's "Penny Lane" is a character/geographical study of weirdly framed but staunchly English archetypes, whereas Lennon's "Strawberry Fields Forever" remains one of the most introspective searches for an elusive but availing inner peace set to music. Moreover, while John could be coyly vague in his songwriting, Paul approached his songs with headstrong maturity. John also used the pop form to roguishly play with words, while Paul mostly got straight to the point.

When Paul first played "Hey Jude" for John in the summer of 1968 at his London flat on Cavendish Avenue, he was unsure of a lyric that he used as a place holder. For a decade, they had worked tirelessly bouncing phrases off each other, changing titles and stanzas, developing new narratives that expanded song themes as two craftsmen do. Paul, in particular, locked in first on melodies that he was worried might flit away, so he would supplant nonsensical syllables that worked; examples include singing the words "Scrambled Eggs" in place of "Yesterday" or

"Ola Na Tungee" as a stand in for "Eleanor Rigby." As John listened, Yoko at his side, McCartney noted that the ambiguous line *The movement you need is on your shoulder* would soon be replaced by something less "crummy" that made more sense. "You won't, you know," Lennon intervened. "That's the best line in it." Recognizing the power of oddly formulated words that might tilt heads and raise eyebrows, a talent his partner excelled at, allowed McCartney perspective. And since each writer's opinion in the songwriting process weighed heavily in final decisions, the line stuck.

Beatles author and Lennon biographer Tim Riley cites, "When McCartney brought him 'Hey Jude,' Lennon was so thrown he could sense this was an earthquake of a song that nobody else could have come up with; a great weaving together of all the things that were going on in their personal and public lives, the life of the world and the life of the culture they participated in. It was the perfect statement for them to make as a single at the end of that summer and Lennon was re-intimidated in that moment by McCartney, and respects the song so much, he pronounces it finished. He doesn't insist on putting his fingerprints all over it. And you can imagine how that impulse was very strong in Lennon, because he knows when McCartney would turn in weak lines or bridges and he'd fix it, saying, 'You need me here.' He didn't do that with 'Hey Jude,' although I've checked the dates, and there are two or three days where they work on the song at McCartney's house in London, and it's not clear exactly what they're doing, but Lennon never came out and said, 'Yeah, I fixed that third verse.' He always told everyone, 'That's McCartney's thing.' He lets stand the public story about the song, which is very revealing about their method and their respect for one another. It's one of McCartney's great moments."

Later McCartney mused, "So, of course you love that line twice as much because it's a little stray, it's a little mutt that you were about to put down and it was reprieved and so it's more beautiful than ever."

"In the history of the John/Paul collaboration, this was a moment between them that they both remembered and they both prized and treasured, and, to me, that's really beautiful," says Sheffield. "*The movement you need is on your shoulder* is about moving forward. I'm not saying it makes a lot of sense as a linear expression, but, for me, it's 'You don't need a hand on your shoulder to push you forward, just follow your shoulder and move forward.' *You* have to lead the movement."

"If you listen to that line in the context of social and political change, it could be interpreted as a call to action," says professor of sociology from Michigan's Grand Valley State University Joel Stillerman. "It could also be taken as a call to personal change to resolve improvements; the responsibility is 'on your shoulders.' It's wonderfully ambiguous."

Adam Duritz notes: "It echoes the earlier line, *Don't carry the world upon your shoulders . . .*, but it's interesting because in that one he's saying, 'When you're hurting, don't assume that you have to bear all this weight yourself, there are people who will share it with you.' But then at a later point, he echoes that same sentiment by saying the opposite—*The movement you need is on your shoulder*, or *you* can do it."

Bob Costas, the host of NBC's *Later*, asked the composer in 1991, eleven years after Lennon's murder, if there was a moment when he's on stage that he feels the emotion of his songs the way the audience does. "Most of the time I don't get that moved, because I'm thinking of words, like an actor in a dramatic part, you're really thinking of your next line," McCartney said. "But there is one moment in 'Hey Jude,' because I hadn't done it in so long, this one line that always reminded me of John, and that used to get me emotional. *The movement you need is on your shoulder*. It would creep up on me and catch me unawares. It was always quite emotional to sing that line."

Singer/songwriter Eric Hutchinson says, "It's interesting, when I try and analyze that line, to me it reads as a more poetic version of something being right under your nose the whole time, the movement is on your shoulder as, 'Hey, look over there . . . there it is' or a bit of a *Wizard of Oz* click your heels three times and go home. There's something almost naïve about it."

"I've never felt the need to intellectualize it beyond being a very novel way of expressing a very simple sentiment, which is the strength that you need to get through this, to survive, even though you don't think you can do it, is within you," concludes author Devin McKinney. "The movement that you need to push this thing out of your way is *literally* on your shoulder, you can do it! I think that's a beautifully magnificent human sentiment—not the strength, but the *movement* you need is on your shoulder is just enough off a conventional rendering to make it magical. It's so lodged in our memories, it has us talking about it all these years later. And it was John's brilliance that he told him not to change it. He knew that the product of your unconscious is telling the truth."

Then you begin to make it better

The answer to Professor Riley's question of what Lennon and McCartney were doing in those days after *the movement you need is on your shoulder* stayed in the song forevermore can be found in their acute faculty to mesh their distinct voices, strategically imbued into "Hey Jude." Lennon's nasal solemnity harmonizes beautifully with

McCartney's angelic croons from the start, taking early cues from the Everly Brothers and a host of doo-wop masters: the Drifters, the Five Satins, the Ink Spots, and the Del Vikings—whose "Come Go With Me" was McCartney's first record purchase. Intertwining their voices, sometimes switching the roots and thirds and fifths of chords within the same phrasing, provided a richness to their initial, less experimental work and later seamlessly adorned the Beatles' musical evolution. This is evident in "Hey Jude," as much a McCartney vehicle as any of the band's songs, as Lennon's subtle but crucial harmonies punctuate lines such as *Remember to let her into your heart* and the final *Hey Jude, don't make it bad / Take a sad song and make it better*. Riley duly writes in *Tell Me Why*: "It's their best duet since 'If I Fell,' not only for its sense of shared experience but for its similarly effortless intricacy—the harmony is just as affecting as the melody it complements, Lennon's presence on the last verse makes what would have been a great solo more of a *band* experience, strengthening the power of what would have been a solo tour de force."

Riley expounded on this to me: "It is just so slyly beautiful what Lennon does in that song. He doesn't participate until the final verse, where he does this very subtle backup harmony, and then he leaps up on top of McCartney and takes the upper harmony, . . . *then you can start* . . . That is the *only* time I can identify in the whole Beatles' catalog where Lennon sings *on top* of McCartney. So, it becomes this perfect Beatle moment—along with all the other layers of meaning. It's similar to what McCartney does for John on 'Don't Let Me Down' the next year, this beautiful counterpoint that you don't even notice. It is Paul and John shadowing the other very respectfully."

Music journalist Steven Hyden writes in his 2020 "The Best Beatles Songs, Ranked" for *Uproxx*: "If the backstory here is messy and incoherent, it's only because the deepest and most meaningful relationships of anyone's life typically unfold in strange and unpredictable ways. You love each other, but you're destined to drift apart. You hate each other, and yet your family-like bond makes it impossible to stay mad. I think about all of this during the last verse, when John gingerly sings with Paul about taking a sad song and making it better. For me, it's the tear-jerkiest moment of the Beatles career."

"'Hey Jude' may be very Paul, but then you get this John harmony underneath it," adds Eric Hutchinson. "This is what makes the Beatles *always* so creative. There is a duality in it."

The Lennon/McCartney songwriting craft, at first, was not so unique; framed in the classic verse-verse-chorus-bridge-chorus structure found in the origins of trite popular music, it would quickly blossom into ranges untried in the form, culminating in McCartney's brash experiment to write a song with no true chorus until the end, an ending that the Beatles could evidently not contain. "Hey Jude," a song of comfort and finding and accepting love, was a nod to their past, present, and future. Teen songs of love, pining, loss, and lust of the early 1960s evolved into questions of existence, spirituality, and introspection. Sitting across from each other, working—as Lennon told *Playboy* in 1980—"eyeball to eyeball" in close quarters for hours, these emotionally scarred young men imagined stardom, transformation, adulation. They imagined the Beatles.

The movement you need is on your shoulder

Not long after joining John's little group back in 1957, McCartney brings in his young friend, barely fifteen years old, rough-and-ready

George Harrison, to enhance the guitar sound. Soon the lads will drop the English skiffle music fad, played on washboards and badly tuned guitars, in favor of the electric dazzle of rock and roll. By 1960 they are a well-oiled unit, seeking a more appropriate name. The Quarrymen become Johnny and the Moondogs, and then Stuart Sutcliffe, an art school chum of Lennon's, whose plunking away at a bass he could barely fathom earned him a place in the band, considered a mash-up of Beat in honor of beloved American Beat writers like Jack Kerouac, Allen Ginsberg, and William Burroughs, and Beetles, an homage to Buddy Holly and the Crickets. This eventually becomes the Beatles.

Underaged but undeterred, joined by the dour but handsome Pete Best on drums, they are booked in the German red-light district of Hamburg, playing for ten hours a day, seven days a week in a grueling trial by fire—over three months, some five to eight hundred hours—getting tighter and more intense as a performing unit. It is here in the squalid environs of sweaty clubs among the German demimonde that the band learns to extend songs for an hour at a time, laying on a groove and playing to the crowd, evoking singalongs with Ray Charles' "What'd I Say" and Jerry Lee Lewis' "Whole Lotta Shakin' Goin' On." The seeds of *Na . . . na . . . na . . . na na na na* are being sown.

"I'm assuming if you're a band playing in Hamburg every night and you need to fill five hours of set time, there's a couple times where you're like, 'Let's just go around and around and around,'" says Eric Hutchinson. "And that's sometimes where the magic is in a song. In the case of 'Hey Jude' or any song, you would do a groove like this in the studio, but the Beatles, who we know are all about brevity, might fade it out at two-forty-five just as it was getting interesting. The idea that they just let it run makes it a daring choice for a pop single, but not for a band *finding its groove*."

Keep people singing, give them a show, is the order of every day into night. "Mach Shau!" the rowdy German audiences would howl. On stage, these hormone-raging teens with greasy hair, leather jackets, and tight-fitting jeans hobnob until dawn with drunken servicemen, gangsters, and prostitutes, learning to drink, take speed, and stumbling into sexual awakening. Mostly, they learn to entertain an audience with wild abandon; they figure out how to perform as one, have each other's backs, and stay the course. Somewhere about this time, John and Paul receive their iconic Beatle haircuts—most likely inspired by the style of young German existentialist, art student, and photographer Jürgen Vollmer—during a quick trip to Paris, transforming the duo into a visually homogeneous unit. Back in Hamburg, Astrid Kirchherr, another of the band's first photographers, catches Stuart Sutcliffe's eye and soon their sort-of bass player quits, making way for Paul McCartney—having purchased his signature Hofner violin bass during the band's second German stint—to settle on the instrument that will define him. Playing basic guitar riffs and having to fill in the workload for subpar musicians, McCartney, already gifted with natural musical skills, develops one of the most uniquely melodic bass styles in rock and roll. Moving from guitar with a piano background, he revolutionizes its place in songwriting and accompaniment.

The band returns to England as conquering heroes, building their bona fides around Liverpool. Then, after backing established rocker Tony Sheridan as the Beat Brothers on record, they begin working in the now legendary Cavern Club, where Rory Storm and the Hurricanes, with beatnik-bearded Richard Starkey a.k.a. Ringo Starr on drums, rules. Soon they will replace Best with Starr's steadier approach. Well versed in showmanship and tight from the German experience, the Beatles become the Cavern's house-band, playing some 290 shows from the winter of 1961 into 1962.

Thanks in no small part to Paul McCartney's discoveries of various music styles across generations as a youth, the early Beatles' repertoire was spectacularly diverse. It included hokey show tunes, Marlene Dietrich's "Falling in Love Again (Can't Help It)" and Roaring Twenties staples, "The Sheik of Araby" and "Ain't She Sweet," and even foreign fare, "Bésame Mucho," a song Paul learned from his father. McCartney delivers one of his finest early vocals on "Till There Was You" from the hit musical, *The Music Man*, featured on the Beatles' second EMI album *With the Beatles*. Their rock-and-roll palette, laid before them from their worship of Elvis Presley and Little Richard, ranged from New York City's famed Brill Building teen hits written by Carole King and Gerry Goffin to rhythm-and-blues numbers by Jerry Leiber and Mike Stoller to an embrace of the Phil Spector classic, "To Know Him Is to Love Him," which developed their glossy three-part harmonies.

The days Paul spent with the family around the piano singing the classics was a wonderful precursor to the Beatles' embrace of Broadway tunes, girl groups, church hymns, Delta blues, and Liverpool shanties, all of which found their way into John and Paul's early writing. Learning these indomitable hooks, clever uses of slang, changes in keys, how to build verses into bridges and then into easily identified refrains—all became the foundation for one of the most prolific and successful songwriting partnerships of the latter half of the century.

In their 2019 study of the Beatles' oeuvre, *What Goes On*, musicologists Walter Everett and Tim Riley point out that because Paul and John could not read music, they relied on their ears—McCartney's preternatural abilities since childhood—to tap into hundreds of songs from every genre. They conclude: "Musicians can learn so many songs so quickly and thoroughly only if they have already deeply assimilated many aspects of song structure, poetic practice, and melodic/harmonic voicing and function."

"John and I wrote together something like three hundred songs," McCartney recalled to David Frost on Al Jazeera in 2012. "We would meet up, sit down to write, and three hours later we'd have a song. And never, *never* did we have a dry session. We never left saying, 'We can't figure it out.' We always wrote a song. And I look back on it and think, 'That's pretty amazing.'"

"It's crazy to think of John and Paul writing together as teenagers, because when I think about so many of my friends who are professional musicians now growing up playing music together at fifteen years old, and to watch someone become the musician that they become as an adult, is a really profound experience," says Kiley Lotz. "They were these inseparable creative partners, and then being in a band is such an intimate thing; it's like a marriage, it's becomes your family. And that can also be tough. It's really interesting to think of these kids as the Beatles, who are now understood as one of the greatest bands of all time."

By the mid-sixties, and from then on, McCartney expanded his musical frontiers first with Lennon, and then alone, inside and beyond the Beatles. While relying on the approbation of his partner for a solo excursion, as in "Hey Jude," he found a singular voice as an expressive balladeer ("Michelle," "Here There, Everywhere," "Fool on the Hill"), an unflinching rocker ("Can't Buy Me Love," "I'm Down," "Paperback Writer"), an experimentalist in independent film (avant-garde–inspired Super 8 films and the Beatles' *Magical Mystery Tour*), art (investing in and forming the *International Times* and London's Indica Bookshop and Art Gallery), and soundscapes (tape loops and editing techniques for the Beatles' "Tomorrow Never Knows" and the unreleased, "Carnival of Light" as well as the film soundtrack for *The Family Way*). While he could pick out songs and carry his own on piano as a kid, and later during frantic moments on stage in Hamburg, the kid who watched his father's emotional resurrection on the instrument took proper piano lessons in his early twenties that helped shape his composing—"For No One," "Lady Madonna," "The Long and Winding Road" and, of course, "Hey Jude."

"While I don't think the Beatles would ever first be thought of as a piano band, they did center many of their finest later songs on piano, especially Paul," says Hutchinson. "And 'Hey Jude' is a throwback to all that stuff McCartney loved because he listened to it with his dad, sort of this old Broadway and Brill Building songwriting style. It's funny that the guitar became so synonymous with rock and roll because just as many of the early stars played piano; Fats Domino, Little Richard, Jerry Lee Lewis, and the piano is very heavy in a lot of those Chuck Berry songs, and Paul and John loved them all. I'm sure it also had a huge effect on later rock artists like Elton John and Billy Joel. Pretty much anyone that's ever tried to write a pop song on piano owes something to 'Hey Jude.'"

Beyond the music that first sustained and later completed him, what never left Paul McCartney was the empathetic nature of his mother's love. Although he could be calculating in professional relationships, serially unfaithful with women before marrying Linda, and just as mean-spirited as John in that Liverpudlian school-boy way, it was Mary's spirit that shown brightest in Paul. He drew from it when interacting with fans, many of which he invited into his Cavendish Avenue flat for tea. "Paul was at his best allowing ordinary people to share in and enjoy his celebrity," Howard Sounes observes.

Mary's sense of empathy was on display when Paul demonstrated compassion to his contemporaries in need. When Rolling Stones' founder Brian Jones was in trouble with the law over drug issues and even members of his own band seemed to discard him, McCartney invited him into his home. McCartney was also the only rock star to write to art dealer Robert Fraser when he served his drug sentence in 1967. In the mid-eighties when Fraser was dying of AIDS, Paul and Linda spent time by his side. Perhaps only rivaled by the gregarious Ringo Starr, Paul was the Beatle most amenable to the press. One in particular was the chain-smoking, straight-talking Judith Simons, a journalist with the *Daily Express*, who had covered and befriended the group as it gained popularity in the early 1960s. Simons became something of an older sister figure to Paul. For years, Simons would tell anyone who listened that she was the inspiration for "Hey Jude," and Paul, even though he knew better, never refuted it. In fact, on her ninetieth birthday he wished her salutations in an email that began, "Dear Judith, or should I say Hey Jude."

Michael Lindsay-Hogg, the director of several Beatles music clips, including the legendary "Hey Jude" music video and eventually the last Beatles' film, *Let It Be*, emailed this recollection of McCartney to me: "Paul was and is a man of real charm, in that he really connects to whomever he talks to. He is tough but enthusiastic and interested, looking for take as much as give. He knows who he is: one of the greatest songwriters and musicians of the twentieth century, a member of the most famous group of all time. But I found him always good to be with and talk to."

As noted, Mary's care for Paul and his brother and her dedication to nursing appears in one way or another in much of his work—most notably in the aforementioned "Lady Madonna," the other Beatles' #1 hit of 1968 released five months before "Hey Jude." Using the Madonna or Mary, Mother of Jesus, as one of his ready characters—another Mary—McCartney wrote one of pop music's first tributes to the sacrifice of motherhood. He had hinted at his understanding of the older generation with his "Your Mother Should Know" from *Magical Mystery Tour* the year before. He told Barry Miles: "I always hated generation gaps. I always feel sorry for a parent or a child that doesn't understand each other. A mother not being understood by her child is particularly sad because the mother went through the pain to have that child, so there is this incredible bond of motherly love. So I was advocating peace between the generations. In 'Your Mother Should Know' I was basically trying to say your mother might know more than you think she does. Give her credit."

Well into his post-Beatles' years, McCartney's two biggest solo hits resounded with humanistic themes of brotherhood and togetherness: the nostalgic "Mull of Kintyre," equaling the American popularity of "Hey Jude" by remaining nine weeks at #1 on the UK charts in 1977, and the painfully sweet "Ebony and Ivory," a duet with the inimitable Stevie Wonder, which spent seven weeks at the top of the *Billboard* charts in 1982. Neither song was particularly connected to the zeitgeist; the bagpipe-adorned "Mull of Kintyre" could not have been more tone-deaf to the late seventies punk period and "Ebony and Ivory" came along many years after songs of racial harmony were in vogue. It did not matter, for the art of song had a special connection for McCartney as a healing measure in his life. He originally wrote "Hey Jude" to comfort his friend's son; the song also provided solace to those in a youth culture clamoring for a glimmer of hope from the Fab Four, who had brought a needed exuberance in the early 1960s that endured for the remainder of that transitional decade.

"Almost all of the songs from his solo career speak to Paul's sense of 'rallying the troops,'" notes Beatles lecturer Scott Freiman. "Everyone knows someone who is always trying to make people feel better, trying to resolve fights. I won't say Paul was *exactly* like that, but he certainly was the guy in the Beatles who worked to keep the band going, telling them, 'Hey guys, let's put on a concert, let's do a movie, let's do this, let's do that' and that extends to his role for the fans of the Beatles and his solo work, where he does love those healing songs and getting everyone to sing along at his concerts. There is something psychologically built in him to want that attention, to want to lead, get people moving, and inspire people. I think 'Hey Jude,' even though it started out as a song to comfort John's son, Julian, became very quickly a song to John, a song to himself, a song to the audience. *Take a sad song make it better* is a really beautiful sentiment that has meaning well beyond just talking to Julian."

"'Hey Jude' is the ultimate song of comfort, of not giving up and throwing caution to the wind to go for it, even if it doesn't work out, showing vulnerability in an age of macho man bullshit," says Kiley Lotz. "I don't know if you can offer that to people without having had some experience that you lived through and then seen the other side of, which doesn't necessarily require being older. Some younger folks have endured so much and find themselves on the other side creating."

"It is an interesting angle to cite Paul's empathy, because he is not known for his empathy in the studio or in his personal relations," Walter Everett wrote to me. "It's in the music that it appears more readily. His 'Here Today' (from 1982) is a very touching tribute to John Lennon, as was his ukulele accompaniment to 'Something' as an ode to George Harrison. And 'Calico Skies' (from 1997), a very pretty folklike tune, is a fitting and loving tribute to Linda."

"I try to maintain a separation between the artist and his art," says Devin McKinney. "Is Paul an empathetic human being in his daily life and his dealings with other people? Many times, I'm sure he's been the biggest bastard in the world. But when we talk about Paul being empathetic, we're filtering that through the feeling that we get through his music, and his music is among the most empathetic that's ever been recorded. And that is *real,* regardless of whether he talks shit about someone or if he slept around on Jane Asher or if he didn't do the right thing in his personal life at every point. That's biography, not *the art.* You look at his music, and empathy is the organizing principle of his creativity. Music is the only reason we're even talking about his private life, that's where the empathy blooms, and that is *absolutely* real. I don't think anyone could deny that Paul is an enormously empathetic person in his art."

"Earlier in their career, John and Paul were writing for themselves, while a bit later they also had to think of selling songs," reasons Professor Halpern. "So, it's difficult to separate the motivations, but you can certainly write about loss and grief without *actually* feeling it yourself. I think it's a mistake to assume that artists, whatever medium they're in, are actually feeling an emotion or they're trying to capture it, because that's what art is. You can't merely deduce that every piece of art or music is written because the person is tortured or happy. That could be the case, of course, but true artists try to *capture* other people's experiences."

"I agree with the idea of empathy, but I'm not sure that the empathy is conscious on Paul's part," says Dr. Auxier. "That is, I don't think it would matter to him much whether he's aware of it. It's just the way he is, and it's just the way he writes. But he has tremendous insight to go with that empathy, and 'Hey Jude' is a perfect example. Listening to his vocal, you can imagine Paul seeing into Julian's insecurity, and it's the kind of advice you could give to a six-year-old. It also works just as well for somebody who's twenty-six having the same struggle to find a new love and avoid making his world a little colder."

"The fact that it was so easy for Paul to sing this song for Julian, when it was something that was so impossible for John to do, is one of the fascinating spiritual elements of the song," concludes Rob Sheffield. "And 'spiritual' may be a difficult and slippery word to talk about when we discuss music, but with this song, it's really hard to avoid the fact that Paul is displaying a level of compassion that was very unusual for somebody in the Beatles' scene, especially John. Try to imagine another sixties rock star, Mick Jagger or Keith Richards, doing something like that on their day off! For any twenty-six-year-old male to reach this level of instinctive empathy and maturity is honestly tough to imagine."

Shaken by the death of his beloved mother, a sensitive, bright-eyed, and determined Paul McCartney found consolation in music and almost immediately understood it like few others around him, save the troubled kid with a similar desire to see in rock and roll a guiding light—two Liverpool lads finding two others to set a course for fame and fortune. Early drafts of the line on the original lyric sheet for "Hey Jude" read: *She has found you, now go and get her* instead of the later form *You have found her* . . . The subtle but crucial difference between the two provides insight into the origin of a song about a boy dealing with a broken family, but might indeed also be about its composer, his songwriting partner, their mothers, and the new women in their lives. It says that sometimes fate, love, connection, in life and music, comes *to* us, and we only need to be receptive to it. But then Paul changes it to a theme of discovery, as he *discovered* music as a way to rise from the ashes of tragedy, and then *discovered* the Beatles, as a vehicle for his art. The power and prominence, the inspiration and joy that John, Paul, George, and Ringo would provide a generation and beyond is a story found in the musical notes and underlying message of "Hey Jude." And while John Lennon would eventually honor Julia with his first-born son, whom he named Julian, and Paul McCartney named his first-born daughter, Mary, the memories of their mothers live on in their music, which they share with the world.

CHAPTER FOUR

Don't Be Afraid

Jules as John as Us

When I write, I'm just writing a song, but I think themes do come up. You can't help it. Whatever's important to you finds its way in.

—Paul McCartney, *Conversations with McCartney*

During the hour-long ride out to Weybridge, Paul McCartney sings to himself, perhaps *for* himself, and for his songwriting partner and his son, whom he describes as "a fragile little kid."

Hey Jules . . . don't make it bad . . . take a sad song . . .
and make it better . . .

Paul recalled in *Anthology*: "It was optimistic, a hopeful message for Julian: 'Come on, man, your parents got divorced. I know you're not happy, but you'll be OK.'"

McCartney expounded on his empathy for children caught in circumstances beyond their control in *Many Years from Now*: "I always feel sorry for kids in divorces. The adults may be fine but the kids . . . I always relate to their little brain spinning round in confusion, going, 'Did I do this? Was it me?' Guilt is such a terrible thing and I know it affects a lot of people and I think that was the reason I went out. And I got this idea for a song, 'Hey Jude,' and made up a few little things so I had the idea by the time I got there."

As Paul pulls into Kenwood Estate, Cynthia Lennon is surprised but pleased to see her old friend, whose obvious concern for her and Julian's welfare leaves her touched. "It made me feel important and loved," she writes in her memoir, *A Twist of Lennon*. "As opposed to feeling discarded and obsolete."

In grand McCartney fashion, the smiling "cute Beatle" gets down on one knee and hands Mrs. Lennon a rose, exclaiming, "How about it, Cyn? How about you and me getting married?" The two have a great chuckle about that. Cynthia then recalls Paul sheepishly sharing his shame about being caught in bed with another woman—not even Linda—by his fiancée Jane Asher that lands as a final coffin nail to his engagement. This is, of course, unnervingly similar to John's being discovered by Cynthia. "Paul blamed himself [for the breakup] and was heartbroken," she remembered later.

The two old friends also commiserate on the emotional rollercoaster ride that is John Lennon—his charms, his moods, his mean-spirited barbs and random but cherished kindnesses. It's over for Cynthia. And how much longer will it last for Paul? There is a part of him, beyond the glib and grinning exterior, that knows his creative and spiritual partnership with John is tenuous at best. In many ways, it always has been. Perhaps John finding Yoko and him finding Linda is pulling them further from each other.

"They both needed to have strong partners, one way or the other," says author Peter Ames Carlin. "They had been each other's strength from their teenaged years all the way until 1968. When that was losing its emotional effectiveness, and the connection between the two of them began to fray, they each found a woman to replace the bond."

For well you know that it's a fool / Who plays it cool / By making his world a little colder

For the barely six year old Julian, the visit is akin to any of Paul's trips to Kenwood or the holidays they shared—playing with Uncle Paul, his father nowhere to be found.

"He told me that he'd been thinking about my circumstances all those years ago, about what I was going through," Julian Lennon, a pop star in his own right, told *Mojo* magazine in 2002. "Paul and I used to hang out a bit—more than dad and I did. We had a great friendship going and there seemed to be far more pictures of me and Paul playing together at that age than there are pictures of me and dad."

Six years before that interview, an anonymous bidder paid twenty-five thousand pounds for McCartney's scribbled "Hey Jude" recording notes. It turned out to be Julian Lennon, who years later still cherished his relationship with his father's partner. "Every birthday and every Christmas, he sends a card," recalled Julian. "He's never missed. I find that amazing."

"Julian Lennon was sort of the forgotten child," says Adam Duritz. "After John and Yoko had Sean, he became the *real* Lennon child. Everybody forgot about Julian until he put his record out in the Eighties, so as the years passed 'Hey Jude' must have been even more meaningful to him."

"It's weird how Paul is modest about the kind of emotional generosity that other people around him notice," says author Rob Sheffield. "It was very easy for him to be generous to Cynthia and Julian in ways that they remembered for the rest of their lives. Whereas it was very difficult for John or anybody else in the Beatles' circle to consider doing anything like that. I can't even begin to process that Paul, with all the other distractions and temptations available to him on a summer afternoon, spent it going to check on the two of them. That's a mind-blowing anecdote that can't be fully explained, this instinctive, impulsive warmth and compassion on Paul's part. It's not an emotional gesture a twenty-six-year-old male is usually capable of making, and for Paul it was just another day."

Singer/songwriter Dan Bern adds: "When you consider what we think of as John and Paul's relationship, and later with the breakup and everything around that time, that Paul is singing this comforting song to John's son, there's something *really* sweet about that."

McCartney has told the story in several interviews over the years that once when he was playing tag with young Julian, Lennon pulled him aside and asked him how he was able to do it. It made Paul sad because he knew of John's difficult upbringing as an only child and how affection had not come easily for him, whether giving or receiving. Years later, after the breakup of the Beatles and the ensuing public acrimony between the two, when Paul visited John, his friend ran up to him to give him a hug, which at first startled McCartney. Then as John repeated, "Touching is good," it gave him pause. "If I ever hug anyone now, that's a little thing that sticks in my mind," Paul told Barry Miles.

"He was right, but the thing is, I actually knew it more than John did, he was only saying it because he was discovering it. I don't think he had a lot of cuddling, certainly not from his mother, because he wasn't even allowed to live with her."

In the absence of tangible social expressions, Lennon chose to pour his deepest feelings into music. Just two months before Paul's visit to his family, John, wrestling with guilt over never being there for his son during the height of Beatlemania and then leaving his family so abruptly, penned a lullaby for Julian, "Good Night." Even then, he balked at singing it, handing it over to Ringo. Years later Julian admitted to author Steve Turner in his *A Hard Day's Write: The Stories Behind Every Beatles Song* that he never knew the song was for him.

And so, Paul knows what he has to do for Julian, because John cannot. As the songwriters help to complete one another's compositions, adding something the other is incapable of imparting musically or lyrically, McCartney steps in for his childhood pal. The visit is also a reflection of Paul's love for John's mother, Julia, for whom Julian was named. Spending time at Julia's house in the first year of their partnership, Lennon's mother would dote on his young friend, empathizing with his having lost his own mom. Julia was also, like Paul's dad, quite adept at making music and encouraged both John's and Paul's early pursuits. A long-time friend supporting the family of his brother-in-arms is rewarded tenfold, for that hour-long ride sparks perhaps the finest song in the plethora of great ones written by Paul McCartney.

"I've always been a massive Beatles fan; their music is just in a different league for me, emotionally speaking," young songwriter Jesse Epstein of Imaginary Future emailed me when I reached out to him after viewing his unerringly tender version of "Hey Jude" on YouTube. "I grew up listening to them since I was a baby, and I think their songs just seeped into my consciousness. So, they just feel different to sing. With 'Hey Jude' in particular, I've always loved the place it came from, and knowing that Paul wrote it to comfort John's son is just so moving. There's a real softness there in the message of the song that I wanted to emphasize in stripping it down. When I sing it, I imagine hopefully comforting a child of my own one day."

Jackie McLean, composer-performer in the husband/wife band Roan Yellowthorn, emailed me a similar sentiment when I shared with her the origins of "Hey Jude": "All my life, I have been looking for fathers. I find them in men who are older than me. Who believe in me. Who want me to succeed. Who show me kindness and care. You can't have enough surrogate fathers, really. It's a search I'll likely continue all my life." Jackie McLean is the daughter of acclaimed singer/songwriter Don McLean, whose songs, especially the lengthy "American Pie," recall McCartney's sense of melodic and lyrical sentimentality. Jackie's public honesty about their severed relationship casts a greater light on her response to the song. Much like Julian, she finds comfort within it that was lacking in her dealings with her own father. "Once I learned that Paul McCartney wrote 'Hey Jude' in order to comfort John Lennon's son, it became the song of a surrogate father to his surrogate child," she wrote. "A song of comfort. Of reassurance. Of hope. It's a song of encouragement. Of imploring. You can feel Paul's soul shining through in the warmth of his voice and the earnestness of his words. You can feel how much he cares. You can feel the love in the song. It permeates the words and melody. I can hear a surrogate father in this song speaking to me—telling me that I can get through this moment. That everything is going to be all right. And I believe him."

"When Paul sings, *You're waiting for someone to perform with . . .* he's addressing a signature moment of loss in someone's life, a sudden division when your parents get divorced," notes Adam Duritz. "You're not the family unit you used to be, and you're not the full person you used to be either. It could be very easy to go through the rest of your life feeling like you're missing something, that you're waiting for that something to complete you, and you don't have to. The song says, 'You're enough.' And it's not even about necessarily being sufficient alone, it's that you're sufficient to love someone too, that you are enough for everything the world will ask of you."

"I know it's about Lennon's son, but that's not what I think about," says singer/songwriter Seán Barna. "I've always heard this song as a pep rally. Every stanza is a vague gem of advice—we know, or can reasonably discern, the literal meaning of the words as they are put together, but we never know why the narrator chose to say any of it. In other words, immortal songwriting."

Kiley Lotz agrees: "The universality of, 'You're gonna be okay' is timeless. That encouragement to acknowledge our own personal failures or fears of inadequacy is something we can all be pushed to embrace, especially in the digital age where we're trying to present the best versions of ourselves all the time. Even for musicians, not only are you a musician now, you're a fucking internet influencer! I didn't sign up for that. I'm a person, and songwriting for me is trying to connect with personhood for myself and trying to understand the things that I don't understand. And for that 'Hey Jude' reminds me that I don't know how to write a song like that yet—a song of comfort without an air of self-deprecation or apology. I certainly don't feel like I'm in a position to tell someone else that it's all gonna be okay. I'm still struggling with that myself. And 'Hey Jude' is so important for songwriters for that reason. We know that we can embrace that honesty and it can be good without being cheesy or contrived. And also, it tells us, 'Who gives a fuck about being too cheesy?' All these things you start fretting about don't matter."

And in 1968, with no smartphones or handy digital recorders to capture it, the nascent melody of "Hey Jules" has to stick. Noting his and John's edict that if they couldn't recall a song, it is likely not good enough to finish, Paul relies on its strength.

"It's funny how melodies would come to Paul in the car, because most of my songs come to me when I'm in the car driving," says Lotz. "It's always during a lengthy drive by myself where I find myself humming it over and over again, so I won't forget it and by the end of the trip if it doesn't stick then maybe it wasn't meant to be or it wasn't that good. I think driving makes you focus on the immediate and relaxes another part of your brain that allows you to have ideas easier. It's as if it's happening to you instead of making it. If you remember it, then maybe you have something."

McCartney indeed remembers it and has something. Something special. Returning from his altruistic sojourn, McCartney retreats to the top floor music room of his Cavendish Avenue apartment to work out the chords on what he refers to as his "magic piano," a small upright model manufactured by the respected Alfred Knight company, which had the proud distinction as the only other model displayed in Steinway Hall alongside the manufacturer's own renowned pianos. It has served Paul well over the past year as he has composed all of his growing number of keyboard-driven tunes on it—"The Fool on the Hill," "Martha My Dear," "Lady Madonna."

McCartney recalled to his biographer Barry Miles: "It had a lovely tone, that piano, you just open the lid and there was such a magic tone, almost out of tune, and of course the way it was painted added to the fun of it all."

Duly impressed with the psychedelic paint job that Dudley Edwards, Douglas Binder, and David Vaughan had done on a Buick 6 sports car owned by Tara Browne (the Guinness heir whose later fatal car accident formed the first verse of "A Day in the Life"), Paul commissioned the celebrated pop art collective to perform the same visual expression on his beloved "magic piano." The three artists had come to prominence during the Swinging London days of the mid-to-late 1960s. In addition to customizing cars, they transformed furniture and wallpaper into far-out colorful expressions of the time. Their psychedelic murals appeared in the London boutiques of King's Road and Carnaby Street, which brought them to the attention of the rock community. The Beatles would eventually retain their services to transform their own Apple fashion boutique, as the band had indeed transformed the Western world, and so Paul, a man inculcated in London art circles, wished to give his piano the same allure.

Staring out the window of his home, McCartney's hands glide over the keys of his "magic piano," and the crude but memorable melody formed in his car begins to take shape, as does his emotional promise to Julian that he could find *better* in the darkest of times.

This warm ballad with a most notable ending will soon manifest itself in the grand theater of the Beatles, an unfathomable machine of power and influence as the pop world has ever seen.

CHAPTER FIVE

Let It Out and Let It In

A Very Brief History of the Beatles: 1963–1968

Excitement wasn't in the air, it was *the air.*

—Greil Marcus, "The Beatles,"
The Rolling Stone Illustrated History of Rock & Roll

Thousands of books, articles, theses, and psychological and social treatises have been rendered on the Beatles as a uniquely cultural global force. Some of them even mention that they composed and performed music which, when discussed with hushed reverence, oft times reaches beyond mere historical perspective. "With the Beatles it feels like with every passing generation you try to give your kid some kind of classical music background," says Dan Bern, who has taught classes and spoken at symposiums on songwriting. "In terms of rock music, or pop music, twentieth-century music, the Beatles feel like getting a grounding in Beethoven, the classical undertones of *everything*."

"Young kids today really respond to the Beatles," notes sociology professor Joel Stillerman. "Because, well, people still respond to Mozart and Beethoven."

"When I was a kid, I was obsessed with the Beatles, the energy of it was contagious," recalls Kiley Lotz. "These people were making history, creating things that didn't exist before, which was so exciting to me. The idea that you can make something totally new that no one has heard before is so compelling. I don't think I would have wanted to start writing music, if not for my parents' love of the Beatles. Some of the first songs I learned on piano, like 'Eleanor Rigby' became a part of my life."

"I started to rethink the incredible impact of the Beatles since the movie *Yesterday* came out," notes philosophy professor Randall Auxier. "Its premise is that this young musician has a temporal experience and wakes up in a world where nobody knows the Beatles and spends his time trying to recollect every Beatles song, so he can become a star by taking them as his own. And the argument of the movie is that these songs are so great that it wouldn't matter when and where you put them, they would be hugely popular at *any* time. And when Ed Sheeran makes an appearance in the film as himself, I get to thinking, is Ed Sheeran even possible without the Beatles? Never mind Sheeran, what about the Rolling Stones and David Bowie or any pop music? Could you *actually* have as rich a musical culture *without* the Beatles?"

Tim Riley, Beatles author and associate professor and graduate program director at Emerson College in Boston, shared with me how he explains this very point to his students: "Many of them were born between 1999 and 2003, so most of them know the biggest pop culture phenomenon in their lifetime is *Harry Potter*. Okay, so take *Harry*

Potter as a touchstone that *everybody* knows and multiply that by about a thousand, and you haven't even come close to the impact of the Beatles in the sixties. You could not get through a day from 1964 to 1970 without hearing a Beatles song, seeing a Beatles image on TV, or seeing something about them in magazines and newspapers. It is impossible to describe how big it was."

"And it only lasted a few years," says Adam Duritz. "The Stones last *fifty* years, the Beatles last ten? And they have just as many songs that we can all hum, maybe *more*. Way more, actually, what am I talking about? No one comes close."

Ten years of music that continues to delight us today, which is covered distinctly in Rob Sheffield's *Dreaming the Beatles: The Love Story of One Band and the Whole World*. The author expresses their enduring legacy to me this way: "There was a time in the seventies and eighties when people thought of the Beatles as something that happened in the past. It's funny how in recent years it's just become clear that the Beatles are not something that happened, the Beatles *happen* every day. And it's not limited to one moment, or one country, or one generation, or one culture, or one language. The Beatles are everywhere in ways that are just weird and uncontrollable and it just never stops. Even the Beatles themselves in their most arrogant, egomaniacal moments wouldn't have imagined this."

Beatles expert Scott Freiman perhaps sums it up best: "There's no other band or other artist, Frank Sinatra, Elvis, Queen, Prince, where every note of every song is known so well and that you can get an audience from five to eighty-five in one room all enjoying the same music."

Then you can start to make it better

Beginning in earnest during the autumn of 1963—when the term Beatlemania had first surfaced in the British press, much of it spurred on by the band's October 13 appearance on the popular *Sunday Night at the London Palladium* variety show, reportedly drawing fifteen million viewers while thousands more were captured on camera stampeding woefully unprepared constables outside—the Beatles phenomenon began to swell into something of a secular religion. "You could actually taste the noise," is how Radio Luxembourg DJ Jimmy Savile describes the moment before he introduces the band to a typically piqued Beatles' audience. Andrew Loog Oldham, the Beatles' first publicist and later manager of the legendary Rolling Stones, framed the experience in *Stoned: A Memoir of London in the 1960s*: "The roar I heard was the roar of the whole world . . . the noise they made was the sound of the future."

One year after the band released its first UK single, "Love Me Do," a rather pedestrian introduction to what would be in the ensuing months the most radical expression of popular music ever, the Beatles ruled the world with songs that, according to authors Walter Everett and Tim Riley, "sprang from some collected dream-life, a mass Jungian unconscious, instantly creating its own possibilities, contexts for new realties, reviving unselfconsciously dormant spirits."

Powered by an unfathomable succession of smash hits; "Please Please Me" (#2), and three chart-toppers, "From Me to You," "She Loves You" and "I Want to Hold Your Hand," four mop-topped, suit-wearing, boot-kicking lads from Liverpool dominated the realm of entertainment. Twenty-three-year-old John Lennon—guitar, harmonica, and lead vocals; twenty-one-year old Paul McCartney—bass and lead vocals; twenty-year-old George Harrison—lead guitar and lead vocals; and twenty-three-year old Ringo Starr—drums and, yes, lead vocals would move swiftly beyond chart supremacy to alter the machinery of the music business; shift the parameters of Western culture in fashion, comportment, and social experimentation; and, in the process, redefine pop stardom.

When inducting the Beatles into the Rock and Roll Hall of Fame in 1988, Mick Jagger of the Rolling Stones, who would emerge in the wake of Beatlemania and the resultant "British Invasion" of the early sixties pop world, called them a "four-headed monster." And so they were. Dressing in unison, singing in unison, bobbing and *whooo-ing* and bowing in unison, the band was a singular, impenetrable, visual and aural monolithic force, impeccably groomed in tailored suits as suggested by their manager, Liverpool entrepreneur Brian Epstein. They were also a well-oiled performing engine from hundreds of hours of agonizing gigging. By the time this juggernaut reached America's shores in February of 1964, cementing its influence on coming generations with their appearance on the *Ed Sullivan Show*, which attracted an estimated seventy-three million viewers (thirty-four percent of the nation), they summarily annihilated the *Billboard* charts. In April of that year, the top five songs in the United States belonged to the Beatles.

The Beatles in America was a transformative generational moment, a pivot toward an upward youth trend that was palpable. As the year that many historians have marked as the one that framed the perception of the "sixties" began to unfold in the wake of this grand spectacle, the Beatles ushered in the bright future promised during the atomic age.

As in England—where the Beatles served a similar distraction in October of 1963 when British prime minister Harold McMillan was forced to resign in disgrace in the wake of a sex scandal in his cabinet that stunned the nation—America was ready for the Beatles; in part, the hysteria that embraced their initial arrival in New York City was a joyous reaction to brazen foreigners beguiling a nation still in stunned horror from their young president having been struck down in his prime by an assassin a little over two months before.

Perhaps the truest diversion of Beatlemania was in its tangible healing. Shaken by the Civil Rights Movement (the Beatles refused to play to segregated audiences, causing venues in the South to relent) and still mired in 1950s conservatism, America was rescued by four kids from Northern England who paid homage to the stateside originators of rock and roll, many of them African American artists who were forgotten or simply unrecognized for their immense contributions to the genre. Reviving interest and building upon their legacy served to congeal the power of Beatles music beyond imagination. "One of my hats is as a historical sociologist, so I'm always interested in the incipient things that were happening before an event that helped make that event possible," says Professor Stillerman. "And while the Beatles seemed new, they were not particularly countercultural in the kind of music they were playing or the way they represented themselves. They seemed, at first, to be squeaky clean and less sexually provocative as Elvis before them, at least not intentionally. But when we consider what *produced* the sixties as a cultural phenomenon, we first accept the demographic changes, but there are also cultural precursors that were already on the scene but existed more as subcultures than as mass popular phenomena—jazz musicians in the 1940s, who were innovators in music, fashion, experimentation with drugs, and the way that they inspired the Beats up through fifties rock and roll and the creative production and fandom in the 1960s. The Beatles absolutely benefited from that seedbed of cultural activity and would at first revive and then exponentially expand it, along with other art forms, over the next few years."

Scott Freiman adds: "The history of the times, and the fact that so much of it was about change, the Beatles' immense popularity meant they were both caught up in it, and, in a lot of ways, its leaders as well."

In his thoroughly enjoyable *Magic Circles: The Beatles in Dream and History,* Devin McKinney writes, "At certain points in the sixties, the feelings people had for the Beatles and for the world around them came together and formed a magic circle, a sphere of fantasy within which mutations of thought were formed, the unimaginable was imagined, and action was taken."

Author Peter Ames Carlin surmises: "Are the Beatles a function of the media? Are they a function of the times? There's part of me that believes in the way artists can channel light beamed down through the universe, that they're not necessarily in control of, and the Beatles, together, channeled and created a light that was so overwhelmingly powerful that teenybopper girls would have orgasms watching the Beatles play, which when you think about it you have to ask: Does that happen? I mean, a lot of other bands have been really powerful, but does *that* happen? I'm not in the demographic, so I can't tell you, but the fact that the Beatles could be so intense that unsophisticated children would have *that* visceral a reaction, while on another level a classical music critic in England is also writing about the Aeolian cadences in their music is hard to fathom."

While teenage girls scream, prompting observant teenage boys to start growing their hair and looking for those fancy Beatle boots, the press, smitten by the band's wit and bravado, hail their every move. Celebrities clamor to be near them. The business world quakes. Promoters, television shows, radio stations—anything with a cash register comes calling. Their likenesses, as Professor Riley recalls, were ubiquitous. Beatles merchandise—wigs, lunchboxes, combs, plastic guitars, buttons, games, models, pillowcases, and on and on and on—came from everywhere. In July of 1964, a feature film was released. Unlike the cheap crap being peddled to exploit the band, *A Hard Day's Night* was actually quite good, and John, Paul, George, and Ringo were good in it. Film critics, ready to pounce, were charmed. It's noir flamboyance, cheeky dialogue, and groundbreaking cinéma vérité shifted the foundation of pop art. It would earn over a million and half dollars and receive two Academy Award nominations.

The initial stage of Beatlemania was a winning streak never before conceived of nor duplicated in the annals of show business. No more a stupefying example of this may be the band's first album, *Please Please Me,* beginning a thirty-week run at #1 on the British charts, only to be dislodged by its sophomore release, *With the Beatles.* For two years between 1963 and 1965, eighty-two of ninety-three weeks, a Beatles album reigned. This continued unabated through the rest of the decade with another three movies, an animated television series, a phalanx of singles, thirteen EPs and twelve albums, not including a ludicrous number of compilations, foreign releases, and so forth. There was the Beatles and then there was everything else.

Most of the everything else was the aforementioned "British invasion" that sailed into chart success on the enormous Beatles' wave; Gerry and the Pacemakers, Herman's Hermits, the Dave Clark Five, the Small Faces, and dozens more made up a quarter of the *Billboard* charts starting in 1965 and remained there for the rest of the 1960s. Many of these groups simply imitated the Beatles' hair, fashion, sound, and demeanor, launching a burgeoning rock movement that by decade's end would become the biggest moneymaker in entertainment, youth or otherwise.

But by 1966, this all left the band exhausted, hounded, and isolated. Peter Ames Carlin succinctly describes one Beatles' tour of America as "a portable riot; hysterical and loud, far beyond reason, perpetually on the verge of destruction." The only way to escape was to cease appearances and concentrate on expanding their musical notions, which had proven time and again to rise above the vacuity of fame. "Yesterday" with its string quartet and, later, the addition of the sitar on "Norwegian Wood (This Bird Has Flown)," the experimental backwards tracks on "I'm Only Sleeping," strange reverb-induced epics such as "Tomorrow Never Knows," and somber elegies like "Eleanor Rigby" would be impossible to perform live, especially during a time when the band could barely hear itself on stage amid the din of shrieking adolescents. Lennon bemoaned: "Beatles concerts are nothing to do with music anymore. They're just bloody tribal rights."

It also appeared that the whole deal had become too monumental, as the band began receiving backlash for its once enviable brashness—lowlights include Lennon remarking that the band was "bigger than Jesus," which resulted in the burning of their records in the American South; the unintended snubbing of Philippines' First Lady Imelda Marcos, which caused an international furor so great they barely escaped the country alive; and the rather unsubtle admission to the playful use of illegal substances that cracked open the counterculture façade and mainstreamed psychedelics. The bizarre undercurrent of Beatlemania featured death threats, mauling by fans, being mercilessly pelted on stage with their favorite candy, and having the sheets in their hotel rooms shorn and sold on the black market. There was constant stalking at their private residences, as fans spat at their families and girlfriends for their preferred status inside the sanctum. Infirm children were led backstage for blessings. There was no life, normal or otherwise, outside the bubble.

The Beatles needed a respite, and they had much to reflect on in the winter of 1966. They'd laid waste to the construct of a music business once run from office buildings first in New York City—Tin Pan Alley and later the Brill Building—and then in Los Angeles, with its high-rise record company towers and gleaming teen-idol factories. Venerable songwriters like Irving Berlin, who hated rock and roll and was not shy in stating it, as well as songwriting teams that had once worked tirelessly to control the pop music world in cramped, smoke-filled rooms were now being replaced by the voices of youth culture, which exploded with the baby boom after World War II. From 1941 to 1961, more than sixty-five million children were born in the United States alone. At its apex, a child arrived every seven seconds. They had now come of age and openly welcomed contemporaries singing songs that reflected their times.

"The social subject called a teenager didn't exist prior to World War II," notes Professor Stillerman. "And with postwar prosperity, they had leisure time and access to disposable income for radios and record players, so they can start drawing on influences beyond the nuclear family and school, which leads them to challenge authority. This made young people very receptive to popular music, which greatly contributed to a push for change that went on from the 1950s through the sixties into the seventies—cultural change, in the universities, in foreign policy, in our relationship with the environment, in sex roles, and so on."

Professor William Boone of North Carolina State University, lecturer on the history of pop music explains: "The Beatles made middle-class white kids feel like they could have their own band. They saw the Beatles on the *Ed Sullivan Show* and decided, 'This is not something I can just watch on a stage, this is something I can *do*! Me and my three friends in the suburbs have something to say.' And when the Beatles moved in a more artsy direction, well, they can do that too. 'We can be artists! We're not just suburban kids with guitars anymore, we're *artists*.'"

This art had a unique perspective for Beatles fans, as Professor Alexander Shashko of the University of Wisconsin points out: "One of the things I cover in my classes is the distinction between the Beats and the early rock and rollers and how they're both challenging the conformity of Cold War containment culture in the 1950s, and yet in terms of who they were and what they aimed for, they were different. The Beats wanted to drop out of society to live in an alternative fashion, while those in rock and roll wanted to *make* it, and by doing so wanted to get out there and change what was considered popular and shift what was at the center. This is later reflected in the politics of the late 1960s when the Beatles released 'Hey Jude.'"

Scott Freiman adds: "Here you have the Beatles as generational spokesmen, who start out as nice clean-cut guys, even though they really weren't underneath, and as they start to move forward—longer hair, facial hair, psychedelic clothes—they're bringing a whole generation with them. And while I wouldn't necessarily say that they were the innovators behind all of it, in fact they were often times jumping on the rails as the train was already moving, but because of their position they *became* leaders for these movements. They didn't discover meditation, but when the Beatles do it, everyone suddenly gets interested in it. And that I think it is a big part of their story."

As Lennon pointed out to journalist David Sheff in 1980: "Whatever wind was blowing at the time moved the Beatles, too. I'm not saying we weren't flags on the top of a ship; but the whole boat was moving. Maybe the Beatles were in the crow's nest, shouting, 'Land ho,' or something like that, but we were all in the same damn boat."

The Beatles, especially musically, had developed the uncanny ability to tap into their times while simultaneously pushing movements forward, acting as both a sounding board and as prophets for where the growing counterculture might go. From the exuberant expression of young love in "She Loves You" (1964), to societal anxieties in "Help" (1965), to reflections on mind expansion in "She Said She Said" (1966), to a sense of universal philosophy in "All You Need Is Love" (1967), the band presented its single and album releases as grand proclamations. Critically acclaimed and smash-hit albums, *Rubber Soul* and *Revolver*, shifted the axis of rock and roll forever. Everett and Riley write in *What Goes On*: "A key to the Beatles' protean imagination lies in how they kept ascending new summits only to redefine them as springboards, not endpoints."

"The Beatles are a lasting statement for their times and beyond, and the reason their music is still relevant today, is the pure fact that the Beatles were just *that* good," says Dr. Boone. "The music was so well written and so well put together. Look at the trajectory from '63, '64 to '68 and listen to how their music evolved. They were absolutely fearless in what they were willing to try. That's how you go from 'I Want to Hold Your Hand' to 'Tomorrow Never Knows' in three years! It's the quality of the work that deserves to stick around."

The Lennon/McCartney songwriting output was so prolific, even the second- and third-rate material they whipped off for Brian Epstein's stable of artists like Cilla Black, P. J. Proby, and Billy J. Kramer and the Dakotas made or topped the charts. For the first time, a pop act's publishing was put on the London Stock Exchange, and the Beatles were such a boon to the British economy Buckingham Palace announced they would receive four MBE (Member of the Order of the British Empire) medals handed to them personally by Queen Elizabeth II.

For the remaining years of the decade, the Beatles would deftly move from marking new ground and reflecting its culture to becoming its center. The crowning achievement of this is *Sgt. Pepper's Lonely Hearts Club Band,* a genre-altering psychedelic epic that held the world in its sway during the summer of 1967. From its very inception, and for decades to come, the album would be hailed as the greatest artistic achievement of the period. Once again, the Beatles had dismantled what had come before—the long-player used for filler around hit singles—and turned it into something else entirely. Some called it high art. Others, marketing. Still others, bombast. Nearly everyone called it genius. *Sgt. Pepper's* featured a high-design concept cover, its lyrics printed on the back, and music within that defied comparison. It was Paul McCartney's idea to take a band that could no longer adhere to the restrictions of Beatlemania and give them a new identity; and the rest of the group followed suit, their appearances morphing into the styles of Swinging London with mustaches, granny glasses, and flowing paisley Carnaby Street clothing replacing the monochrome four-headed monster.

"This was sunset on the mop tops," cites Tim Riley. "The front cover of *Pepper* is a graveyard. It's over. It's a new chapter. 'We have mustaches . . . deal with it.'"

During this new incarnation, the Beatles expanded on themes beyond the usually trite confines of a pop song, exploring different character narratives—in some cases several in one song, as in "She's Leaving Home," a McCartney composition that imagined a young girl running away from home, with Lennon's added parental responses. As in their most recent albums, in which the subjects for songs ranged from illicit affairs ("Norwegian Wood"), financial woes ("Taxman"), loneliness ("Eleanor Rigby"), Hindu tenets ("The Word"), and quotes from the *Tibetan Book of the Dead* ("Tomorrow Never Knows"), *Sgt. Pepper's* investigated a variety of themes: identity, "Fixing a Hole"; mind-expanding drugs, "Lucy in the Sky with Diamonds"; advertising, "Good Morning, Good Morning"; charity, "With a Little Help from My Friends"; mythology, "Sgt. Pepper's Lonely Hearts Club Band"; aging, "When I'm Sixty-Four"; Eastern philosophy, "Within You Without You"; mundanity, "A Day in the Life"; spousal abuse, "Getting Better"; and lust, "Lovely Rita."

Each songwriter developed his own persona—Lennon, acerbic and fanciful; McCartney, playful and romantic; while Harrison swung from deeply philosophical to haranguing. Inspired by fellow sixties maverick Bob Dylan to take a more studied approach to popular music messaging, they had returned the favor by influencing his swerve into electric music. Another composer from whom the Beatles had taken inspiration, Brian Wilson, the creative force behind America's Beach Boys and their groundbreaking album, *Pet Sounds,* would state that *Sgt. Pepper's* had "eclipsed the whole music world."

"The idea of pop culture being talked about fifty years later is a product of the Beatles' mid-sixties output, especially *Sgt. Pepper's,*" says Dr. Boone. "People expected their pop culture to be trendy and disposable.

The Beatles were on the forefront of redefining this idea of 'What is pop?' *Sgt. Pepper's* is an *artistic* statement, and because it was celebrated as such, for us now, we put it on the same par as a classical piece by Arnold Schoenberg. The sixties were the first time that rock musicians claimed that kind of space for themselves, and the broader culture went along with it. Combined with the cultural shift throughout the decade, these lofty assertions allowed people, the counterculture specifically, to look at things that way. From JFK to the Civil Rights Movement to Vietnam, there was a major cultural shift that seemed revolutionary, and along with it is the Beatles breaking totally new musical ground that resonates even today."

Beyond its influence, there was an immediacy to the Beatles' music. Due to their spectacular hold on the charts and extraordinary success as generational spokesmen, the entirety of their support group, from record company, EMI, to its studio, Abbey Road, hopped to the band's whims. Sometimes within mere weeks, Lennon and McCartney could bring in a song, the band would convene around intrepid producer George Martin, and crank out a world-class recording. A single was due? It was duly written and recorded, then pressed with grand efficiency, packaged, and sold to the world in record numbers. The best example may be "All You Need Is Love"—the Beatles' contribution to the June 25, 1967, "Our World" live broadcast, the first-ever international, satellite television production. Beamed to nineteen nations, the two-and-a-half-hour event was seen by an estimated four hundred million viewers, the largest television audience ever. It needed an anthem. Lennon's song of positivity fit the bill. It was recorded in the first weeks of June, mere days after the monumental release of *Sgt. Pepper's,* and debuted two weeks later; then it was released as a single two weeks after that. Within the month, it was #1 everywhere.

The eventual escape from Beatlemania and the maturation of the band's innovations translated to their personal lives, as Lennon, Harrison, and Starr decamped to the London suburbs. McCartney dabbled in a pivotal relationship with Jane Asher, moving into her parents' London home in early 1964 and residing there for three years, immersing himself in upper-class notions before settling into his bachelor pad on Cavendish Avenue, a mere stroll from EMI Studios in St. John's Wood.

Along with domesticity, there were business concerns; accountants, publishing, merchandising, promotions, studio costs, royalties—and while most of this was handled by the band's manager and tutor, Brian Epstein, the band members had become more aware of their positions of financial power, just as they had come to voice their opinions in the studio over their mentor, George Martin, who had successfully manned the producer's role at EMI Studios for all of the Beatles' recorded material. By the end of 1967, although the four-headed monster was loping forth unimpeded, there were signs that it could move in several directions at once.

One year to the day before the release of "Hey Jude," August 27, 1967, Brian Epstein was found dead at his London home of an overdose of barbiturates. "I knew that we were in trouble then," John Lennon told *Rolling Stone* in 1970. "I didn't really have any misconceptions to do anything but play music and I was scared. I thought, 'We've fuckin' had it.'" When Epstein pulled the Beatles from relative obscurity, massaged their image, and engineered their ascent to stardom, his authority over the band's enterprise was absolute. In an instant, as with Paul and John's beloved mothers, he was gone. "Brian's death uncorks this giant, familial dysfunction," says Tim Riley. "Virtually every decision made after Epstein's death appeared as if a knee-jerk whim with no foresight."

The band kept making groundbreaking music and remained a cultural guiding light but, for the balance of its historic run, the Beatles were a rudderless ship that sometimes ran off course. The first public missteps occurred when *Magical Mystery Tour*, a televised film conceived originally by McCartney but embraced by the push-the-boundaries aesthetic of Lennon, flopped; the press turned on the Beatles for the first time. Soon afterward, leading into 1968, other factors would cause acrimony, paranoia, and fractions within the band that would never again fully coalesce, leading to a growing public perception that the Beatles' pristinely harmonious image was fraying.

This included the Beatles following guru Maharishi Mahesh Yogi to his ashram in Rishikesh, India, to take part in a three-month Transcendental Meditation retreat in February 1968, which ended badly when the Maharishi was accused of seducing young women. While Harrison bristled at the accusations, it was McCartney who, in the absence of Epstein, nestled into the role of group spokesman, telling the world, "We made a mistake. We thought there was more to him than there was." Lennon later told *Rolling Stone* that when Maharishi asked why they were leaving, he replied, "If you're so cosmic, you'll know why." The heretofore unchallenged forerunners of the youth culture looked duped and summarily disillusioned by the fact that there was no "there . . . there," when for the past few years they had sung about a "there" with rapt enthusiasm.

In May, Lennon and McCartney traveled to New York for the public unveiling of the Beatles' new business venture, Apple Corps. Formed several months earlier as a plan to create a tax-effective business structure, centering on record distribution, film production, technological advancements, peace activism, and even education, they described it to

NBC's *Tonight Show* audience as "a controlled weirdness" and likened the setup as "rather like a Western communism."

"Apple was part of the sixties ethos—we can do this better than our parents," says Tim Riley. "The people we've worked for our whole lives have done nothing but screw us over and underestimated us and packaged us wrong and if we get control of that end of it, we can finally make sense of it in a way that we could be proud of."

The ill-conceived enterprise, which included a pitch to the creative world that anyone could show up at the Apple London offices with notions of stardom, began almost immediately hemorrhaging money. The underqualified staff hosted elaborate parties and made useless purchases stemming from decisions inspired by the nearly three-thousand-year-old Chinese Book of Changes, the *I Ching*. "It's a classic story of creatives trying to take over the business without knowing how to run a business," says Riley. Eventually, the erratic spending turned into outright looting of the offices. The closing of the Apple Boutique turned into a ransacking by fans. Although Apple would more than soldier on as an entity for both Beatles and ex-Beatles music, its public failures became a symbolic requiem for the love generation and another glaring example of the Beatles' sudden fallibility.

Insularly, when the Beatles began working on what would be the White Album in late May of 1968, John's new love was suddenly a constant presence. Yoko Ono, a strong, highly opinionated woman, eviscerated the band's male-dominated construct, and Lennon's insistence that she remain there became an emblem of the slow erosion of their once immutable solidarity. "Yoko was a gifted and tough-minded artist who earned her stripes in the avant-garde and who, if she'd stayed in that world, wouldn't have been judged for her disinclination to be cute and cuddly," says author Devin McKinney. "Her coolness would have added to her aura—though not as much as if she'd been a man. As it was, she made a partnership with someone who was worshipped almost beyond human scale, whose words and actions were seen, and were often meant, as challenges to his fans and to his fame. So, she entered a spotlight where millions rather than thousands felt free to condemn her, often in racist and misogynist terms. And she stood up to all of it, even later when her husband was murdered before her eyes."

"Lennon sees the only way to break through his relationship with Paul and his immersion in the Beatles is to just tear a hole in it," says Riley. "And he thinks; 'I have just found the most beautiful tear in the universe. And its name is Yoko Ono.'"

Exacerbating matters, Lennon and Ono started dabbling with heroin. The Beatles' use of drugs is well documented. In the early days, band members used speed/uppers in the Hamburg clubs to manage the arduous hours and later in the studio for energy and focus. Then in the mid-sixties, marijuana opened up their creative horizons, and by the mid-to-late sixties, experiments with cocaine and especially LSD had taken hold. But heroin was a singular statement by Lennon to further remove himself from the inner circle. Although Ono is quoted in Peter Brown's *The Love You Make* as first trying the drug with Lennon while in exile as "a celebration of ourselves as artists," Lennon later excused it as an emotional reaction to the contemptuous affront his affair with Ono had engendered within his band. "We took H because of what the Beatles and their pals were doing to us," Lennon remarked. "They didn't set down to do it, but things came out of that period. And I don't forget."

The mood of the White Album gradually became bleak. Each member of the band spent time in separate studios creating their songs, sometimes merely using the others as a backup band, if using them at all. Patience frayed, and sometimes paranoia set in, as each member accused the others of not giving it his all for *his* song. Loud screaming matches prompted the band to excuse the engineers from the room. Time was wasted on needless takes and retakes to sate egos. After a month of this, McCartney confronted Lennon, accusing him of sabotaging the sessions. Lennon lashed back, refusing to act anymore as Paul's "sideman" for what he deemed crowd-pleasing musical treacle which he mocked as "granny music shit." The band's guiding principal, George Martin, had to excuse himself from the proceedings, instructing his assistant Chris Thomas, all of twenty-one years old in his first sessions, to babysit for a while. After weeks of constant bickering, lead engineer Geoff Emerick quit the project.

Take a sad song . . .

The four-headed monster was being felled by each part moving in different directions and sometimes viewing the other three as adversaries. On a deeper psychological level, this fracturing was a painful reminder of their exclusive union. As Scott Freiman notes: "Only John, Paul, George and Ringo experienced 'becoming the Beatles,' which no one in the world could possibly understand. This created a deeper connection. They were inseparable, because, at first, they *had* to be out of sheer survival starting out and then dealing with immense fame. Only they could conceive of what was happening to them; not managers, family, wives, or anyone else. Those types of things *never* leave you."

As 1968 unfolded, it became a time of reflection for the group. At the dawn of the year, the first official Beatles biography, compiled by

British journalist Hunter Davies, was released, and with the advent of Apple, talks began regarding a full-length band documentary. For the first time since their meteoric rise, the Beatles were considering their legacy and the need to forge a firsthand narrative of what had transpired during the wildest of rides. Perhaps looking to the past to better understand their current conflicts was a significant sign that they understood the end was in sight.

This may have been part of the nostalgia McCartney felt when he took his ride to Weybridge to serenade a broken family. With John Lennon mired in heroin addiction and seeking refuge with Yoko Ono, George Harrison and Ringo Starr feeling disregarded by the band, and the growing responsibilities within Apple Corps, it had fallen to Paul to rally the troops. His ability to process conflict in life's narrative—as he had done as a pragmatic boy faced with trauma—seemed to drive him to push the band into new ideas, take charge in Apple's offices, and answer for the band's missteps in the press. And while this forge-ahead method would prove flawed by the beginning of the following year when the idea of the band continuing on no longer appeared plausible, in the summer of 1968 the Beatles were still a viable musical entity with now three solid songwriters producing quality records.

"Hey Jude" is one of those records and, of course, it is Paul McCartney who writes it. He is, after all, still fully immersed in the Beatles and is, in many ways, its shining avatar.

As biographer Philip Norman observes in his *Paul McCartney: The Life*: "There were already fears that the Beatles mightn't last forever; an awareness that their life together maybe hadn't brought the supreme happiness we all presumed, and that strange discontents and doubts were starting to gnaw at them. But one, at least, seemed to stand for continuity. Paul still maintained a flawless Beatle cut, wore the latest Carnaby suits, attended West End first nights, signed autographs and kept smiling."

And so, McCartney, cornered by accusations of taking over the group, losing his songwriting partner and brother-in-arms to a mercurially strong woman, and preoccupied by his own adoring new love, hopes to quell it all with the same medicine that has worked since his mother's death twelve years earlier. He puts it all into song.

And anytime you feel the pain
Hey Jude, refrain

CHAPTER SIX

And Make It Better

Composition

It's easy to forget how much craftsmanship goes into great songwriting. It is inspiration, but it's also craftsmanship, and "Hey Jude" is just a perfectly crafted song.

—Adam Duritz

Fleshed out in a roots-blues-gospel exercise and embellished with plenty of his long-developed balladry and show-tune skills, Paul McCartney begins crafting "Hey Jude" as he has done hundreds of times with other melodies since his early teens—drawing from the vast library of music from his childhood, mixing in the warmth of his Irish/Scottish heritage, and relying on the sponge-like qualities that readily educe fragments of pop songs that have always worked before.

It begins with a simple message: *Take a sad song . . . and make it better . . .*

"That is the key line for me in terms of understanding Paul McCartney," his biographer Peter Ames Carlin states emphatically. "Paul is really singing about something that's close to his own bone when he goes to a music metaphor. Because he *radiates* music. I'm reminded of his 1982 song 'Take It Away' from *Tug of War*. 'Take it away' is what you say to a band when you're asking them to play. But on the other hand, that's also what good music can do to bad feelings, take them away, because we can get swept away in rhythm and melody, and *that's* the power of music. And Paul is *all* about the power of music. He is the living embodiment of it. It is and has been what his entire existence is about. When he goes to the music metaphor it is coming from a deep place for him."

Working with a verse/verse/bridge/verse/bridge/verse/conclusion pattern, or in *aababac* form, McCartney extends the normal eight-measure verse in his opening stanza to nine measures, exquisitely leading into the first bridge with its *Anytime you feel the pain . . .* melody, stretching it to eleven measures long. Playing steadily in 4/4 time, Paul then adds one exception—measure nine is in 6/4 time. This adjusted time signature settles tenderly in a short but effective piano interlude that introduces a hint of *na-na-na* that brings the composition back to its opening verse: *Hey Jude . . .*

Dr. Tom Koch, musicologist at North Carolina State University, explains: "The bridge's phrase structure is completely different; whereas in the verse the melody itself stands on its own, in other words, you can sing the melody without the piano part and it could stand on its own, here I'm not so sure that the melody in the bridge is as effective without the accompaniment of that beautiful descending line *And anytime you feel the pain / Hey Jude, refrain / Don't carry the world upon your shoulders.*

That goes all the way back to Bach; a classical structure where you have a descending bass line. The classic 'walking bass' we see in jazz and pop music really goes back to the baroque over four hundred years ago."

"*Anytime you feel the pain* . . . is the most succinctly perfect McCartney melody *ever*," says singer/songwriter Eric Hutchinson. "It rotates and comes back around to the beginning so effortlessly."

This melody, according to musicologist and author Walter Everett, borrows crucially from the sublime pre-chorus of the Drifters 1960 #1 hit, "Save the Last Dance for Me." The group's honey-voiced lead singer Ben E. King sings the rising lilt, *But don't forget who's taking you home / And in whose arms you're gonna be* that Paul affectionately mirrors with *Remember to let her into your heart* bending back down slightly to *Then you can start to make it better*, a structure also crafted by songwriters Doc Pomus and Mort Shuman into their chorus: *So darling, save the last dance for me.*

The echo-chamber creativity of the Lennon/McCartney team has made a fine living working from the template of the best of their forebears, specifically themes of expressing advice. A woman who needs to be reminded of how much she is loved does not escape McCartney's pop sensibilities when addressing his Jude. "I think there are some songs where you're meant to hear the quotation, and it's a deliberate reference that if you're not getting it, you're missing it," notes associate professor of music theory at Indiana University Frank Samarotto. "And then there are other times where it can be tricky. For instance, George Harrison's 'My Sweet Lord' was definitely referring back to the Chiffons 'He's So Fine,' taking a secular song and making it into, for him, a sacred song."

Irrespective of his discovery, Everett notes in his densely evocative second volume of *The Beatles as Musicians*, "The 'Hey Jude' melody is a marvel of construction, contrasting wide leaps with stepwise motions, sustained tones with rapid movement, syllabic with melismatic word-setting, and tension ('don't make it *bad*') with resolutions ('make it better'), all graced, of course, by the composer's gift for a natural tune."

Dr. Koch concurs: "Paul is not simply playing chordal roots in the bridge, he's actually making a melody with the bass line, as he often did when playing the actual bass on other Beatles songs; his sense of melody and countermelody comes out here. And that's the part about the bridge that is so intriguing and takes the ballad part of the composition into another sphere, it's really *two* melodies going on—there's a real melody at the top that he sings and there's the bass descent that is acting like its own melody. We don't hear that in the verse. The verse is primarily root-position chords, but his bridge adds a whole new dimension of two melodies going on simultaneously."

"You can tell you got a bass player playing the piano here," cites Dr. Auxier, who in addition to his work in academia is also an amateur composer and has played bass in professional rock and soul bands for thirty years. "It's in the sophistication of the left hand. Most piano players will use the left hand as accompaniment, whereas the bass player will think of it as rhythmic *and* melodic."

Everett also references in his book that for the first notes of the opening verse (*Hey Jude . . . don't make it bad . . .*), McCartney either borrowed or subconsciously nicked English composer John Nicholson Ireland's 1907 liturgical piece "Te Deum (pronounced tay-dayum) Laudamus in F major." Everett explained in an email: "When I first heard 'Te Deum,' it made a lot of sense to me. Almost nothing is known about the music Paul McCartney sang as a boy at St. Barnabas, or his playing in a bell choir in those days, but it can be sure that Anglican anthems like Ireland's were represented."

Everett was alerted to these similarities by his longtime friend, John Deaver, currently the director of music and organist at Trinity Episcopal Church in Covington, Kentucky. Deaver met Everett at the College–Conservatory of Music (CCM) at the University of Cincinnati (where he is a part-time teacher today) in 1977, when the latter was studying for his master's in music theory and the former was entering his second year of his doctorate. "It wasn't until the early eighties when I knew that Walt was writing a book on the Beatles and it was through my working with Ireland's 'Magnificat' that I sent him a note saying, 'I think I found the origins of 'Hey Jude.'"

It was during rehearsals for the canticles "Magnificat and Nunc dimittis in F" when one of Deaver's altos, a young student by the name of Mary Lee Nixon, alerted the choir that she had discovered a melody within the "Te Deum" that the whole pop world had embraced nearly two decades earlier. There it was—the opening notes to *Hey Jude . . . don't make it bad . . .* written a half century ago in the opening of a 1917 canticle by another British composer fifty-one years before.

A canticle, from the Latin, is a Christian hymn of praise with lyrics taken from biblical texts. "Te Deum" is translated as "We praise Thee, O God." There are eight such canticles which are determined by the musical tone of the day and hundreds of iterations of the title "Te Deum." Deaver explains; "'Te Deum' would be sung in the morning service and the 'Magnificat and Nunc dimittis' would be in the evening service. It comes from *Morning Prayer from the English Book of Common Prayer*

1662, which is still the official prayer book of the Church of England, which here in the States is the Episcopal Church."

The spiritual connotations of a former choir boy choosing a morning canticle, the origins of which date back to the fourth century, as a starting point for a melody to embrace a new love and lend sympathy to a young boy in peril, are stark.

Before speaking with Deaver, I listened to several versions of Ireland's melody and it is indeed eerily similar to the first half of Paul's intro. Yet for the second half of the phrase, where Ireland moves down the scale, McCartney moves up, as Paul doubtlessly searched the volumes of his encyclopedic musical mind—harkening back to his childhood living room with aunts and uncles and then his early days with John Lennon as a teenager—to combine a church hymn with a soulful classic like "Save the Last Dance for Me."

When I broached McCartney's choice of chording compared to Ireland's with Dr. Koch, he noted: "Yes, in general the pitches and rhythms are the same as in Ireland, but Ireland's E♭ chord at the end of the phrase isn't the same as Paul's (C7 sus4). And if someone suggests that Paul is unconsciously tying that E♭ chord to the outro of 'Hey Jude,' I think that's pushing it."

Having analyzed theories on tonal music and currently writing a book on the subject, Professor Frank Samarotto expounds: "We can imagine a first idea of 'Hey Jude,' maybe literally or not, as something immediately discarded—where it would go, *Hey Jude, don't be afraid, dah dah dah dah dah* . . . which is kind of boring, but then he adds the little melodic turn up to the high F note, which is not part of the chord underneath, and a funny note to go to. Paul is not only vocally beautiful on the word *song*, but he twists and turns the melody around and makes it better. Instead of going down . . . let's try going up . . . and hint at the big ending. The music *tells* you that you're feeling okay; there are possibilities, there's something coming up and it's going to be good. Paul has musically planted it there. And this is the way I approach music; do the notes really speak? If it's not in the notes, no matter how good a singer you are, it's not going to come out. It's nice to hear great singing but a beautifully crafted composition gives you those sorts of possibilities."

McCartney, subconsciously or not, draws from a melody he most likely discovered in childhood and enhances it for his song of empathy and hope. "I think in all composition the composer is drawing from everything he or she experiences," adds Deaver. "Each person has preferences for sounds that they like more than others. I think that the theme of the 'Te Deum' is so strong, and it comes back so many times, that it just stuck in Paul's mind."

Professor Andrea Halpern, who's psychological discipline is memory, lends her expertise to the subject: "The human mind is amazing, and once something is encoded into memory, we can't prove it's ever lost. Most of our memories are retrieved without conscious awareness from everyday life, so we don't know that Paul didn't consciously remember the melody. It's not at all unusual for people to use throughout life things they learned as small children. Case in point; language. All the language you use as an adult is built up throughout your life; you have no memory whatsoever of having learned what the word 'judicious' means, but you use it. And so, our entire musical corpus may very well be available, and in a composer's memory sometimes things are used deliberately. Of course, there are many examples of classical composers deliberately revisiting a theme that they'd done earlier in their life and building upon it. Paul may have done this deliberately or not.

We can't know unless he introspects for us and tells us, but to recall a piece of music from his teenage-hood subconsciously would be completely reasonable. That's something from youth that could have certainly remained with him, especially in someone who is music oriented. Music is his expert field, and we remember things particularly well in our expert field."

Dr. Koch agrees: "The melodic phrase is so good I'm not surprised it appears elsewhere. Composers tell me that not infrequently they will write a phrase that they find out later belongs to a piece they've never heard."

"I've read how the Beatles owe a melodic debt to this song or that melody, but that's not how people write," says Adam Duritz, who has written seven albums of material over a thirty-year career, including a myriad of hits and an Oscar-nominated song. "No one is sitting around thinking about some classical piece and then writing a new song, it just happens that there are melodies that have commonality with others, little bits of here and there."

Professor Samarotto adds: "Sometimes you can't always lock something down in terms of history, but it's at least a possibility . . . and why not? I always say that the similarity is the 'amen chord' in 'Hey Jude,' the flat-seven chord seals it for me. I believe that he heard the 'Te Deum' and that he sang it somewhere."

Pressing Deaver further on the chances a young boy in a 1950 Liverpool Anglican choir might have either heard or sung the "Te Deum," he did not hesitate to answer in his measured tone: "I think there's a strong possibility, yes. My gut feeling says at least seventy-five percent or higher, because it is a highly regarded piece within music circles, and the music is still very accessible. In other words, it takes a good choir but not a great choir to sing it, so most parish choirs could and *would* have performed it. And if Paul did, then I think, for most people, if we learn something as a kid it stays in our mind but might change a little bit, so we kind of put our own take on it. I think that's what happened with Paul."

Since the opening notes from Ireland match those found in McCartney's "Hey Jude," which is the very melody that first came to him while driving to comfort Julian, its seminal impact from when he was around the same age as Julian may have ignited something deep within him. "It was probably a popular piece with the boys, and being incredibly melodic, it just *became* a part of him," concludes Deaver. "He could have gone home humming it, but then twenty years later when he wrote those notes, he had no idea he was doing so almost verbatim from John Ireland."

The composing tradition of using distant melodies to begin a phrase is, in Dr. Deaver's estimation, a long and curious one. "I teach organ, so I'm aware of today's composers for the organ and how some of them will pick an early twentieth-century French style and then they'll put some German dissonance in and it's an amalgam of different national styles, but they make it their own. Stravinsky while composing 'Petrushka' heard a melody outside his window and he included it in the piece. He had no idea the source of the melody—actually a popular tune of his day."

Here is McCartney, alone in his Cavendish Avenue upstairs music room, pulling from the sources of his distant youth, his adoration of rhythm and blues, and mindfully aware—like with "Yesterday"—that the magic of songwriting can sometimes lead the composer to believe it has come from many places all at once. It is just as magical for, years later, Professors Deaver, Everett, Samarotto, and Koch, and even a young singer named Mary (hmmmm . . . another Mary), to find the origins of that confluence of ideas in an inspiring song of providence.

"'Hey Jude' is a gift from the gods of songwriting that comes after you've cranked out a ton of really good songs, and then all of a sudden, you have a miracle fall in your lap," says author Tim Riley. "It's nothing anybody can predict. All of a sudden, the gods say, 'You are the quality of songwriter that deserves a giant gift . . . and here it is.'"

Deaver left me with this: "Pop music isn't my forte, but the Beatles were among the best, and 'Hey Jude' sticks around because it is a great song with a melody I can always recall, which is part of its lasting success. I think while it may have started with Ireland's opening melody, McCartney put his stamp on it."

Hours after discussing this, Deaver then emailed me this note: "The canticle ends with the words 'O Lord, in Thee have I trusted: let me never be confounded,' which is an offer of hope and consolation."

"'Hey Jude' is about literally lifting up a voice in song as Psalms commands in the Bible," concludes University of Evansville's associate professor of writing Katie Darby Mullins. "You don't think you have the voice for it? That's just another part of the magic. Everyone has the voice for it, as long as they are open and turning toward joy."

This then brings us to McCartney's decision to change *Hey Jules* to *Hey Jude*, which he later claimed was inspired by the Broadway hit musical *Oklahoma* and a character's name, Jud—interestingly, a character who does not fit comfortably in his milieu and pines for a woman. McCartney's previous work had incorporated many characters that jumped from the page, like the denizens of "Penny Lane," the haunting

"Eleanor Rigby," grandchildren Vera, Chuck, and Dave in his nostalgia number, "When I'm Sixty-Four," or the two songs he'd recently worked on with the band, Western-flavored "Rocky Racoon" and Desmond and Molly from the bouncy "Ob-La-Di, Ob-La-Da." There is also a Christian-related subtext to the name Jude that may have entered into the song's theme, as McCartney had been baptized a Catholic and, although there were no discernably strict adherences in his household to its tenets, when considering the origins of the "Te Deum" from his time in the boys' choir, it is hard to believe he did not understand the primacy of the saints in the faith.

McCartney biographer Howard Sounes told me: "I don't think Paul was or is particularly religious, but then again we don't live in a particularly religious era, do we? Yet it is part of his general biographical background—he did later compose the 'Liverpool Oratorio' which has religious connotations; oratorios are usually religious. I didn't find any evidence of him being a churchgoing religious person, although I'm sure he possessed a vague sort of Christian faith that shows up in his music, like 'Let It Be' or songs like that."

In his fantastic, *Can't Buy Me Love: The Beatles, Britain and America*, author Jonathan Gould notes: "It is hard to imagine that the son of Mary McCartney would have been unaware that in the Roman Catholic church, Jude is the patron saint of lost causes, a connotation that not only fits with the hymn-like feel of the music, but also places the song in the unusual position of offering solace to a saint."

St. Jude, Judas Thaddaeus, is said to have been one of the twelve apostles as depicted in the New Testament of the Holy Bible. These were the devoted disciples of Jesus, a first-century Nazarene preacher who, after his execution by the Roman Empire, was purported to rise from the dead and as such was deemed to be the Son of God, the Christ, and became the impetus for the Christian religion. Although sometimes identified outside of Catholicism—a Roman expansion of Christianity in the third century—as Judas, his distinction as Jude came from early Christian Greek-to-English translations of the New Testament in an effort to avoid confusing the faithful. It was an important qualification, since the great villain of the Jesus story is Judas Iscariot, the apostle who betrayed him prior to his crucifixion. Thus, Judas became Jude.

St. Jude's likeness in Roman and Byzantine art usually includes a tongue of flame above his head depicting the visiting of the Holy Spirit, a mysterious part of the Holy Trinity along with God and Christ that is part of Christian tradition. In secular terms this spirit might be defined as inspiration or a spiritual awakening, imbuing the subject with a divine wisdom. In Catholicism, St. Jude is the patron saint of desperate, impossible, and lost causes. McCartney's Jude listens as the song's narrator tells him that he too can accept the spirit of love and find acceptance in companionship, but only if he is open to it—much like religious doctrines counsel the giving of oneself over completely to a greater power. The power for Paul is the love of the right woman. In this spiritual way, echoed in the Maharishi's proverb, "The heart always goes to the warmer place" he can *take a sad song and make it better*.

Oh, and one last tidbit on St. Jude. The penultimate book of the New Testament titled the "Letter of Jude" or "Epistle of Jude" is attributed to him. It has twenty-five verses. Counting the major verses (6) and the full *Na . . . na . . . na . . . na na na na . . . Hey Jude* stanzas (19), you get twenty-five. Cue eerie music.

"This all strikes me as synchronicity in the Jungian sense of the word," says Dr. Auxier with a smile. "Which is to say, under no circumstances did Paul intend *any* of this. Paul probably knew the book of Jude, I've taught it, I teach Methodist Sunday school, and I've studied the book very closely. It comes from the Johannine community, which becomes ultimately the Eastern Orthodox Church, not Roman Catholicism. And I never saw anything in the book of Jude that reminded me of the song whatsoever, nor is there any basis in the book of Jude for the tradition of making Jude the patron saint of lost causes."

An interesting sidelight to all the vague religiosity behind "Hey Jude" comes to a head when McCartney innocently decides to paint the title of the song onto the window of Apple's boutique in London but is met with protests from Jewish leaders who recall the German harassment of *Juden* painted on shop windows before the war. One dissenter actually calls the utterly clueless Paul up and threatens violence. "One thing is for sure with the name Jude," concludes Dr. Auxier. "All of the tribes of Israel are absorbed into Judah, and that's where we get the word Jew. And so, you've got this very rich sort of Hebrew association with the name Jude."

The final aspect of spiritual overtones found in the composing of "Hey Jude" is in its arrangement. Steeped in the church sermon tradition through the Jesuit priests inspired by the rhetorical genius of Aristotle: "Tell them what you are going to tell them, tell them, then tell them what you told them," Paul incorporates the Beatles' standard methodology of repeating the first verse for the third in order to better drive the point home and imprint itself on the listener. Although this was an effective songwriting technique, McCartney later admitted it was mostly the result of having difficulty finding the right lyrics to complement his first two verses, so he preferred to simply repeat the first. In doing so, he makes a small revision in singing *skin* in place of *heart* in the final verse which is what likely caused his partner to flub the line and shout the infamously recorded expletive.

Having rendered the gospel-tinged message of inspiration and comfort into his ballad, when McCartney reaches the coda, he is conjuring all of his instincts as a songsmith—his early days at his father's piano playing singalongs with his beloved aunties and uncles, the soulful surrender to the rhythm and blues he adores, and all those extended jams in the sweat-drenched Hamburg clubs... *Na... na... na... na na na na.* Quite suddenly the ballad transmogrifies into a universal chorale, or as Mick Jagger remarks upon hearing it, a completely new composition attached to the end, akin to what Paul and John had done with his middle section for "A Day in the Life."

"There is this theory among musicologists of *organicism* occurring especially in the nineteenth and the eighteenth centuries, which applies to composers like Brahms and Beethoven, where the ideas that the parts aren't just arbitrary but belong together the way parts of an organic body belong together; every part informs every other part," explains Professor Samarotto. "The composition of 'Hey Jude' is two parts of an organic whole, it's not just a case of 'Oh, I like the melody in the first and I like the melody in the second,' the melody in the first part gives way to the next one like a bird flying off into this wonderfully ecstatic space. It's *the change* that does it. We can't imagine the first part of the regular song without the *Na-Na-Na* part, but if we could, I don't think it would have gotten very much notice at all, it would have just been a B-side song somewhere buried on an album—nice but no big deal. It is the way Paul builds it up, so that when you're hearing that first part, you're saying, 'I'm waiting for a kind of ecstasy, almost sexual ecstasy, really, to come to pass.' And does anyone ever get tired of singing *na-na-na na-na-na-na*?"

Professor Koch adds: "Think about the progression of the song—notice how he starts out very calm, as if he's talking to a child or he's like one of those preachers that begins his sermon very calm, 'Let me tell you a story . . .' and by the end of the sermon, there is sweat on his face. He is swept up by the spirit of it."

"I think the song overcomes your state of mind," says songwriter Kiley Lotz. "If you're in a cynical place, it might not feel so good, but if you're in a place open enough to hear it, then the triumphant payoff is amazing. But the interesting thing about 'Hey Jude' is before you can get cynical, Paul presents that first chord with just the vocal. It's an intentionally simple presenting of raw fact. He's not trying to win you over with some sort of glittering, overly arranged thing right from second-one. It's a leveling person-to-person conversation. And then by the end, it is a musical catharsis, like being in church singing about your troubles being relinquished, this communion idea. This is what happens by the end, you go from feeling solitary to being part of the whole. If not for that opening person-to-person level at the beginning of the song, maybe the cynics wouldn't give it a chance."

"When Paul gets to the build-up of the notes up the scale it feels like you've been waiting the whole time for it, because the rest of the song has been in a gentle meter," says Professor Samarotto. "But then he provides the strongest beat we've gotten to so far in the whole song at the end."

"It's an invitation to participate," notes NC State's Dr. William Boone, who is also a songwriter and guitarist who's played professionally with Black gospel artists for almost two decades. "It takes nothing to join in on that chorus, if you want to call it that. I like to call it a vamp, in the gospel tradition. It's *instant* participation, like in Black Pentecostal churches even today; if the spirit gets really high, they'll use a singalong to go to that place where you don't *need* words. I think the Beatles were already doing that with the *Yeahs* and *Ooohs*. It's a pop music trope, but 'Hey Jude' really takes it into the transcendental place, like Little Richard's *A-wop-bop-a-loo-bop* where you're not saying words but tapping into something deeper, more primal, more immediate. 'Hey Jude' provides a pretty clear message first and then you get to that part at the end where Paul has moved *beyond* needing words anymore—now we can all just *na, na, na* which is more meaningful then if he tried to write anymore lyrics. The *na na na* says more than any words he could've put there."

Adam Duritz observes: "The melody is good enough that he doesn't even *need* words. You see some of that in a Cocteau Twins record where words pop in and out, but the melodies and music are so beautiful it doesn't matter, but this isn't a bunch of different melodies sweeping in, it's a *single-line* melody, which is so good that a bunch of people can just sing it together and it can go on for four straight minutes at the end of a song when you've already sat for three fucking minutes. It may be the greatest vamp in music history."

In this way, McCartney is "borrowing" from himself. During the last few months, he had perfected the singalong chorus in the infectious "Ob-La-Di, Ob-La-Da" and, having recently attended the premier of the Beatles' fourth film, *Yellow Submarine*, he listened with satisfaction to the mostly industry-insider audience singing like giddy children to his short but effective ditty, "All Together Now." Presaging the universal message of "Hey Jude," the song's title flashes upon the screen in several languages repeated over and over like a Maharishi mantra, *All together now . . . all together now . . . all together now . . .*

"All Together Now" quite literally demands participation, as Paul uses a child-like melodic rhyme to touch the core of innocence, something he fears has been stolen from young Julian much like it had been for John and him after the deaths of their mothers. Mostly, his aim is to help Julian feel less alone. As long as music was there for young Paul, he was never alone.

And so, as author Jonathan Gould rightly notes, McCartney's use of *na*—usually expressed as a negation, as in a child's refusal to understand, obey, or commit—is transformed in "Hey Jude" as an "outsized gesture of affirmation." Taken alone, it is merely *Na!* But together, the mighty *Na . . . na . . . na . . . na na na na* is impenetrable, a strength in numbers, musical legion.

"One of music's purposes is to bind a culture together," cites Bucknell University's Professor Andrea Halpern. "I begin my psychology music class by having my students read an essay on 'Functions of Music,' wherein the author talks about the role of music in culture from different angles—the family culture, religious culture, etc. So, yes, a song having a commonality, especially in a time when there's radio and songs can be widely distributed to millions of people, it can evoke a communal feeling. You sing hymns and Christmas carols together, because they're fairly accessible. Musicologically speaking, 'Hey Jude' is accessible that way. It's 'We Shall Overcome,' essentially, isn't it?"

Tim Riley adds: "The idea that the refrain is longer than the song itself is a conceptually daring achievement. It's hard to even imagine the structure of a song like 'Hey Jude,' and say, 'Okay, write a song where the refrain is longer than the body of the song itself and actually upstages it.'"

"I tell my students, songwriting is being good at capturing the muse," notes Professor Aaron Keane. "Paul McCartney worked his ass off when he was young, so that when the muse hit him, he *had* it. And that's what 'Hey Jude' sounds like to me, the culmination of a creative spirit. My wife calls it a 'mommy song,' a song that you'd sing to your baby or you'd make up on the spot. But obviously its developed; Paul worked it and nuanced it, and so it turned into this very clever musical thing."

"It's as painfully sincere and vulnerable as any song ever written—a mantra that promises things might be hard now, but they would get better," says Katie Darby Mullins. "Even more promising, if the 'Jude' of the song can remain open to love, life could hold riches and joy beyond what he can imagine now in this young and broken state. It doesn't take a life-long cynic to roll their eyes a little at the message: *remember to let her into your heart / then you can start to make it better* sounds so much like what contemporary culture is referring to as 'toxic positivity.' Many Beatles songs were based, literally and figuratively, about love as an all-powerful, all-moving force: it is, of course, all you need."

"I hear 'Hey Jude' as a song in the American songbook tradition," says Dr. Koch. "You talk about Gershwin, Jerome Kern and Irving Berlin, this is a song in that tradition. The way it's structured is very proportional and balanced that way. And like those songs we can all sing not only the verse and the bridge, but particularly the ending part; but this one is unique because it doesn't have a built-in singalong chorus *until* the end. You have to wait for it. But what an ending!"

Again, from *The Beatles as Musicians,* Walter Everett surmises: "A wordless four-minute mantra with a grandeur that seems to suggest that, given the proper understanding and encouragement, Jude has found his courage and moves on with grace and dignity."

The minute you let her into your heart
Then you can start to make it better

McCartney is so jazzed by his newest composition and its well-designed audience-participation coda, he yearns to perform it for someone outside of the Beatles.

Relegated to not plying his trade in front of fans, something he's become less enthused about, he decides *Na . . . na . . . na . . . na na na na* needs an audience, and so, according to music journalist Chris Hunt's February 2002 essay in *Mojo* magazine, "The Story of Hey Jude," McCartney tests his latest composition "on anyone too polite to refuse."

"Hey Jude" reinvigorates the healing joy of music in the twenty-six-year-old Paul McCartney. The kid who snatched "I Lost My Little Girl" from thin air at fourteen excitedly careens into an Abbey Road session looking for someone for whom to debut his latest creation. The lucky audience is the Barron Knights, a British comedy/musical troupe named after its cheeky bassist/vocalist Barron Anthony. Peter "Peanut" Langford, the Knights keyboard/guitarist, recalls the Beatle telling the stunned group, "'I've just written this song, would you like to hear it? It's hopefully going to be our next single!' He actually forgot the words too."

Soon after, still bursting with excitement, McCartney interrupts his own session producing the Bonzo Dog Doo-Dah Band's "I'm the

Urban Spaceman" to try the song out on them. Neil Innes, a comedy writer and musician, who went on to work with the infamously brilliant Monty Python and later even played a John Lennon character in the 1978 Beatles satire, *The Rutles: All You Need Is Cash,* recalls: "He was just enjoying singing and playing it, like you do when you first write a song. You want to go through it in public to see if there might be something else in there. It was at that demo stage."

Finding himself in the Northern England town of Yorkshire during another session producing the Black Dyke Mills Band's rendition of his instrumental "Thingumybob," McCartney stops at the village of Harrold in Bedfordshire and performs "Hey Jude" at a local pub. Beatles' press agent Derek Taylor was on hand and shared his memory of the evening in the *White Album's 50th Anniversary Super Deluxe* box set booklet: "In the pub, Paul got to a piano and a singalong was started—he'd always been good at that sort of thing—and he said, 'Well, here's a new one,' and he played 'Hey Jude.' Taught them how it went: 'Na, na, na, na, na, na, na.' so they were all at it! That was the premiere of 'Hey Jude.' It was an unbelievably wonderful night. We didn't leave there until dawn was coming up."

Nearly a month later, on July 23, the day after signing to Apple Records and months before McCartney would compose their first #1 single, "Come and Get It," the Iveys—soon to be Badfinger—are treated to an impromptu "Hey Jude" performance. This time, unlike "forgetting the words" for the Barron Knights, trying out a "demo" for the Bonzos, or even a pub singalong, Badfinger bass player Ron Griffiths vividly remembers Paul walking deliberately over to a grand piano and announcing, "Hey, lads, have a listen," before launching into a fully realized performance. Griffiths recalls, "We were gobsmacked."

All of this woodshedding of a song with the magnitude of "Hey Jude," even for a master craftsman at the height of his creative powers, is understandable, especially when considering where McCartney's band had arrived in the summer of 1968. The nod toward St. Jude may have also underscored his seeing the Beatles as his own "lost cause." McCartney's band has been slowly drifting apart for some time, and despite everything he's tried, it is becoming apparent there is almost nothing he can do about it. His song expresses a similar frame of mind.

Don't carry the world upon your shoulders
For well you know that it's a fool
Who plays it cool
By making his world a little colder

Professor Alexander Shashko concludes: "So much of what the Beatles write in their music is in some way shaped by what is happening directly around them, about what is happening in the studio, about their relationships with one another, even when they wrote in coded language it was part of the story, and there absolutely has to be that kind of sense of both lament and desire in 'Hey Jude' for Paul to keep them together."

It could be argued, and I would like to try, that "Hey Jude" is the last time the Beatles would make a lasting, impactful statement in a single song that defined their times and their enormous cultural influence. Its universal appeal, as demonstrated on the pop charts where they reigned, is one example and—when considering what the band had achieved, where it had been and would eventually go for the remaining sixteen months of its run, and pondering the international civil, economic, social, racial, and generational implosion of 1968—it is a rather important one from a damned important band.

McCartney knows this. He always did. From the time he was bowled over by Elvis Presley and shouted to his friends, "The messiah has arrived!" and found in rock and roll his deliverance, he aimed to share that feeling. In transforming his melody of support for young Julian Lennon, a child he'd taken under his wing, he discovers that it is as much about the hope to be found in a new love for himself and for his long-time chum John as well as a desperate plea to the biggest musical group of all time. In their hands, in their times, its significance will be imprinted forevermore. As a McCartney effort, "Hey Jude" represents a magnificent piece of work that speaks volumes about the human spirit, but when set aloft atop the steeple that John, Paul, George, and Ringo have erected, its reverent transformation will be complete.

CHAPTER SEVEN

Someone to Perform With

Making Magic

The studio was where it was all going on.

—George Harrison, *The Beatles Anthology*

Rehearsals

In the midst of what appeared in public and was certainly becoming a grimmer reality in private—the slow demise of the mighty Beatles—John, Paul, George, and Ringo did what they do best: make music—most notably, a new single. Without the grueling hours of parsing through dozens of songs for an album but instead hearkening back to pre-Beatlemania and the ensuing halcyon days before the experimental studio-tricks and fractious recording techniques: A song. The Beatles. Period. It was an appealing notion for all involved.

"'Hey Jude' and 'Revolution' are the last songs recorded by all four Beatles specifically for a release as a single," notes author Devin McKinney. "It was, in reality, the end of an unprecedented era."

"It came in a moment during a rough period where each Beatle is carving out a space for himself in the band, and here was a song that everyone rallied around," observes Scott Freiman. "The Beatles realize 'Hey Jude' is a great song and put the requisite time and energy into it. Their honed instincts proved correct. It turned out to be their biggest number one."

Having gotten his blessing and settled on an arrangement for "Hey Jude" with Lennon the previous week, a formula that *always* worked, McCartney convenes the band for two evenings; Monday, July 29, and Tuesday, July 30, at EMI Studios to rehearse the song. The Beatles play "Hey Jude" twenty-five times over those two days, six of which are taped for posterity, including three completed versions and one short film of the proceedings.

Two of these takes are officially released. Take 2, clocking in at 4:21, winds up on *Anthology*, volume 3, in 1996. Take 1, a longer pass at 6:44, appears on the 2018 release of the *White Album's 50th Anniversary Super Deluxe* box set. Take 6, only available in studio logs, falls in the middle at 5:25, as the band begins to find the longer groove that would eventually be the song's aim. Take 9 would end up in a lo-fi mix for filming during day-two of rehearsals. The final run-through, Take 25, wherein Paul finds his eventual vocal phrasing, stretches "Hey Jude" to 6:23; *Na . . . na . . . na . . . na na na na* slowly but surely expunging the bad vibes from the grueling White Album sessions.

You're waiting for someone to perform with

The first night kicks off at 8:30 PM with engineer Ken Scott manning the session. Scott, who had first worked with the Beatles during *Hard Day's Night* and would go on to a stellar producing career, sits in for George Martin, who's broken from working with EMI exclusively and branched out into his Associated Independent Recording (AIR) company so he can work with other artists in a myriad of studios. Also absent is Geoff Emerick, a permanent fixture behind the board since the experimental *Revolver* sessions, who left under a barrage of band infighting. And so, Scott is assisted by newcomer John Smith. According to the wonderfully researched *The Beatles Recording Reference Manual*, volume 4, by Jerry Hammack, Paul McCartney plays a nineteenth-century Steinway "Music Room" Model B grand piano, while also working out a guide vocal. Lennon plays his prized 1964 Gibson J-160E acoustic guitar and, on early runs of the song, George Harrison switches between three electric guitars, a 1961 Fender Stratocaster, a 1964 Gibson SG, and 1965 Epiphone Casino. Ringo rounds out the foursome on his signature 1964 Ludwig Oyster Black Pearl drum set. Mark Lewisohn's seminal work, *The Complete Beatles Recording Sessions*, notes that the band doesn't break until four o'clock the following morning.

From the released takes and existing bootlegs, the musical comradery and playful banter, especially between John and Paul, denotes a respite from the anxieties of the previous months. McCartney playfully octave-hops on the opening *Hey* . . . in Take 1. Take 2 begins with Lennon shouting, "From the heart of the black country . . ." cueing his partner to croon, "when I was a robber, in Boston Place, you gathered 'round me with your fond embrace," Boston Place being the location of Apple's soon-to-be defunct electronics laboratory. The remark could well be a swipe at Magic Alex's fraudulent "expertise" in "creating" unhinged experiments like disappearing paint, a flying saucer, and a seventy-two-track recording deck. Here is the sturdiest element of the Beatles on display, what had bound them through tough times in Hamburg to the heights of overwhelming success—their keen Liverpool humor. On both takes, Paul sings with exaggerated vibrato during the *na, na, na* refrain, while encouraging John to sing along. According to the accompanying book for the *White Album's 50th Anniversary Super Deluxe* box set, Take 3 ends with a reference to the aborted open to Elvis Presley's 1955 recording of "Milkcow Blues Boogie," as John similarly halts the beginning of the pass by exclaiming, "Hold it, Paul. That don't *move* me!"

A film crew moves in for a portion of the July 30 sessions to record footage for a documentary titled *Music!* produced by the National Music Council of Great Britain. This marks the first time the Beatles permit cameras into the inner sanctum while they develop a song. The cameras capture what the audio from the previous day hinted—while these are the same men who are enduring the contentious White Album sessions, there's a discernably lighter air about these proceedings. Paul, headphones tight to his head, keeping one off his left ear, sits at the piano dressed in a patterned knit button-down shirt establishing the tempo. He leans in to sing tentatively but is clearly comfortable about where the song will go, although closeups reveal that he's still reading from a handwritten page of lyrics. To his left, sits John, also sporting headphones behind a baffle, his signature mid-1968 straggly hair, and granny glasses. Ringo, stylish in a purple shirt, shaggy-haired with hip moustache and sideburns, drags on the last puffs of a cigarette before coming in on the hi-hat. When he does, he is joined by John's soft strumming.

As the band kicks into *And anytime you feel the pain / Hey Jude, refrain,* Ringo develops his extended drum fills, creating a dramatic flair to each section. Lennon bobs his head contemplatively, eyeing his lyric sheet, then looks over at his partner, as Paul brings it back to the verses with his distinct if not thus-far choppy piano interlude. It is a treat to see a Beatles classic in its nascent stages—McCartney content with the band's version of his composition while his distinguished partner, in rapt concentration, looks back at the sheet to see where Paul is going.

For the second verse, Ringo, the heads of his drum set draped with towels to dampen the sound, eases into more of a shuffle than appears on the final cut—another valuable insight into how the Beatles' drummer hones his unique backbeats to anchor early run-throughs, allowing the other members to find their bearings and work out parts to solidify their unique sound.

"There are so many things about the music of 'Hey Jude' that people so rarely point out or rarely even notice, for instance, more than anything else, it's a drummer's song," notes author Rob Sheffield. "It is the main reason it's impossible for people to cover it. For me, the only version that I think is as good is Wilson Pickett's, because Roger Hawkins, the famous Muscle Shoals' drummer, is playing on it. It's not a song that one guy with a voice and a piano or guitar can do. It's a band song, and so much of that depends on Ringo, who holds down the groove all the way through."

"My first obsession with 'Hey Jude' was in high school as a young drummer," recalls singer/songwriter and classically trained drummer,

Seán Barna. "Why did Ringo immediately start playing the ride cymbal instead of the hi-hat when he entered? Shouldn't that be reserved for later in the song? In the chorus maybe? Why am I getting emotional over a tambourine shake?"

A closeup during the final verse reveals only three needles on the famed EMI board bouncing to the sound. Up in the control room, George Harrison is shown mouthing *Hey Jude* . . . along with Paul. As the camera pulls back, we can see he is seated with engineer Scott and a returning George Martin, who listens intently. The reason for this is a growing tension between McCartney and Harrison about an "answering" guitar line that the latter was adding during the verses which Paul did not fancy.

Devin McKinney recounts, "George wanted to do these country western fills after every line in 'Hey Jude,' and Paul is saying, 'Well, no, that's not the way to go.' And, well, of course, he was right. If you listen to 'Real Love,' which the surviving three Beatles recorded years later, George is filling in after every vocal line that he probably wanted to do in 'Hey Jude.' Now, I love 'Real Love,' it's one of my favorite Beatles records, but I'm not crazy about the tendency for George to add little answering guitar licks after every vocal line, and listening back to 'Hey Jude,' it would have *destroyed* it. So, you can say Paul is a control freak, but his judgment was exquisite, and he knew what was right, every time."

However, unlike the filmed spat that ensues in the *Let It Be* sessions the following year where a frustrated Harrison barks at Paul, "I can play it or not play it, whatever it is that will please you, I'll do it," things are subdued right away. This is in evidence when Paul struggles to sing *Better... better... better... better...* and the camera finds Harrison laughing with delight and some measure of teasing. Putting a capper on this tiff, Harrison would go on to either pay tribute to "Hey Jude" or more likely tweak his old bandmate with "Isn't It a Pity," a song on his 1970 solo album, *All Things Must Pass* that both laments their rocky relationship and honorably re-creates its celebrated refrain.

Back downstairs, the three-piece unit does a one-measure pass through the three chords that act as the foundation for the soon-to-be-famous coda before singing along. Even Ringo, laying on his ride cymbal, joins in. John, with his striped dress shirt, black vest and white sneakers, enthusiastically bellows the refrain. Paul exclaims, "Come on children . . . sing!" while trying out different vocal descants that will eventually adorn the final recording. Ringo throws in occasional drum fills, as John pouts his lips and bobs his head, adding more background shouts. Here is the birth of *Na . . . na . . . na . . . na na na.* Watching the Beatles sing it for one of the first times, discovering its cohesive spirit, is endearing. And having traveled all the way from the early days after Paul's mother's death, his weeks and months recovering from the grief with song, then finding John, the Beatles, and all the rest, the band can feel it too.

Friend and colleague of Professor Tom Koch from North Carolina State University, Professor Aaron Keane is a longtime producer and engineer of pop, rock, and television media. When we spoke about the Beatles' recording of "Hey Jude," he was adamant about their organic preparations which are not followed as closely today, as many of the artists he's recorded prefer to build tracks piecemeal. He found this film particularly intriguing as it presented what he called "the Beatles arranging in real-time." He continued: "While I don't do pop music much anymore, if I were a producer today, I'd be looking for ways of getting back to the immediacy of a live performance, the fundamental aspects of how the music is made. I think that's where a lot of the humanity lies. The way 'Hey Jude' was made celebrates that intimacy. It is part of its lasting charm."

When the filmed take concludes, there remains a joyous air in the room. John playfully sings in falsetto, "Boogie-woogie . . . Boogie-woogie!" Ringo complains his pants keep getting stuck on his bass pedal. "Take 'em off," John snickers, then turns his attention to Paul, and in one of those classic Lennon asides that balance adoration with derision, says, "I felt closer to it that time, I must admit I felt *closer* to it." Paul, appearing drained and still contemplating the song, affects a more serious tone. The camera captures Ringo running both hands down his face as if exhausted. The film finally fades with John's broad smile and laughter.

If Ringo is tired, then he is in for a long evening. Day Two of rehearsals features Takes 7 through 25—the filmed version was only Take 9, as noted in Lewisohn's book. However, filming is soon halted, as Ken Scott comments in the *Sessions* book: "The film crew was supposed to work in such a way that no one would realize they were there, but, of course, they were getting in everyone's way and everyone was getting uptight about it."

The footage eventually airs on American television on February 22, 1970, while moviegoers in Britain see it in October of 1969 as an accompanying film with the Mel Brooks movie *The Producers*. McCartney loves the results and is inspired to have the next album's sessions captured and turned into a full-length feature. That, of course, will become *Let It Be,* released in 1970, essentially acting as the band's epitaph. Its director, Michael Lindsay-Hogg, will soon play a key role in the "Hey Jude" saga.

Unlike the preponderance of the *Let It Be* sessions, the lightened, stripped-down, and casual mood of these rehearsals translates into the band returning to its musically diverse personality, as they exuberantly perform a de facto trio riff on Louis Armstrong's classic "St. Louis Blues." This prompts Harrison, recalling the Hamburg days, to begin tossing out requests over the studio talkback. "Two crates of beer if you do 'Twist and Shout'!" Lennon, once the group's unquestioned leader, cries out, "Boys!" reminding the lead guitarist of the popularity of the Shirelles B-side they'd habitually performed on stage. Later, they stumble into a version of Ray Charles' 1959 hit, "Don't Let the Sun Catch You Cryin'."

One could be romantic about this mood shift and claim that Paul's empathetic theme of support and positivity in "Hey Jude" strikes a chord in a discordant band. Maybe, I would like to think, the communal underscore of *Na . . . na . . . na . . . na na na na* means as much to the bickering Beatles as it might to a world fast becoming unhinged outside the studio doors. Even John, convinced Paul is providing him a lyrical benediction to embrace Yoko and find his own way through song, is moved to eagerly dive in. One might also consider the lightened air as the band merely embracing the professional accord that work is to be done, and with cameras present, there is a public persona of unity to uphold. But the most practical answer to the cordial atmosphere may simply be that the density of the time-consuming double-album sessions has sucked some of the life from the one element of their profession that the Beatles adore, recording new music. Also, as stated above, laying down a single in rapid fashion is a nostalgic reprise of fond memories of cranking out the hits while always experimenting. "Hey Jude" returns the Beatles to their roots, and those roots, it turns out, are strong.

"'Hey Jude' captures the communal spirit of the Beatles," says author Rob Sheffield. "It's a shared fantasy of the Beatles being friends as adults. It's definitely not a kid song. It's certainly one of the very few McCartney songs where he's singing as one man to another man, because Paul McCartney has basically no interest in men. It's something he and John have in common; neither of them is interested at all in what men have to say. In fact, the song's recording very much depends on all four of them pulling together, to make that fantasy real at a time when it was very difficult for them to capture that spirit."

"You could say, they knew this was the beginning of the end," says singer/songwriter Eric Hutchinson. "And they were just trying to hold on to it as long as possible."

As the seven-hour, July 30, rehearsal (8:30 PM to 3:30 AM) wraps up on the morning of July 31, George Martin takes a rough stereo mix of Take 25 to arrange the orchestral score. This, and what will transpire at Trident Studios the very next day, is likely the reason a bootleg exists of the take. Martin, still unsure of the song's length, decides to accentuate its coda with the kind of layers McCartney has included in his arrangement. Martin later recalled: "I realized that by putting an orchestra on you could add lots of weight to the riff by counter chords on the bottom end and bringing in trombones, and strings, and so on until it became a really big tumultuous thing."

Recording

The Beatles move quickly to get "Hey Jude" down, as they did in their grand productive days of single-in/single-out. Within weeks, Paul's kind gesture to John's son has gone from a quaint melody to a structured song, then to a band arrangement and rehearsals, and on Wednesday, July 31, the group and its producer move the 2.6 miles (or 4.8 kilometers), about a sixteen-minute drive from EMI Studios on Abbey Road, to the SoHo district of London and Trident Studios with its eight-track recording capabilities.

The entourage arrives in the afternoon, the session booked from 2:00 PM until 4:00 AM. The band's general practitioner of all things, Mal Evans, ceremoniously presents studio head Norman Sheffield with provisions for meals and marijuana plants to be placed in the studio at the band's behest. Sheffield lets Evans know they have a well-stocked kitchen but acquiesces to the pot plants as décor. Sheffield is rapt with excitement over having the biggest band on the planet consider his five-month-old space for recording a new single. He opens his delightful 2013 studio memoir, *Life on Two Legs,* noting the band's casual dress: John in "a tee shirt and waistcoat," Paul in a "scruffy wool jumper," and George's "floral shirt and pinstripe trousers." He has no memory of Ringo's ensemble. Poor Ringo.

His brother, Barry Sheffield, is tasked to assist George Martin with using the mix-down of Take 25 as the basis for that day's session. This means a tape recorded on Abbey Road's antiquated four-track deck has to be transferred onto Trident's modern eight-track machine. Not surprisingly, this doesn't work. No matter, reinvigorated by the new surroundings and a chance to lay down a new song on eight tracks, it's decided to start from scratch.

For the final recordings, according to Sheffield and corroborated in *The Beatles Recording Reference Manual*, volume 4, McCartney plays the studio's one-hundred-year-old Bechstein grand piano. Lennon once again strums along on his Gibson acoustic guitar, although a second Martin D-28 may have been played. This time, Harrison, figuring a part that works for Paul, is back on electric guitar, using the same allotment as in earlier rehearsals, as is Ringo on his usual Ludwig drum kit. Being together again in the same room—not "four musicians with four backing bands" as will be derisively written about the White Album sessions—and finding themselves in fresh environs to record a brand-new song further enhances the heightened temperament and reminds the band of what it could still accomplish as a mighty foursome. "A party spirit spilled into the icy atmosphere," Bob Spitz describes in *The Beatles*.

The sonic result speaks for itself, and its mastery arrives without delay. When considering how dozens of takes on individual songs—and in some cases over one hundred—for their current White Album project are bogging things down, the Beatles record just four takes of "Hey Jude" on this day, and that even turns out to be overkill. The very first one is unanimously selected as the master.

This singular and pivotal moment in Beatles lore is evident in how the take comes together. The original arrangement during the two days of rehearsals has the band settling on the iconic cold open vocal: *Hey Jude . . .* followed by just piano during the first measure. A single tambourine will later be overdubbed for the second verse. Next, Ringo will come tumbling in with a heralding drum-fill before laying into the backbeat. However, fully engaged in the moment of recording a new song, *his* song, McCartney starts the take completely unaware that his drummer is on a bathroom break. Hearing this, and knowing he has two measures to settle in, Ringo tiptoes slowly back to his kit and, on cue, lays into his part impeccably. This is what you hear on the record.

"He couldn't have timed it better," Sheffield writes in his memoir. "Everyone collapsed with laughter in the control room upstairs." Paul later remarked that he could feel Ringo's sudden presence as he played, but instead of halting, he hoped for the best. He receives it. Paul told Barry Miles in *Many Years from Now*: "I think when those things happen, you have a little laugh and a light bulb goes off in your head and you think, 'This is the take!' and you put a little more into it. You think, 'Oh fuck! This has got to be the take; what just happened was so magic!' So, we did that, and we made a pretty good record."

"You can hear a smile in Paul's vocals," notes Rob Sheffield. "It's around the one-minute mark, because Ringo emerges from the bathroom to get back to the drums in time. Everybody has their favorite Beatles moment where you can literally hear them smile while they sing. This is mine."

Ringo recalled years later, "It felt good recording it. It just clicked. That's how it should be."

"Ringo always said, 'When there was a good song, they were all in, because they loved each other, and they loved what they could do together, and they loved being Beatles,'" cites author Peter Ames Carlin. "When they had a good track to work on, they were as happy as they could ever possibly be. You can *hear* that on 'Hey Jude.'"

The band, hardly distracted by Starr's timing, glides effortlessly through a pristine take. For all intents and purposes, except for a few key instrumental, vocal, and orchestral overdubs, the core of the most popular of Beatles songs—a monumental and record-breaking hit, with its outlandishly inspired and extended ending of industry-challenging length—is done in one pass, the *first* pass. The Beatles, *together*, relieved to be outside of Abbey Road and away from personal and public distractions, triumphantly return as the Four-Headed Monster. "Hey Jude" captures this moment in time. On tape. The Beatles crushing it.

"I think the nature of recording everybody all together has a huge effect on the sound," says Aaron Keane. "They're looking at each other and feeling the arrangement in real time, and there's a huge difference in how the performance *becomes* the recording instead of the other way around, as the Beatles had recently been doing. Performance makes a bigger difference than what technology can do. Sure, you can record different tracks, you can isolate things and manipulate things more later on, but with being able to record the band playing the song, which eight-tracks allow you to do with some room to make sure it sounds good, the act of recording very much comes out of the live performance at that time. The Beatles are *playing* the song. At Trident, the recording of 'Hey Jude' became all about playing the song."

"There's a point when, after the bridge, the band *releases*," notes Dr. Auxier. "And instead of having choppy strumming on the acoustic guitar, all of a sudden you have the full ring. It's the same thing on the bass, which Paul is mainly driving with his left hand on piano. Instead of little breaks between the notes, they all go legato. And that last verse, when the full band opens up and becomes whole, you can hear Ringo start for the first time in the song laying into that groove. You can clearly hear him shout *Oh!* right before they bring it home on the recording."

"It's a little bit loose, but its charm is that it's not a perfect recording, it feels *live*," says Eric Hutchinson.

"It's a very austere production," says Rob Sheffield. "It could have been maudlin and cloying, with a little more softness, but it has that George Martin touch of austerity. Martin always made sure nothing was maudlin while he was doing it."

Dan Bern notes, "The songwriting idea is that everybody would sing that extended bit at the end. Well, in lesser hands, it could have come off as 'Kumbaya,' which everybody loves to bash, or sassed or fey or precious in its, 'Let's all sing along now!' Instead, it has an *edge*. I think that is probably partly why it was so big at the time and why it's continued to feel relevant. It's not soft. It's not easy. There's a grit to it."

"In the 'Hey Jude' recording, you have these wonderful expressions of a group trying to stay together and *always* falling into sync, in spite of the fact that reality is pulling them apart," says Devin McKinney. "This session is a paramount example of this. You read their quotes about it, they all loved 'Hey Jude.' John always said it was one of Paul's best songs. They were *all* into it, and they *loved* working on it. It was the right song at the right moment to achieve this unity."

"The muse is what keeps the Beatles together, and they all sense intuitively that despite all the dark static that surrounds them, they have more to say together and there's more ensemble magic yet to happen," concludes Tim Riley. "And they keep chasing it, even though they're not getting along so well, they keep finding these grooves, and the groove just keeps rewarding them. What are you going to do, walk away from a groove like that? It's a once in a lifetime groove. They have ears. There are no other four musicians in the world who know how to hit a groove like that. It is a slice of magic. And they all love it. And they all need more of it, even though making it happen gets more and more costly."

Like clockwork, the next day, Thursday, August 1, around five in the afternoon, the band works on overdubs. McCartney puts down the final lead vocal and his sultry bass track. He decides then to make a last-minute change of the lyric *she has found you* to *you have found her*. Hammack notes in *Recording Reference Manual* that some of Paul's guide vocal recorded during the previous day's backing track run-through bleeds into the main vocal track at certain points in the final mix—most notably at 1:43, 2:17, 2:57, and 3:07, and additionally during the coda. In fact, if you listen closely to the right channel, you can hear Paul's initial free-association melodic vamps that he then alters further into the ones we hear more clearly in the mix further along. Later, Lennon and Harrison join the overdub session, adding the *ahhhhhs,* as John also interposes his crucial harmonies to key lines, and in the process blurts out his now infamous *Fuckin' hell!*

All four Beatles then add the vocals and handclaps that make up *Na . . . na . . . na . . . na na na na.* Ringo, the tardy impetus for the miraculous first-take/final-take, lays down his tambourine part. John and George also record electric guitar passes that, while appearing lower in the final mix, add to the song's dramatic build. This is true of another piano part added by Paul and the extant lines, *Let her out and let her in . . . Hey Jude* that he sings during the third verse. McCartney then clears his head, and channeling his childhood hero Little Richard, works out his final improvised throat-shredding shrieks. Three hours later they are done. And just in time.

And you know you can make it, Hey Jude you gotta break it!

At 8:00 PM the orchestra arrives. Mark Lewisohn's *The Complete Beatles Recording Sessions* cites thirty-six instruments used—ten violins, three violas, three cellos, two double basses, two flutes, two clarinets, one bass clarinet, one bassoon, one contrabassoon, four trumpets, two horns, four trombones, and one percussion instrument. Each musician is paid the normal union fee of twenty-five pounds, while only two musician names are noted: Bobby Kok on cello and Bill Jackman on flute, the latter previously having played baritone sax on the Beatles' latest single, "Lady Madonna."

George Martin's young assistant Chris Thomas, who is also present on this day, remembers: "The studio at Trident was long and narrow. When we did the orchestral overdub, we had to put the trombones at the very front so that they didn't poke anyone in the back!" Since all eight tracks of the tape were filled by the time the musicians arrive, the orchestra is recorded on tracks three and six at the point in the song where they are needed. This means that George's electric guitar on track three, as well as John and George's electric guitars on track six, are wiped at the point in the song where the orchestra arrives.

"When the horns come in it is absolutely crucial to the song's success," says Dr. Auxier. "I've done some work as a recording engineer and I can tell you that this is a conscious decision. Even at nine years old, because I was playing trumpet at that time, when the trumpets come in on the *na-na-nas,* that's when I *knew* Paul was going to start his *Judey-judey-judey*. George Martin, a trained orchestrator, creates this build. He uses the arrangement the band has delivered him to accentuate the drive of the build-up with the strings and, crucially, those horns."

"The designed layering becomes a timbral cue, which makes the repetition interesting, and not just different, but more complex," notes psychology professor Andrea Halpern. "The musical color changes with the instruments being used, altering the spectrum of the waveforms that you're hearing, essentially creating different sound quality with each pass through the repetition."

When recording wraps, Martin asks if the musicians would consider laying down additional backing vocals and handclaps during the coda for a double fee. According to Norman Sheffield, there is initial dissension in the ranks, some of whom are "looking down their noses at the Beatles." McCartney ensures their cooperation by demanding: "Do you guys want to get fucking paid or not?" All but one finally agree. According to Martin, as he recounts in his 1979 memoir *All You Need Is Ears,* the lone dissenter puffs, "I'm not going to clap my hands and sing Paul McCartney's bloody song!" The producer continues: "The only time we have had real objections from an orchestra was during the recording of 'Hey Jude,' the biggest-selling single of all." During the first few takes, McCartney is so underwhelmed by what he deems a painful lack of energy in the vocal performance, he promptly does his best to rouse the makeshift chorale by standing on the grand piano and conducting another take.

The orchestral booking is officially logged at Trident as concluding at 11:00 PM, but further documentation shows the Beatles and Martin keep working until three the next morning. Again, according to Sheffield's account "an amazing stereo mix" is made and everyone in the

Don't Be Afraid—Paul McCartney with four-year-old Julian Lennon in the Summer of 1967. "The universality of 'You're going to be okay' is timeless."
CENTRAL PRESS / STRINGER

Survivors—Paul in 1964 with his father and namesake, James. Their love for piano and song delivered them from the grief over Mary's death. "It must be in the genes." PICTORIAL PRESS LTD / ALAMY STOCK PHOTO

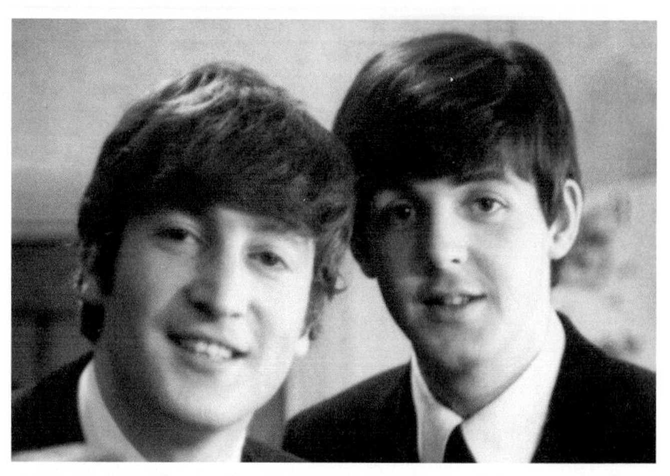

A Mystical Bond—Paul and John creating dreams. "The memories of their mothers lived on in their music, which they shared to conquer the world." VAL WILMER / REDFERNS / GETTY IMAGES

The Four Headed Monster—The Beatles at the height of Mania. "The sound of the future." MARKA / ALAMY STOCK PHOTO

Newly in Love—Paul and Linda in May of 1967 at Sgt. Pepper's *launch party. "You have found her, now go and get her."* KEYSTONE PICTURES USA / ALAMY

A Renewed Creativity—John and Yoko in July, 1968. "Remember to let her under your skin." TRINITY MIRROR / MIRRORPIX / ALAMY STOCK PHOTO

So Cosmic—The Beatles and the Maharishi Yogi, 1967. "The heart always goes to a warmer place." PICTURELUX / THE HOLLYWOOD ARCHIVE / ALAMY STOCK PHOTO

Patron Saint of Lost Causes—St. Jude Thaddeus, from "Christ, the Apostles and St. Paul with the Creed," Hendrick Goltzius, ca. 1589. "Accept the spirit of love." ARTOKOLORO / ALAMY STOCK PHOTO

An Offer of Hope and Consolation—John Nicholson Ireland, whose 1907 canticle "Te Deum," likely sung by McCartney as a choirboy, comprises the opening notes of "Hey Jude." "It just became a part of him." HISTORIC IMAGES / ALAMY STOCK PHOTO

Seamlessly Adorned—The Drifters, the soulful refrain of their 1960 chart-topping hit "Save The Last Dance For Me" worked its way deep into McCartney's melodic structure for "Hey Jude." "You're meant to hear the quotation." PICTORIAL PRESS LTD / ALAMY STOCK PHOTO

News At Home—A couple digests the grim daily news reports from the Vietnam War—"A less-than-noble and seemingly unachievable cause."
IANDAGNALL COMPUTING / ALAMY STOCK PHOTO

"Na . . . na . . . na . . . na na na na"—Surrounded by a diverse chorus of revelers, the Beatles film a performance of "Hey Jude" to premiere on David Frost's Frost on Sunday *in the UK and eventually* The Smothers Brothers Comedy Hour *in the US—"The communal Beatles hymn."*
MARKA / ALAMY STOCK PHOTO

jam-packed control room, including the Beatles, is "over the moon." His state-of-the-art studio has been properly christened. "I knew the equipment we'd installed was the best in both London and the UK by a mile," Sheffield writes. "But even I was impressed by what came out." Equally enthralled is George Martin, who has spent the better part of his world-class career at EMI Studios, crying out; "Nobody touch anything!" An awed Lennon asks, "Can you play it louder?" Barry Sheffield counsels against this, lest anyone have their ears blown off. This sparks laughter all around. Sheffield also recalls McCartney running to a phone to call his friend Peter Asher. In his memoir, Asher believes it was Paul's bass session on the inaugural James Taylor album, an album Asher was producing, which inspired the Beatles' session at Trident. "Peter come 'round here and have a listen to this!" Paul gushes. Norman and Barry Sheffield's studio is now officially on the map.

Later that day, Friday, August 2, a final mixing session begins at 2:00 PM with Martin and Barry Sheffield. On Tuesday, August 6, the same engineering team meets again in the control room of Trident Studios from 5:30 to 7:30 PM to put together the first mono mix of the song. This is done in a most unusual way for the time, combining both channels of the stereo mix made from the previous session instead of going back to the original eight-track tape. Nevertheless, the mono mix is considered suitable and taken back to EMI the following day as a possible master for release as the Beatles' next single.

The next evening, Wednesday, August 8, a mere eighteen days before its US release (twenty-two in the UK), the final mono mixing/mastering session of "Hey Jude" begins in EMI Studio Two at 6:40 PM where something of a reversal of misfortune is discovered when trying to transfer tapes between studios again. Just as the final Take 25 from

Abbey Road that George Martin had hoped would stand as the foundation to "Hey Jude" a week earlier at Trident was unusable, this time the Trident master tape mixed to acetate proves problematic due to the recording sounding murky when played back on EMI's equipment. Ken Scott immediately determines there is virtually no high end to the sound. He recounts in Mark Lewisohn's *The Complete Beatles Recording Sessions*: "I got in well before the group. Acetates were being cut and I went up to hear one. On different equipment with equalizing levels and different monitor settings, it sounded awful, nothing like it had at Trident." He shares his concerns with Martin. After reviewing it himself, the producer concedes that the amazing mix from only hours before that had had everyone agog at Trident now sounded terrible. Norman Sheffield, who at first had taken this incident as a slight on his studio, argues that it's simply "sour grapes" for the behind-the-times EMI Studio: "They didn't know what to do with our tracks; and besides I didn't really care what they thought. I knew George Martin and the Beatles were happy and so was I, because I knew what it meant for us."

Upon arrival at Abbey Road, McCartney does not take the news well, as Scott's account attests: "The look that came from Paul towards me . . . if looks could kill, it was one of those situations." McCartney knows what this song, these sessions, this organic rebirth of the Beatles means to him and the band. They invested so much in the "magic take" that had floored everyone at Trident, and now it seems it might have all been for naught. When the other Beatles arrive, a conclave forms on the studio floor. Scott, terrified he'll be blamed, can only guess what they're saying. When everyone reconvenes in the control room, it's agreed that they'll give it a listen. They all hate it. Although it is hardly his fault, upon hearing that everyone concurs that it's a disappointing mix, Scott still shares years later: "I wanted to crawl under a rock and die."

Perhaps when considering all of the serendipitous timing regarding the inspiration, composing, recording, and eventually the release of "Hey Jude," there is no luckier break for McCartney, the Beatles, or their disgruntled producer than the random visit to Abbey Road that crack engineer Geoff Emerick decides to make that day. Martin, likely pacing the halls contemplating various methods of equalization to save the "magic take," runs into his trusted second in command and asks for his assistance.

In his book *Here, There and Everywhere*, Emerick, having recently retreated from the Beatles' heightened troubles, recalls: "George opened the control room door and I saw four very unhappy Beatles gathered around a flustered Ken Scott, who was tweaking the controls of a piece of outboard equipment that we called a Curve Bender. George said, 'I've got a visitor here who might be able to help.' Paul was the first to spot me; he broke into a big grin and gave me a wave from the back of the room. 'Ah, the prodigal son returns!' John called out brightly. Even George Harrison gave me a warm handshake and said quietly, 'Hello, Geoff. Thanks for stopping in—we really appreciate it.'"

The crestfallen group plays Emerick the song. He then surmises the recording quality poor with "no top end whatsoever." This assessment echoes exactly Scott's concerns, as Emerick remembers him swearing that it all sounded fine at Trident. "I went by Trident to see the Beatles doing 'Hey Jude' and was completely blown away," Scott is quoted in Lewisohn's *Sessions*. "It sounded incredible."

Having assisted in recording the most astonishing music ever put to tape at Abbey Road, Emerick has a different take than the confident Norman Sheffield: "Obviously something at Trident had been misaligned, and the only hope of salvaging the mix was to whack on massive amounts of treble equalization." Emerick continues in his memoir: "I walked over to the console and Ken motioned for me to sit down. John Smith rewound the tape repeatedly while I worked at the controls. Eventually we got it to sound pretty good, although the track still didn't have the kind of in-your-face presence that characterizes most Beatles recordings done at Abbey Road . . . I might not have done anything that Ken himself wasn't doing—I think that all they really wanted was my stamp of approval. All four Beatles thanked me profusely as I left."

The accompanying booklet in the *White Album's 50th Anniversary Super Deluxe* box set explains: "It was discovered, in time for later Beatles recordings at Trident that part of the problem was due to the studio's American tape machines being set to the US equalization curve NAB, while (EMI) used the UK standard CCIR. To resolve this in the future, Trident tapes were always copied at Abbey Road with the correct NAB setting during playback." In other words, Emerick is proven correct. It's not that Trident's equipment is bad; its US calibrations just don't match up with EMI's board. This also comports with Norman Sheffield's memory of having the eight-track machine that is the envy of the Beatles shipped directly from the States.

And so, the final mono mix and mastering of "Hey Jude" is made on this day and will be released three weeks later, eventually becoming the Beatles' longest running #1 in America, a colossal hit worldwide, and by the longest shot, the most popular song of 1968.

"The most important part of the sound of 'Hey Jude' is that dry mix," cites Kiley Lotz. "His voice is right up front, which I love about that time period of music and engineering, it makes you feel as if Paul is sitting right next to you singing in your ear; 'Don't be afraid. Don't let it get you down. You can do this.' And you don't even realize you're being carried through to this big finale, because you had someone holding your hand the whole time. When he sings, *Don't you know that's it's a fool* . . . all these little variations on the theme gets you excited. You're thinking, 'Oh, that was cool. I wasn't ready for that one.' You are so familiar with the hooks that when he sings something different or the harmonies come in your pupils get wider and wider."

It'll be another fifteen months before there'll be a true stereo mix of "Hey Jude." George Martin, joined by engineers Emerick, Phil McDonald, and Neil Richmond in EMI Studios Room 4 between 2:30 and 5:15 PM on December 5, 1969, will also work similarly with its B-side, "Revolution." Both songs round out a hodgepodge of Beatles A- and B-sides from 1964 through 1968 that make up the 1970 US album release, *Hey Jude*. No one seems to notice that this paean to length is five seconds shorter than the mono mix. Weirdly, no matter where you listen to "Hey Jude" today on a bevy of streaming services or YouTube, you are likely to see it appear from 7:06 to 7:09; the latter of which it appears in the wildly popular Beatles' *1* collection.

Pleased with the results of the original mix, McCartney leaves the studio that evening with an acetate copy under his arm and makes his way to a party held by Mick Jagger at Vesuvio's nightclub in central London where the Rolling Stones are celebrating the completion of the band's

Beggars Banquet album. Once put on the club's state-of-the-art speakers, any trepidation regarding its sonic splendor evaporates for Paul. Vesuvio's co-owner and drug dealer for the Stones, Tony Sanchez, describes the scene in his book, *Up and Down with the Rolling Stones*: "The slow buildup of 'Hey Jude' shook the club. I turned the record over, and we all heard John Lennon's nasal voice pumping out 'Revolution.' When it was over, I noticed Mick looked peeved. The Beatles had upstaged him."

If the immense popularity, the ensuing critical accolades, and the bevy of lists cited earlier are any indication, the Beatles have recorded perhaps their finest record. Meanwhile, the world it is to greet beyond studio machinations and the cushy surroundings of the rock star elite rages in historic tumult. As the Beatles revert to their default position as studio wizards, a killer rock band making unprecedented pop music to rescue themselves from a malaise of drug abuse, professional strife, and inner fighting, their generation is quite literally coming apart.

CHAPTER EIGHT

Anytime You Feel the Pain

The Violent Global Tumult of 1968

The political and cultural tidal waves gathering force through the mid-sixties crashed down on Western Europe and North America during the mythic year of 1968.

—Craig Werner, *Freedoms*

The world is on fire. Literally. Figuratively. Symbolically. Politically. Emotionally.

The year 1968 is the most contentious and violent year since World War II had come to an end. The threat of nuclear annihilation hangs heavily as the Cold War between the communist bloc of Russia and China and the Western democratic world escalates daily. The Vietnam War, its senseless bloody nexus, has become an untenable fiasco. There are street riots fueled by economic, cultural, and generational strife in Paris, London, and Mexico City, while political unrest in Czechoslovakia leads to a Soviet invasion. In America, volatility reaches such dangerous proportions that comparisons to Civil War times are routinely evoked. Revolution, both cultural and political, replaces the peace and love edict that had taken hold only a year before. Race riots, war protests, domestic terrorism, and counterculture uprisings overrun campuses and cities. Mind-bending, gut-wrenching, history-shaking assassinations of cultural and political leaders crack the country's very foundation, where splits within the ranks of the New Left and the emerging modern conservative movement widen. Throughout 1968, there are splinters within fissures and gaping holes in the reasoning of it all.

Professor and lecturer, at the University of Wisconsin–Madison's Department of Afro-American Studies, Alexander Shashko: "My sense of 1968 is that it is a moment when a lot of the contradictions of the 1960s really came to the fore. The Summer of Love from 1967, the Civil Rights Movement from a few years before, this new nascent wave of feminism, the early stirrings of the modern environmental movement buy into this utopian sense of possibility that the American experience can be perfected. There is this idea, especially from a younger generation, that America can aspire to and reach ideals that it hadn't lived up to in the past. This is not only a movement on the Left. You have the rise of Evangelical Fundamentalism happening at the same time, which has both utopian and dystopian elements to it. By the time you get to 1968, there is this sense of, 'Well, if we're going to try to perfect the world, it also means combatting the system that is preventing us from doing that.' And that means a growing cynicism about the institutions that run the country as it already exists."

Professor of sociology, at Grand Valley State University in Michigan, Joel Stillerman: "The way that young people were challenging universities, which was built on the Civil Rights Movement before that, and the ensuing global activism in [19]68, was the direct result of the post war demographic bulge that was straining the resources of universities. Many of these young people finishing college were feeling status inconsistency, because they have this college degree but their prospects for employment were not necessarily great. You have a generation of the overqualified, something occurring in many different places around the world."

Professor emeritus of Afro-American Studies, at the University of Madison–Wisconsin, Craig Werner: "Factualism, everybody fighting for their own corner—whether discussing the lifestyle-oriented hippies and the political New Left—is difficult to discern by 1968, because they overlap. There certainly were hippies that didn't want to mess with politics, but 'the drug culture' also participated in underground political movements. On the far left, the radicalization of the counterculture resulted in splits between the Maoists and Trotskyites, while you have anarchists basically operating under Jerry Rubin and his PR machine. It was a confusing ideological rabbit hole that seemed to lose its moral and practical grounding to embrace extremes."

Professor Stillerman concludes: "One of my colleagues, says, 'Sociology is the study of people doing things together that refuse to do things together.' This explains the events of 1968 fairly well."

Confronting and reflecting the furor of 1968 becomes a moral imperative and a lucrative exercise for inspired works of art in the literary and film worlds, and, of course, in music. A call to arms stands beside escapism to create some of the most lasting statements of the era. Rising above it all is a piano ballad by a Liverpool songsmith, whose empathy for the moment and instinctual passion to express the human spirit soon puts the Beatles front and center once again. In the middle of a summer of dark premonitions, anarchic violence, and tragedy, the world, especially in America, pauses to sing: *Na . . . na . . . na . . . na na na na.*

"I think the impact of 'Hey Jude' was very different for Britain than it was for America," notes author Tim Riley. "It was quite wrenching for Americans that spring and summer—the assassinations, the Chicago National Convention, the riots, and the emergence of this very stark culture war that we're *still* in the middle of."

To fully comprehend the emotional currency of "Hey Jude" is to face 1968 as an inexorable cataclysm of all that the Beatles had wrought in the modern world, a schizophrenic dream of change simultaneously retreating into innocence. According to Todd Gitlin's *The Sixties: Years of Hope, Days of Rage*, there had already been a place for the Beatles' most beloved melodies to soundtrack the times. From Berkeley, California, where students burst into choruses of "Yellow Submarine" at a 1966 protest march to the Pentagon anti-war protestors the following year in which the flower children trade in *Yeah! Yeah! Yeah!* to sing *All you need is love . . .* as if a unifying prayer. The streets now own the music.

"It is the whole 1960s picture in the microcosm of one year, in the sense that the best and the worst of everything came together at this one synchronous point in history," notes author Devin McKinney. "And the Beatles' music that year becomes a microcosm of creativity and history, and the way the two interact. The individual talent or the entity, in this case being the Beatles, meeting with social and political forces over which they have no control, but yet are compelled to respond to create within. And that's where it all happens, this collision of history and creativity. In the sixties, you have some of the most amazing history ever made, which happens to be the framework in which the Beatles, one of the most, if not *the* most creative, forces of the twentieth century happen to be doing their thing. So that's the collision, and it happened in 1968 in a much more concentrated and violent form."

"As bright and embracing as it is, the opening assumption of 'Hey Jude' is we're in crisis, we are in deep doo-doo here, and we need to find our way back to our best selves, to our best hopes, to our fondest dreams," says author Tim Riley. "And that's what's so great about the song in aesthetic terms; it delivers the listener to a better place every single time, so it's kind of a recipe, a giant musical algorithm for input crisis/output hope, and the proof of it is in the lead vocal to the song that starts from singing completely alone to singing with this giant chorus that spins out into infinity of never-ending reassurance and hope."

"But in the end, what Paul is offering in 'Hey Jude' is all you're going to do is make it better, so it's not going to *solve* the problem," says professor of philosophy and communication studies, at Southern Illinois University Carbondale, Randall Auxier. "And I think that really helps, because it's a sort of backing up, saying, 'I can't solve your problems for you, but here's a list of things you can do to make it *better*.'"

"I think Paul is at his best operating on a subconscious level," McCartney biographer Peter Ames Carlin surmises. "It makes perfect sense for Paul to have written a song that was subconsciously about trying to create ease and get away from the tragedy and the horror of the year and float off on a melody. Think about him being in L.A. at the Capitol Records conference for Apple a couple of weeks after Robert Kennedy was assassinated in the beginning of June. He had to have experienced the tension and grief from that event and channeled it into 'Hey Jude.'"

"When I was in college, we would learn about form and structure, but I always felt it was outside of its historical context," says musicologist Tom Koch of North Carolina State University. "When we would talk about Beethoven, it's almost as if Beethoven existed in some vacuum, so much so as he didn't appear to be a real person living in Vienna and having to put up with everything else all the other Viennese had to put up with, so I always liked to know how music fits into a certain context. It helps me think about the music in a different way."

Don't carry the world upon your shoulders

While the arrival of a new Beatles anthem "Hey Jude" in August seemingly galvanizes pop culture, it doesn't take long to foreshadow the looming darkness of 1968. Despite sexual liberation, drug experimentation, and the generational pull of music and fashion celebrated during the Summer of Love, events throughout 1967 begin to sow the seeds of political and social divisions that will soon crack wide open. The advent of the Yippies (Youth International Party) in America dramatically shifts back-to-the-garden maxims to a virulent call for revolution. The Black Panthers emerge from the nation's Civil Rights Movement to challenge, both rhetorically and tangibly, the status quo with a militaristic stance. The SDS (Students for a Democratic Society), advocating for participatory democracy, grow to over a half-million strong—the largest-ever student activist organization in US history; a radical "action faction" breaks from the SDS and evolves into a domestic terrorist group, the Weather Underground. Urban riots spring up in Newark, New Jersey, and Detroit, Michigan, over economic and racial inequalities. In an already-combustible Middle East, the Six-Day War between

Israel and Egypt, Syria, and Jordan erupts, while a military coup turns Greece into a right-wing dictatorship.

Devin McKinney writes of 1967 in *Magic Circles*, "Sticks were swung, teargas lobbed, and many of those who had attempted to live out some version of the *Pepper* principle—who had, with the Beatles, helped dream its birth, fashion its parts, sanctify its significance—were shown how wrong they'd been to believe in anything but the immovable butt of the American institution."

At the center of the storm is the war in Vietnam, a heretofore little-known country in Southeast Asia, which reaches its bloodiest period in 1968. The US attempt to stem the tide of Communist expansion in Asia has gone from its early military advisory days in 1958 under President Dwight D. Eisenhower to an escalation in 1963 of one thousand strong under the John F. Kennedy administration, to twenty-three thousand at the behest of Lyndon Johnson in 1964 and, after ground troops are introduced to the fray in 1965, bloats to four hundred and forty-eight thousand by 1968. In the year's first days, one of the rudest of awakenings to the utter senselessness of the conflict occurs on the eve of the nation's Tet celebration, a Vietnamese ancestral holiday that also welcomes the lunar New Year. Later known as the Tet Offensive, the North Vietnamese military attacks one hundred cities and many US strongholds and embassies. By the end of this monumentally strategic setback in early March, nearly four thousand US forces are killed, with the total wounded approaching twenty thousand.

The mood of impending defeat falls hard on American morale. In early February, newspapers all over the world publish photographer Eddie Adams' eventual Pulitzer Prize–winning image capturing the horrific execution of a shackled Viet Cong insurrectionist by a brigadier general in the middle of the street with a revolver; the impact of the bullet entering the victim's brain. Soon after, Associated Press reporter Peter Arnett sends to press the most symbolic sentiment yet expressed during the elongated battle, after frantic and confused US troops torched the tiny Vietnam village of Ben Tre. An anonymous officer in charge reasons, "It became necessary to destroy the town in order to save it." The quote reverberates beyond the already motivated and mostly coalesced anti-war movement and into middle America where the shouts of "Our country right or wrong" are rapidly being drowned out by genuine concern that the sacrifice of so many young lives, the growing number of which are coming from their hometowns and immediate families, is for a less-than-noble and seemingly unachievable cause.

Professor Werner: "By '68 you have guys coming back from Vietnam every day with a completely altered view of the war and sharing it with us. I grew up in a military town called Colorado Springs and I played in a band that performed for a lot of GI audiences there and you always had guys coming back, as '68 unfolded, saying, 'This thing is fucked up.' One of the most telling comments I recall was from a guy from rural Wisconsin, and this was no hippie, when I asked, 'How many of you guys were opposed to the war?' And he thought about it for a minute and said, 'By the time we got back, after a year, *all* of us.' So, I think one of the most under-recognized aspects of what happened after Tet was it not only changed the narrative back home, but also GI opinion. It wasn't just the anti-war movement anymore. It was *everywhere* in America."

Tim Riley observes: "It's beginning to dawn on people, starting with Tet, the reality of 'What the fuck are we doing there? Somebody *must* be lying.'"

This rising skepticism of the war effort is cemented in the most crucial way by "the most trusted man in America," *CBS Evening News* anchor Walter Cronkite; after returning from Vietnam, he concludes his February 27 broadcast questioning the government's faith in the "silver linings they find in the darkest clouds." He reports that it appears "now more certain than ever, that the bloody experience of Vietnam is to end in a stalemate," which he's come to believe is "the only realistic, if unsatisfactory conclusion." Before solemnly signing off, Cronkite unflinchingly looks into the living rooms of America and states, "It is increasingly clear to this reporter that the only rational way out then will be to negotiate, not as victors, but as an honorable people who lived up to their pledge to defend democracy and did the best they could."

Many conclude that with those few words, spoken with the gravity of absolute confidence, the final epitaph of Lyndon Johnson's presidency has been written. Only four years before, Johnson made history by signing the Civil Rights Act and, after winning sixty-one percent of the national vote in November, as part of his Great Society initiative, he signed the Voting Rights Act. Both legislative achievements were the culmination of decades of marches, protests, martyrs, dramatic standoffs, negotiations, and hard-fought political bravery. Vietnam has tragically eclipsed all of it. Professor Werner: "Lyndon Johnson's decision to escalate Vietnam was the most devastating aspect of the 1960s. If Johnson hadn't done that, I think his Great Society might've worked, but once he escalated Vietnam, it was screwed."

On March 31, a politically compromised President Johnson makes a somber televised address to the nation, in a measured manner similar to Cronkite's in his broadcast, to announce: "I shall not seek, and I will not accept, the nomination of my party for another term as your President."

The day after Johnson's shocking address, a thousand young men return their draft cards to government offices all over the country. Before the summer is out, anti-war marches, staged events, and insurrections against institutions rise to, again, the greatest number since the Civil War a century before. It begins less than a month later when students take over five buildings on Columbia University's campus and briefly hold the dean hostage, demanding that the university cut its ties to military research. After a week, administrators finally call in the police, who respond with nearly one thousand officers, a dozen of whom are injured in the raid. When the insurrection is over, more than seven hundred are arrested.

On May 17, nine anti-war activists enter a Selective Service office in Catonsville, Maryland, removing nearly four hundred files and burning them in the parking lot with homemade napalm. Although later convicted of destruction of government property and sentenced to jail terms ranging between twenty-four and forty-two months, the actions of those branded the Catonsville Nine spur nearly three hundred similar raids on draft boards over the next four years, prompting a Supreme Court decision that burning a draft card is not an act of free speech protected by the First Amendment.

Finally, the most damaging incident of the war's effect on the home front comes just two days after the song to which this book is dedicated is released. Thousands of anti-war demonstrators, news reporters, and bystanders convene for the Democratic National Convention in Chicago on August 28, 1968. To replace the beleaguered Johnson, the party nominates his pro-war vice president, Hubert Humphrey, but

Democratic delegates in attendance are split on continued US involvement in Vietnam. Eugene McCarthy, a committed anti-war candidate, and others challenge the assumption that the United States pursue the controversial war effort, and fights erupt on the convention floor, inciting the constituency and engendering pure rage on the far left, especially from the angered youth of the nation. A defiant Chicago mayor Richard Daley demands a fierce response to the uprising, deploying twelve thousand police officers and calling in another fifteen thousand state and federal officers to control the protestors in the city's streets, which devolves into an orgy of televised violence as cops club and tear-gas the mob outside. Images of middle-class kids being hunted like wild animals and dragged into police trucks, bloodied and battered, while still others chant, "The whole world is watching!" are splashed across network television in living color. Their anguished voices reverberate in a nation's soul alerted by Cronkite, stunned by the president, and exhausted by a sense of growing terror brought on by two history-altering assassinations.

On April 4, Civil Rights Movement icon, Reverend Martin Luther King Jr., who had culminated the famous march on Washington in August of 1963 with his unforgettable "I have a dream . . ." speech, is gunned down in broad daylight on the balcony of Memphis' Lorraine Motel. The senseless murder of this man of peace, whose historic march from Selma to Montgomery in 1965 became a lasting symbol of the Voting Rights Movement that brought about Johnson's historic legislation, pours gasoline on an already-intense race-based blaze. Over the next week, anger erupts into violence and civil disturbances in more than a hundred cities, leaving thirty-nine dead, more than twenty-six hundred injured, and twenty-one thousand arrested.

"King was killed three miles from my house, which was in an integrated neighborhood, and so my memory of '68 was on the ground in the sense that nobody came to pick up our trash for weeks and weeks, and there was a curfew, and there were tanks in the streets of my hometown," remembers Dr. Auxier. "Granted, I'm only seven years old, but believe me, the adults around me were frightened. It seemed like it was one goddamn thing after another in 1968, and I was thinking the whole world is coming apart at the seams."

On the night of King's murder, Democratic presidential candidate Robert Kennedy, former attorney general for his slain brother John and current New York senator, prepares his stump speech for a packed and racially divergent crowd in Indianapolis, Indiana. State and city officials, aware of the tragedy in Memphis, the news of which has not yet reached the rally attendees, fear reports of King's murder might cause the kind of violent demonstration that has already begun exploding across the nation. The Indianapolis chief of police duly warns the senator that the police cannot provide adequate protection, but an undeterred Kennedy decides to speak to the crowd anyway. Standing on a flatbed truck, head down, voice faltering slightly, Kennedy reads from notes he's cobbled together at the last minute: "I have some bad news for you, for all of our fellow citizens, and people who love peace all over the world, and that is that Martin Luther King was shot and killed tonight." Audible gasps and cries ring out throughout the gathering, as Kennedy forges ahead, calling for calm and respect from his fellow Americans who value and honor Dr. King. He concludes with a resounding call for the times that have befallen a country in turmoil: "What we need in the United States is not division; what we need in the United States is not hatred; what we need in the United States is not violence or lawlessness; but love and wisdom, and compassion toward one another, and a feeling of justice toward those who still suffer within our country, whether they be white or they be Black."

One month later, on May 7, Kennedy wins the Indiana primary, catapulting his burgeoning campaign, which had just announced its entrance into the race two weeks before Johnson bowed out in March. Conjuring images of brighter days of youth and promise from the early 1960s, clashing with the grim visions of his own brother's assassination in November of 1963, Kennedy draws on these personal experiences to connect with constituents. After his emphatic speech the night of King's murder and his ensuing victory in Indiana, the forty-two-year-old senator finds his footing, garnering large crowds at rallies and causing a media stir. As a result, he takes one of the next two primaries and banks the future of his candidacy on the June 4 California primary. After spending countless grueling hours leading up to it, traversing the second largest state in the contiguous United States, Kennedy claims a resounding victory. He has momentum, unlimited press, enthusiastic young crowds, and appears likely to ride all of it to the nomination and perhaps the presidency.

The next night, a jubilant Kennedy hosts a televised presser at the Ambassador Hotel in downtown Los Angeles, finishing by flashing the two-fingered symbol for peace. Minutes later he is shot in the back and neck by a radical anti-Israel Palestinian freedom-fighter from Jordan named Sirhan Bishara Sirhan; Kennedy is pronounced dead at 1:44 AM on June 6 at the Good Samaritan Hospital.

Two towering figures for the civils rights and youth movements of the 1960s are slain in plain sight within weeks of each other. The display of random violence in the streets now extends to the famous and powerful. It is as if anarchy is spreading across the land like a virus. The rage felt in the Black community now expands into liberal quarters, mostly in the entrenched anti-war sect. This sense of taking back the societal narrative also takes root in Europe and beyond, further underlining the furies of 1968.

Student movements in West Germany, Poland, Spain, and Italy are rivaled by those in Pakistan, Brazil, Scandinavia, and Yugoslavia. Workers' rights, anti-war, anti-apartheid, rising food prices, and civil rights issues fuel marches in London in spring; Northern Ireland Civil Rights Association protests to end discrimination and create an independent Ireland spark a thirty-year period of ethno-national political violence waged in communities between multiple groups including British state and military forces, paramilitary, the IRA (provisional Irish Republican Army), and armed insurgents. Mexican student protests against an authoritarian regime leading up to the Mexico City Olympics prompt police and military to kill hundreds in the streets. Perhaps the most famous symbol of protest comes when two medal-winning African American athletes Tommie Smith and John Carlos raise black-gloved fists during the playing of the US national anthem in solidarity with the struggle of oppressed Black people worldwide. Earlier in the year, Czechoslovakia, a Soviet-bloc country, abolishes censorship, stressing the need for greater freedoms. Eventually known as "Prague Spring," it radiates shockwaves inside the Soviet Union. This is March. By late August, Russia has had enough. On the twentieth, six days before the release of "Hey Jude" in the West, Soviet tanks and troops, including soldiers from Poland, Bulgaria, East Germany, and Hungary, storm into Czechoslovakia. The short-lived democratic optimism is over. Of course. This is 1968.

Perhaps the year's most prevalent outburst of collective fury occurs on the streets of Paris, France, on May 6 when youth protests against capitalism, consumerism, American imperialism, and traditional institutions attract press and cameras, and are followed predictably by a police crackdown. A full-scale riot then breaks out between police and more than five thousand university students, garnering sympathy from France's trade union confederations, which are already hurting from the economic downturn. Eventually, eleven million workers go on strike, adding up to more than twenty-two percent of the total population of France, culminating as the largest and most damaging general strike in the nation's history. The organic bonding of these factions leads to battles within the ranks and thus greater rioting. All of this, lasting seven weeks, causes the entire country to shut down, further crippling an already anemic economy. Fearing civil war, the national government briefly ceases to function when President Charles de Gaulle secretly flees to Germany. These protests drive similar movements worldwide, inspiring graffiti, posters, slogans, and, of course, songs and films.

Standing in solidarity with the workers and students, France's most prominent film directors—Jean-Luc Godard, Claude Lelouch, François Truffaut, and Louis Malle—shut down the Cannes Film Festival. Perhaps seen as a rare step beyond their insulated cocoon of fantasy and art, this is not true for Godard, a pioneer of the French New Wave movement and virulent activist. He will soon make *One Plus One,* an overtly political film with combative polemic scenes intercut with the Rolling Stones as they work on the provocative opener for their upcoming album *Beggars Banquet,* "Sympathy for the Devil." Interestingly, Godard approaches the Beatles first, but they decline.

Professor Craig Werner: "Godard's film does a great job at capturing the essence of how '68 operated, how it felt underground with the escalation of violence in every form."

By the summer of 1968, pop culture and art—film, theater, literature, and music—can no longer ignore the events turning everything upside down. In many ways, writers, filmmakers, and musicians have already begun adding to the year's tumultuous narrative.

On April 29, the debut of the Broadway musical *Hair*, featuring nudity, profanity, overt drug use, and a strong anti-war sentiment, causes an uproar. It is also a smash hit, many of its songs finding their way onto the pop charts and into chants of the movement. Off-Broadway, underground theater loudly expresses the times while also heralding the coming of a new age, beginning with the first staged portrayal of the gay lifestyle, *The Boys in the Band*. The San Francisco street theater of the Diggers, the Living Theater in the Paris and New York undergrounds—including renowned artist Andy Warhol's combination of film, live music, and light shows called "happenings"—emerges. Warhol too becomes a victim of the looming violence of 1968, as radical feminist Valerie Solanas shoots him at his Factory in downtown Manhattan three days before RFK is killed. He survives but, as arguably the most influential artist and pop culture commentator of the latter half of the century, Warhol is never the same.

The literary world devours combative author Norman Mailer's trailblazing nonfiction novel *Armies of the Night*, about the late 1967 anti-war march on the Pentagon; as well as Black Panthers' minister of information Eldridge Cleaver's memoir of his imprisoning, *Soul on Ice*; and Tom Wolfe's initial foray into New Journalism with *The Electric Kool-Aid Acid Test* covering author and contrarian Ken Kesey's Merry

Pranksters, a group of societal dropouts roaming the country in an acid frenzy. College campuses are alight with Carlos Castaneda's mystical musings in *The Teachings of Don Juan,* which further cast a spiritual aura around the drug culture. There is a series of swirling free-association essays on the times, *Slouching Toward Bethlehem* by cultural commentator Joan Didion; and *Welcome to the Monkey House,* a collection of playfully subversive short stories by humorist Kurt Vonnegut, who is also completing his seminal anti-war novel *Slaughterhouse-Five,* which will be released to critical and popular acclaim a few months into the following year. Science-fiction author Philip K. Dick's *Do Androids Dream of Electric Sheep?* chronicles the paranoia of a world out of control.

Films of the year also feature themes of doom, revolt, and cynicism. The post-apocalyptic *Planet of the Apes* and an underground classic horror film with cultural underpinnings, *Night of the Living Dead,* provide messages of the times while glimpsing the coming fallout. These are joined by anti-hero tales released in late 1967, *The Graduate* and *Bonnie and Clyde, Hang 'Em High* and *Bullitt,* all of which challenge heroic archetypes. The supernatural horrors of *Rosemary's Baby,* the soulless violence of *Once Upon a Time in the West,* the hallucinatory ruminations of *2001: A Space Odyssey,* and the musical adaptation of Charles Dickens' tragic tale of man's inhumanity to man, *Oliver!,* which will go on to take home the year's best picture at the 1969 Academy Awards, all seek alternative realities in the firestorm.

And as popular music matures, world events work their way into songs. The Rolling Stones' "Street Fighting Man," Sly and the Family Stone's "Everyday People," James Brown's "Say It Loud—I'm Black and I'm Proud," and the aptly titled "Fire" by The Crazy World of Arthur Brown are art imitating life imitating art. The Doors release their anti-war screed "The Unknown Soldier" with a black-and-white film of the staged execution of enigmatic lead singer Jim Morrison by firing squad, while Detroit's MC5 sonic affront is managed by the founder of the radical anti-war White Panther Party, John Sinclair. The usually conservative Motown also chimes in with the Supremes' controversial "Love Child," the song that eventually ends the amazing run of "Hey Jude" at #1 in America. The Temptations take on the ignoring of inner-city poverty in "Cloud Nine" and Marvin Gaye's paranoiac "I Heard It Through the Grapevine" reveal socially conscious and darker leitmotifs that challenge their usual feel-good sixties edict.

"During troubling times, there's a synergy at work between activists in a movement writing music, musicians who are swayed by changes happening around them, and the communities that they live in," says Professor Stillerman. "And then also activists looking to musicians to write songs that make sense of what's going on, acting as a crucial part of an overall organizing strategy."

None of this synergy is happening in a vacuum. Popular music had always been one step ahead of the cultural curve, as Professor Shashko pointed out to me: "Sixty-eight has come to stand for a lot of the societal and generational changes that have really been happening for a decade leading up to it. We tend to fixate on the 1960s as the period in which this change was the most dramatic, but it was already building, and anyone who has studied the history of pop music knows that the revolution starts with Elvis, Chuck Berry and Little Richard and all of those folks well before we get to 1968. By the time we get there the height of the Civil Rights Movement has already come to pass, a lot of things had already been happening leading up to 1968, which I think is always worth noting and recognizing as the context for that year."

Author Tim Riley adds: "In meta terms, it's this great coming of age story where we listen to and participate in all of these people finding their own identity in the context of a group that is just so exhilarating to watch over and over and over again, because as a culture, we're all busy finding ourselves; who we are, how do we fit in? What does this country mean to us? How can we go fight this war we don't believe in? How can these older people be insisting that we do these things when they're feeding us into a meat grinder? This betrayal of the father and son is the central theme of the sixties."

The albums of 1968 also reflect the year's rising conflicts. Johnny Cash's controversial and career-defining *At Folsom Prison* puts country music in the middle of the fight for social justice. The Mothers of Invention mock the counterculture and the Beatles' seeming exploitation of it in their satirical masterpiece, *We're Only in It for the Money*. And the anguished cries of Janis Joplin rattle walls on Big Brother and the Holding Company's *Cheap Thrills*.

In a bold and singular statement, within days of the dawn of 1968, Bob Dylan releases an album of biblical portent and cultural refuge that will dramatically alter the sonic narrative of popular music. *John Wesley Harding* is "the voice of a generation" sending signals from his wooded environs one hundred miles from New York City in Woodstock, New York, where the songwriter had retreated since his reported motorcycle accident in 1966. During this time, Dylan's love for American roots music and its mythos is shared with members of the Band, a group of mostly Canadian (and one American) musicians who'd acted as Dylan's backing band for his controversial move into electric music a few years earlier. In the ubiquitous din of psychedelia and acid rock, both the Band and Dylan turn the clock back to a more romantic time of heroes and villains. In July, the Band releases *Music from Big Pink*, named for the house in which Dylan and the Band met to record hours of what would come to be known as the Basement Tapes, which is circulated as a bootleg almost immediately. These new/old sounds sent sonic shock-waves across the musical landscape, especially in England where they are embraced by guitar hero Eric Clapton, who travels to Woodstock with hopes of being asked to join the Band, and an American electric guitar magician making a name for himself in England, Jimi Hendrix. The latter's cover of Dylan's "All Along the Watchtower" from *John Wesley Harding* six months after its initial release becomes his highest-charting single. Even George Harrison will eventually travel to upstate New York to see for himself how this music is being made.

In Dylan's wake, a return to stripped-down sounds *sans* musical and technological artifice with ancient proverbs and reflections of simpler times works its way into some of the year's more escapist declarations. Irish singer/songwriter Van Morrison blurs the lines of jazz, poetry, and folk in the mesmerizing *Astral Weeks*; mega-successful duo Simon and Garfunkel build a philosophical bridge across the generation gap on *Bookends*; Aretha Franklin breaks new ground with her powerful musical statement, *Lady Soul*, as does Otis Redding with his #1 hit of placid escapism, "Dock of the Bay." The Byrds, a California rock/folk band who turned Dylan's acoustic songs into electrified anthems, is inspired by American country-music enthusiast Gram Parsons to release *Sweetheart of the Rodeo* in August, a signal to future country-rock bands of a new road being forged. *The Kinks Are the Village Green Preservation Society* turns the heavy garage pop of the Kinks into a lamentation for the passing of old English traditions in the wake of the revolutionary spirit of the times. Meanwhile, their hard-rock mantle is being usurped by heavier, less ornamental rock played by new British bands like Black Sabbath and California's Iron Butterfly and Blue Cheer.

And then there is the Beatles, who had written the bulk of what will become known as the White Album in the peaceful mountains of Rishikesh, India, returning the band that started all the artistic experimenting back to their roots of American country music flavors and hard-rocking quartet numbers set against old-fashioned European balladry. This is certainly the mindset of Paul McCartney, who comes to the project with American Western tales, "Rocky Raccoon," singsong paeans to garden living, "Mother Nature's Son," hippie naturalism, "Why Don't We Do It in the Road," prewar piano ditties, "Martha My Dear" and "Honey Pie," tender notions, "I Will," and rock-and-roll fevers, "Back in the U.S.S.R." and "Helter Skelter," and then, eventually, the monumental "Hey Jude."

Beatles expert, Scott Freiman: "Clearly, after they went to India, bringing along their acoustic guitars, they were watching the Band and Dylan as much as the Beatles watched every single artist come out with psychedelic albums after *Sgt. Pepper's*. The Beatles didn't want to be just another one of the pack, so the idea was to largely go back to very little production techniques and write really good songs and let them speak for themselves. 'Hey Jude' is part of that. It is a good song first and foremost. There's nothing flashy about it. For the Beatles, it was a return to just good songwriting."

"Consider both *Pepper* and the White Album reflections of their times, no matter how much different they appear and sound," adds Tim Riley. "While *Pepper* was a reflection of the psychedelic era, the White Album is a reflection of the cacophony and the despair of 1968. Something like 'Revolution 9' could not have happened at any time before the summer of '68. It is a total dreamscape of how people were feeling. By '68, the Beatles may not be charting new territory, but their embrace of the back-to-basics movement is a signal of their greatness; to participate on a completely different level than anyone else and *still* be leaders. It's a very interesting shift."

While the "Hey Jude" / "Revolution" single allows the Beatles to return to more traditional instruments, cleaner recording techniques, and even introspective themes of self-realization, it also symbolizes an aural, lyrical, and even visual (a stark white album cover) stripping away of the barriers of sound, wordplay, and image to arrive at the very essence of the message. Essentially, the Beatles are providing another roadmap, this time to the singer/songwriter era of the 1970s, an expansion on the early 1960s folk movement that once took aim at societal ills but turned those motifs inward. "Hey Jude" can be heard as a template to confessional themes; Paul McCartney's singular statement foreshadowing emotive storytellers like James Taylor, Neil Young, Joni Mitchell, Don McLean, Jim Croce, Jackson Browne, Cat Stevens, Randy Newman, and Warren Zevon to name just a few, who will soon take the mantle of "Hey Jude" and its personal meditation in a time of global panic, cultural strife, and tell *their* stories. This spreads into soul music, as with Motown and Stax songwriters and performers, entering into a period dominated by Stevie Wonder's unparalleled oeuvre, joined by the expanded musical and thematic notions of Isaac Hayes and Marvin Gaye.

Dr. Tom Koch: "When Paul sings that first note a capella, there is a direct audience relationship he's able to form, an intimacy he accomplishes right away, because in rock the band can be an obstacle between the singer and the audience. Look at the great singer/songwriters like

James Taylor, there is no obstacle, you just have one person in front of the stage with their instrument, whether acoustic guitar or piano; their forming a bond with the audience right away, and it's what draws me into the song immediately."

"It is a premonition of singer/songwriters, but there is always this illusion that they are singing directly in the first person about themselves in their own experience," adds Tim Riley. "And while 'Hey Jude' is *bigger* and *better* than that, it does suggest in a personal way where songwriting will be going."

On his own personal journey of love and empathy, on a grander level, considering the pall of 1968, McCartney is also re-creating what John Lennon would later refer to as "the Beatle myth" with "Hey Jude"; the lovable lads from Liverpool coming to whisk you away to a utopian dream. This, beyond anything else, is what the Beatles have come to represent to millions, what author Devin McKinney writes about in his *Magic Circles*: "In their unity the Beatles contained, and in their music expressed the best of their generation's spirit—it's most transformative values, and its largest visions."

McKinney expounded on this point to me: "Obviously, the Beatles coming over after JFK lifted people up, but the important thing at that moment was that they lifted up *the youth,* they were not going to turn into a phenomenon on the backs of Billy Graham or Walter Cronkite, this older generation, they excited *kids*. That's what lofted them, and that's what lofted the sixties. However, 1968 is four years later, and for many of the same kids, it might as well have been a hundred years later. It's a *very* different moment. Everyone's older and tired, everyone wants to feel something a little different, a little deeper, a little more transcendent. And so that's why I think you can make a convincing case that

'Hey Jude' was of and for its time. It was a very different moment from '64 when they first came over, but it might have come out of the same impulse from people who were four years older but felt so much further removed from that youthful time."

Fellow Beatles author Tim Riley agrees, "'Hey Jude' is a revival of the Beatles' utopian ethos, this great giant cosmic accident, where opportunity meets talent and because of timing they become inextricably tied to how the country regathers itself in the wake of the JFK assassination, and then again, four years later, when 1968 comes along. In 1964, it's very difficult to argue that they are a self-conscious answer to JFK, but by '68, I think you could say they are very much conscious of their status and they are trying to position themselves back into that original premise, but as a band that has aged and now *sees* the world."

Out of this mire of despair and upheaval, senseless murder and street violence, emerges "Hey Jude," a humble song of hope and what music journalist David Quantick declares in his *Revolution—The Making of the Beatles' White Album* as "the last great Beatles single." It is not a political statement or a generational call to arms. Just the opposite. It is, if anything, a spiritual calling to look inward to project change outward, as the Maharishi had expressed to Paul, "The heart always goes to the warmer place." In that way, "Hey Jude" reminds the Beatles' audience, specifically in America, of the sound and optimism—Oldham's "sound of the future"—of only a few years ago.

"In its inexorable movement from the personal to the public," writes Jonathan Gould in *Can't Buy Me Love*. "The song itself can be said to open its heart to the world."

However, Paul's songwriting partner, despite admitting at the time "I really thought that love would save us all," has other ideas.

Although John Lennon had commented on the Vietnam War in underground publications and initiated conversations in this direction in private since the mid-sixties, the Beatles had steered clear of being overtly involved in the emerging social turmoil of 1967 by embracing and, in many ways, underpinning the mythical Summer of Love with *Sgt. Pepper's Lonely Hearts Club Band,* which literally had John, Paul, George, and Ringo disappearing into characters and painting new worlds with music. By 1968, at least for Lennon, the global youth uprising, civil rights protests, war, and assassinations has become too much to ignore. "I absolutely wanted the Beatles to say something about the war," he passionately reflected in one of his last interviews.

Constantly challenged by antiestablishment movements to make a stand, and inspired by Yoko Ono's dedication to activism, Lennon's attempt to answer the critics is "Revolution," a musical and lyrical vehicle to tap into the fear and anger he witnessed all around him, especially the Paris uprisings which detonate right before the Beatles enter the studio to record the song on May 30. Tim Riley explains further: "May is the big explosion of riots in Paris; a student demonstration that spreads to the working class and there are millions of people in the streets. And Lennon is adamant; 'We *have* to say something! We must address this! We have too much stature, if we don't say anything, we look stupid.' That's how he understands the Beatles' status."

"Revolution" also features a little of that infamous Lennonesque fun-poking before he'd dare dip his toes ever sarcastically in the boiling waters of discontent: *You say you got a real solution / Well, you know / We'd all love to see the plan.* He told *Playboy* in 1980: "As far as overthrowing something in the name of Marxism or Christianity, I want to know what you're going to do *after* you've knocked it all down."

"Lennon really threads a very interesting needle there," says Riley. "It's probably the song that Beatles scholars argue about the most: Is it pro-revolution or anti-revolution? I think it was Greil Marcus who said that the music encourages revolution while the lyrics counsel restraint, which is the intelligent person's response to the news in the streets; 'Hey, our sympathies are with you and we all want to change the world, but you have to think it through, you can't just overthrow a system.' The impulse to revolution is really tempting, but what happens next? What are you going to replace it with? It's a very sophisticated and complicated idea to put into a hardcore rock and roll song."

"The way people talk about 'Revolution' they completely ignore what John is actually singing in the song," says Rob Sheffield. "John is like, 'You know, there's no need for any kind of political action, and besides, if you endorse political action, people will disagree with you, and that's a bad thing.' *If you go carrying pictures of Chairman Mao / You ain't gonna make it with anyone, anyhow.* Oh, that's a great argument, John. You shouldn't have any political opinions, because what if somebody disagreed with you?"

Professor Auxier: "John Lennon was an intellectual, but he was highly dialectical in his thinking, so for him it was always a personal struggle with the way the world is versus how he wants it to be. His songs reflect what Hegel called the 'labour of the negative,' this constant battle with reality."

This battle is reflected in the Beatles working on several versions of "Revolution"—a slower take that opens side four of *The Beatles* and the sonically belligerent interpretation that will appear as the B-side to "Hey Jude." All distorted guitars and a stringent bellow from John before a single word is uttered, it fits right into the mood and purpose of rock music echoed in the streets. However, when confronted with taking a side, John sings, *But when you talk about destruction / Don't you know that you can count me . . . out.* Lennon injects the ambiguous . . . *count me out . . . in* to the slower album track recorded earlier, but will not be released until November. "I put in both, because I wasn't sure," he later said. Noteworthy is that for the first and more popular single version, Lennon, who claimed to have pained over the lyrics like none he had ever written before, wants indisputably to be *left out.*

Craig Werner: "By 1968, the SDS, still barely a conventional political organization, had gone three-quarters crazy and now embrace terrorist bombing as a tactic, and I think the Beatles are conflicted when looking at all of that and *feeling* all of it the way artists do."

"He doesn't really get off the fence in it," McCartney would joke about his partner years later.

Lennon decides to counter this conundrum by working on the soundscape epic "Revolution 9" with Yoko Ono and George Harrison, featuring a series of seemingly random tape loops of prerecorded stage plays, musical asides, screams, noises, backwards recordings, and sound effects acting as the ultimate statement of what its composer hoped would be the sound and fury of violent revolution—part warning, part call to action. Meanwhile, far from Lennon's chaotically mercurial musical statement, Paul McCartney's A-side ballad about the troubled Jude returns the Beatles to its core influence, as purveyors of positivity, love, and peace. The song, the world, the atmosphere is indeed "bad," but *could* be better. The two Liverpool lads once again finding two sides of a very well-worn coin.

"McCartney's response to 1968 is very different than John's," cites Tim Riley. "McCartney's response is let's do a medium-tempo ballad of encouragement, and it's a pep talk, it's a song of great reassurance. It does have that personal layer, but it's actually a much more self-conscious and culturally aware song about this larger abrasion, about how the world does seem to be cracking, like all the things that we take for granted, all of our assumptions, all of our best hopes somehow seem to be falling away, and where do we stand? Where do we find a center anymore? And there is this very reassuring, Beatlesque promise that the song carries, which is, 'No, we're gonna get through it,' a clarion call to we're bigger than this, we're stronger than this, we have to have hope, and we have to give one another a lifeline in these dark times."

The Beatles, as Mary McCartney's son *would* see it—his sentimentality and empathy shining through—needs to provide succor for the fracturing youth movements. Paul's childhood friend and partner fully understands this, while also envisioning it as his place to make a more aggressive statement, as he does whenever the Lennon/McCartney duo creates.

Scott Freiman: "When it all begins to fall apart for the Beatles and they're each embracing their individuality, one of the things that I think they're wrestling with, especially John, is how do we reflect or comment on what's going on in the world? And so John writes the song 'Revolution' where he is very wishy-washy in saying, 'Look, there might be leaders coming in who are worse off than the ones we have, so be careful what you wish for, this isn't a game.' Consequently, I think Paul was always someone who looked to heal and bring people together; even to this day when he does a concert, it's all about the communal experience, peace and love. So, for him, writing 'Hey Jude' became a way of writing something that was the opposite of 'Revolution,' a healing song, and the *na-na-nas* at the end are, in a sense, bringing the band

and audience together in unison to sing. And in that way, the 'Hey Jude' / 'Revolution' single reveals the polar opposites of its composers; you have 'Revolution' commenting on politics and you have 'Hey Jude,' which is a very healing, communal song. It is what the Beatles did so well, this contrast between the dark and the light."

Rob Sheffield: "When you compare 'Hey Jude' to 'Revolution,' it is John's idea of a conversation, where he interrupts to tell the listener how he's wrong; *You say you'll change the Constitution . . .* 'Well, let me tell you!' It's the quintessential mansplaining cliché, the 'Well . . . !' Comparing the A to the B side reveals how Paul and John approach a conversational song quite differently."

Eric Hutchinson: "It's such a perfect example of how the Beatles worked, a classic Paul and John thing; John hears what's going on, takes a look at the world, and says, 'I hope you're happy,' but Paul is about, 'Yeah, I think everything's gonna be okay.' I think that's probably why 'Hey Jude' resonates so well, because it covers the spectrum of being human, and you know what, there's never a bad time for a song to come along and make everyone feel better. Considering everything that was going on, it makes total sense that people responded so strongly to a complete and lasting message by the biggest band in the world."

Professor Werner: "I think the Beatles hit the dead center of the topical and social commentary of the music of 1968 with 'Hey Jude,' and I also think it's not an accident that Wilson Pickett does a hell of a version of it. It is, after all, a soulful song. It reaches *deep*."

Professor Shashko: "The events of 1968, where 'Hey Jude' fits into the narrative, reflects that period of the late-sixties that bleeds over into the early seventies when you have these competing ideals—this idea that everything is going to hell, but also that we can make it all better, and, in a way that single from the Beatles signifies that."

Indeed, Lennon's "Revolution" is not completely without its own rallying cry for unity. While Paul sings *Let it out and let it in . . .* John is singing, *We all want to change the world* and *Well, you know, we're all doing what we can*, reminding everyone in the refrain, and rather boisterously in the outro: *Don't you know it's gonna be / All right! All right! All right!* Set beside Paul's abstruse *The movement you need is on your shoulder*, which, of course, John absolutely adored, "Revolution" perfectly balances this two-sided dispatch of solidarity. Remember, it was John who held fast against Paul's suggestion to ditch the ambiguous line. Is this *movement* political, cultural, or social? Sometimes it is better, sings Lennon, that change starts from an instinct of solidarity and not artifice.

"The biggest thing that solves the problems that we're still going through now is empathy; getting to know the other person," says Scott Freiman. "I did some work with Palestinians and Israelis years ago and when you get people who are arch enemies to sit together in a room, they talk about their families and their kids and their beliefs and then they can see each other as people, and suddenly you can make progress. And I think, the issues of what needs to be done today with politics, police or education starts with getting people who are different together and understanding those differences. This is what I get when I listen to *The movement you need is on your shoulder . . .*"

"It sounds to me like it's in your hands, this is your call to make, you can *do* or *not do,* and I am *always* a proponent of that idea," says singer/songwriter Stephen Kellogg, who admitted to me when we spoke how he struggled to frame the calamitous events of 2020 into his songs. "I feel like we spend half our lives assigning blame and figuring out what went wrong and then watch it sliding into disappointment often enough. And if 'Hey Jude' is about dusting oneself off, it makes perfect sense that anything that empowers the human spirit is great from my personal worldview. It reminds us that we have more power than we actually admit to ourselves. We're *not* helpless beings. We can affect our own outcome to some degree, if only by the way we choose to absorb events around us."

This duality in the "Hey Jude" / "Revolution" single predictably leads to some confusion for those looking to the Beatles for specific step-by-step guidance and leadership. The critical knives are especially out for Lennon. The political/arts magazine *Ramparts* mocks "Revolution" as a "narcissistic little song," as essayist Michael Wood insists it comes across as an "absurd statement," and the *New Left Review* predictably eviscerates the song as a "lamentable petty bourgeois cry of fear." To Lennon's credit he fires back in letters to publications and willfully engages in debates on the merits of the underground movements. But while McCartney stays out of it, his mega-hit A-side could not be ignored by the same audience.

"Folks on the more activist side of the counterculture, did not love 'Hey Jude,'" recalls Professor Shashko. "They generally found it fluffy and escapist, at least at the beginning, maybe now they have all come around to the sheer power of the song, but to them it evaded the confrontation that was going on. It's especially interesting in the context when coupled with 'Revolution,' because 'Revolution' is also not really a song that is supporting what is going on, at least at its more radical end. The Beatles are these working-class ambitious guys who wanted to succeed. It was reflected in the music they loved and the music they wanted people to hear, and to bring that back to America, and to do that they also wanted to exist in the middle of the political spectrum. It wasn't about revolution in a political sense, so there was some skepticism about where the Beatles were going at the moment among the people that were on that side of the political conversation."

"Interestingly, 'Hey Jude' was never one of my favorite songs, perhaps because of it being too centered that way," admits Professor Werner. "My wife, a big Beatles fan, hated it. But we were in the minority, because I think the vast majority of people that listened to it heard something else. For them, during everything that was going on, it felt like . . . *rest*. Especially for those willing to take the sound as the message, not the lyrical content or the social commentary of the song, and to an extent, so am I, because I think with 'Hey Jude' it's the music that speaks the loudest. It clears your chakras, man. It just makes you feel like a better human being. When I listen to it now, with it not being one of my favorites, I still feel it."

Rob Sheffield argues that "'Hey Jude' doesn't work as an escapist, ameliorating song," returning again to his assessment on its place as a subversive avant-garde statement for the pop charts. "It's not a song that fades comfortably into the background. You could say that if 'The Long and Winding Road' was #1 for nine weeks that year, or if it was 'Yesterday' or 'Lady Madonna,' but 'Hey Jude' is such an experimental record, so arrogant and aggressive in the way it presents its artistic and cultural ideas. I wasn't around in 1968, so I can't imagine how it sounded then with all the conflict, but to me, it does *not* sound like an escapist song, because it's so extreme and so different that it's hard to imagine how it could have sounded on top forty radio at the time, where you're hearing a three-minute song that goes *Yummy, yummy, yummy, I've got love in my tummy* and then this bombastic two-part, seven-minute song that does not fade into the background of your day. It may be easy to think of it as a cozy, friendly, reassuring song, but in practice, it's an *extreme* song that's really disruptive."

Professor Andrea Halpern provides a psychological aspect to how "Hey Jude" may have connected on a subconscious level to the zeitgeist: "There are certain brain circuits that are associated with different emotions, but less than the one-to-one mapping as you might think. Humans have many subtle emotions, and it would be a mistake to associate motion x with brain circuit y in a one-to-one fashion, as many of our emotions are complex. It's a cleaner question to ask, 'What can people detect in an emotional message in music?' There are a number of features that convey a message. This is, of course, culturally determined; you have to be familiar with the culture of that music. Although there are a few features that seem nearly universal—a faster tempo is associated with people judging it to be a happier piece. In Western music, the mode matters—happiness is associated with a major key, while sadness with minor. There are some things we've become acclimated to as little kids, we *learn* it. And then, as a society, we *agree* with it."

Dr. William Boone points out that the communal expression found in the new love/empathy metaphors in "Hey Jude" indeed act as a societal remedy: "Think about another 1960s defining song; Sam Cooke's 'A Change Is Gonna Come.' It also perfectly captures the time, the Civil Rights struggle, but it doesn't say anything about the movement, specifically. There is no mention of Dr. King or marches or voting rights in the lyrics, they're general and vague enough that they could speak to *any* time or *any* type of change. The production of it is so good, the songwriting, and obviously Sam Cooke's singing is so good the music goes beyond the message, beyond any kind of cultural impact, and that allows it to continue to speak."

"I don't think 'Hey Jude' is necessarily part of its era, because it's the sort of stuff Paul writes, and he writes that stuff *now*," adds McCartney biographer Howard Sounes. "He has a breezy, sunny outlook and he's a brilliant songsmith and just superb with melody. 'Revolution' is of its time, but it can't be as good a song, can it? If John Lennon were alive today, I'm not even sure it would be in the set-list, whereas 'Hey Jude' has been a solid gold classic from day-one to today. This is why, I think, ultimately, 'Hey Jude' is obviously a better song."

Stephen Kellogg adds: "It's no surprise to me that the song that becomes massive is not a song about what's going on *right now*, but at the same time it's a huge release of a song that lets us howl at the moon and take a break from the intensity of what's happening, because it doesn't feel like a weightless song. It allows you to fall into it. It needs to be a song with enough gravitas that's heavy enough to meet the intensity of the frequency that we're on right now, but not necessarily *about* what's going on right now. 'Hey Jude' did that in '68 for people who were feeling shell-shocked, who had this PTSD from everything that was happening and felt afraid for the world. And this song comes out, and it's about heavy stuff, but it's *different* heavy stuff that doesn't feel as utterly frightening. And then it has this huge release at the end, this orgasm, if you will, that allows you some release and an ability to just let it all out. So, if I was to try to dissect why the song worked at that time, that would be my assessment, those two things; its weighty enough, but not a political song."

Rob Sheffield concludes: "When you think of songs that are escapist, I think 'Revolution' is the escapist response to 1968. 'Hey Jude' is the one that reflects doubt, conflict, something's in question. 'Revolution' is everything that 'Hey Jude' is not in that it's sentimental, cloying, maudlin, and it sounds very much like a pampered person being astoundingly preachy about luxuries that he enjoys, that the person he's singing to doesn't enjoy. So, to me, 'Revolution' is the one that sounds sentimental, cliched and escapist. 'Hey Jude' is the realist, contingent song."

Regardless of its controversies, the titanic "Hey Jude" / "Revolution" single is the sound of the Beatles making one last stand against the tide of history, a history that they had assisted greatly in shaping. From the moment they took the stage at the London Palladium and launched Beatlemania—and for Americans, the moment Ed Sullivan shouted out their names and they tore into "From Me to You"—the Beatles had been leading up to these songs, especially "Hey Jude," with its multilayered message of hope and inner strength culminating in the singalong to end all singalongs. "I really think that the sixties were an extended serious argument about the meaning of freedom," Professor Werner concludes. "And I think by 1968 it became a physical clash in the streets all over the world that forced us to look at the best and the worst parts of that grand argument." The band, like the world, had faced down its own demons to make the biggest hit record of their career that would speak to millions in a time when a generation looked to the Fab Four for answers to what freedom meant, or as author Jonathan Gould frames it: "'Open your heart,' says 'Hey Jude.' 'Free your mind,' says 'Revolution.'"

Professor Shashko adds: "'Hey Jude' was as popular as it was in 1968 because what Paul was writing at a personal level reflected the kind of anxiety a lot of people were experiencing at a societal level; they were looking for a place of comfort and their ultimate response was that a song doesn't have to be political, per se, to speak to the times, to speak to the moment, the social moment, the political moment, the cultural moment. A song can capture something even if it is not explicitly about a political event or a political movement and it's about saying, 'We're going to get through it.'"

In his *Magic Circles,* Devin McKinney is clear: "As cultural leaders, the Beatles were expected by a good part of the audience to behave in one way; as artists they were bound to behave in another."

Ultimately, the Fab Four's most impactful art may have been as a visual medium—the hair, the suits, the bows, the *ooohs* that shook their heads and in turn shook balconies filled with screaming girls. The Beatles set trends, turning album covers into works of art, providing inspirational and lasting images of youthful optimism. "The mythology of the sixties has replaced the memory of the sixties, which has to do with ways in which this romance with revolution peaks in 1968," says Professor Werner. "This leads inevitably to 'Hey Jude.'"

This, above all, gave the song its extraordinary voice, and it would once again be the sight and vision of the Beatles in their element that would convey the symbolism of "Hey Jude" to its logical conclusion.

CHAPTER NINE

Better . . . Better . . . Better

Shadow & Light

> *It was as though the Beatles were reaffirming their oneness with their audience and each other, instead of just beginning their drift into chaos and bitter enmity. So did the studio audience—and much of the country—join in that night.*
>
> —PHILIP NORMAN, *SHOUT*

It begins on Paul McCartney's face, still reflecting a youthful glow but with eyes weary from experience. He looks directly into the camera, into the same hearts and souls to whom Walter Cronkite had communicated his dire notions of American defeat in Vietnam months earlier. Outside the world is raging, and now, many of the baby boom generation who watched this kid from Liverpool shout and croon and rock and roll their troubles away only five years before once again find themselves looking to him for solace. And he sings . . . *Hey Jude* . . .

McCartney plays it up while also balancing an understated grace, cracking a slight smile when he sings about making it better. Looking momentarily down at the piano and then back to engage the camera, as if millions watching *are* Jude, the composer transforms his second-person ballad into a universal prayer. Underlining this is a close-up of John and George from below, allowing the studio lights to form hallows around their heads as if dramatically poised to bring forth their angelic *aaaahhhs*. Looking off into the distance, Ringo taps his tambourine. The camera moves from him to pan across all four Beatles. There they are. The Fab Four. The legendary group. Playing together. Singing . . . *Aaaahhh*. Then we return to McCartney, making his stand about letting her into your heart and under your skin. *Let it out and let it in* . . . His band, *our* band, testifies.

This is how the film clip of "Hey Jude" begins. Long before MTV and YouTube, it is beamed to the world over two continents on a myriad of television shows from early September to late December. In the final months of 1968, the Beatles would have their visual symbol of solidarity, but it comes, once again, as its recording, at a time of deep turmoil for the band.

On August 22, 1968, four days before the US release of "Hey Jude," the mostly jovial go-along-to-get-along Ringo Starr, who did not have songs to defend, abruptly leaves the studio during the session for Paul McCartney's Chuck Berry homage, "Back in the USSR," which will eventually open the White Album. Feeling his role in the group peripheral and upset at McCartney's constant criticism of his drumming on the track, he sends word that he's quitting the band and heading off to vacation in Sardinia. This had been building for some time, as Abbey Road staff later commented that Starr was usually the first to arrive at the studio and would sit stewing in the reception area for hours waiting for the other Beatles to arrive. McCartney ends up playing many of the instruments on "Back in the USSR" as a result, something Paul is talented and ambitious enough to accomplish but it upsets the rest of the band.

It isn't long before the Beatles miss the soul and feel of Starr's unique style that has anchored the band's sound since he joined six years before. They send him a telegram begging his return and festoon his drum set in a consolatory bouquet of flowers. That's the day they rip through McCartney's raucous "Helter Skelter" a mind-bending eighteen times before the drummer exclaims, "I've got blisters on my fingers!" Of course, it's left on the final recording and becomes an iconic Beatles moment. But before all that, on September 4, the drummer quietly returns to the fold for the promotional filming of the band's next single and its B-side. Back to work for Mr. Starkey, ever the professional.

The wandering Ringo arrives tanned and rested, at the famed Twickenham Film Studios at 1:30 PM to find his kit ceremoniously perched on a riser above his bandmates, just like in the days when he would hover over stages awash in manic shouts of adulation. Twickenham, located in the suburbs of London, is one of the oldest film studios in England, and the site of dozens of British movies, including *Hard Day's Night* and *Help!* The Beatles will return here to rehearse new material the following year, resulting in their final album and film, *Let It Be.*

Clearly perturbed by the current dreariness and carping of his bandmates, enough to resign his position in the biggest musical act in the world, Starr could not help but notice a lighter air of excitement among his mates, along with a bit of trepidation—for the first time in over two years, the Beatles will take a stage and perform together in front of a live audience and then for an expected larger one on television. In just four days, September 8, the clip will debut in London on

ITV network's popular *Frost on Sunday*. Four days after that it will beam across the United Kingdom's most popular music showcase, BBC1's *Top of the Pops*, repeated there again on September 26, and finally it will be played on Britain's Boxing Day, one year after the controversial *Magical Mystery Tour* premier. American fans will eventually get to see it on CBS's hip and edgy *The Smothers Brothers Comedy Hour* on October 13; and then a final airing on West Germany's most influential pop culture vehicle, the *Beat-Club* on November 16.

The plan for the afternoon into evening session consists of pseudo-performances of "Hey Jude" and "Revolution" with the band singing to backing tracks of their recordings, although instruments and amplifiers will be humming beside them. Performing with backing tracks for "Revolution" isn't an issue for the band; a more-controlled staging of a song is how they'd produced nearly all of their promotional clips and feature films. An interesting sidelight is John's addition of the *out . . . in* lyric from the album version, as well as George and Paul singing *badoom shoobie-do- wop*, which does not appear on the final single mix. However, the all-important A-side "Hey Jude," scheduled for broadcast in both the United Kingdom and in America, inspires twenty-eight-year-old American-born director Michael Lindsay-Hogg to turn the session into an event not unlike the Beatles' signature early television performances that cemented their legend.

With input from the band—especially Paul McCartney, who had caught the directorial bug during *Magical Mystery Tour* where he ran things on set and later worked tirelessly on editing—Lindsay-Hogg hopes to present the Beatles' return to the stage to *perform* their newest song. The young director, known mostly for his drama and comedy work on television, had gotten his start in the music business working with British Invasion bands on the highly rated *Ready Steady Go!* He'd become a trusted source for rock acts wanting a new way to promote fresh material quickly, as he had already begun replacing the industry paradigm of live performance with film clips that brought artists closer to their audience without having to endure the demanding weeks and mounting expenses of touring, something the Beatles understood all too well.

In 1966, having quit the road and forced to find other ways to make appearances, the Beatles created filmed performances that would later be hailed as the template for the music video. Although they had always added this element to their oeuvre, it had now become mandatory. For their first post-touring showcases, they tabbed Lindsay-Hogg for staged shorts for the 1966 single, "Paperback Writer" and its B-side, "Rain." Later that year, the Who came calling and Lindsay-Hogg created a playfully humorous clip for their single, "Happy Jack," a black-and-white ad-libbed skit that featured the band in costume acting out the exaggerated parts of their mercurial personalities beneath the music. Marred by drug busts and a disintegrating Brian Jones, the Rolling Stones touring prospects were limited, so this new phenomenon of performing a song for cameras instead of a live audience was their saving grace. The director produced provocative visual clips for their 1968 single, "Jumpin' Jack Flash," and its B-side "Child of the Moon."

After Lindsay-Hogg's work with the Beatles in 1966, Brian Epstein decided to branch out, hiring Swedish director Peter Goldmann to direct conceptual mini-films for the pre–*Sgt. Pepper's* double A-side, "Strawberry Fields Forever" / "Penny Lane" the following year. In both, the Beatles were not lip-synching or even holding their instruments, instead appearing as mystical gurus play-acting in trippy sequences, much the same way McCartney had figured *Magical Mystery Tour.* In fact, it was that film's editor, Roy Benson, who first handed the Beatles a rather unwieldly thirty-eight-page storyboard for a "Hey Jude" clip that would have the band playing in front of a prison. With the return of Lindsay-Hogg, all of that was swept away to present John, Paul, George, and Ringo casually dressed and playing together—coalesced and immediate.

After McCartney heard from Mick Jagger how well the young director had captured "Jumpin' Jack Flash" on film, in early August of 1968 Lindsay-Hogg receives a mysterious package. "A motorcycle delivery guy showed up outside my flat in Hampstead with a brown envelope that he had to put in my hands and no one else's," Lindsay-Hogg recounted in an email to me. He would be one of the first people outside the Beatles' inner circle to hear the acetate of the band's biggest hit and he knew just what to do.

The set Lindsay-Hogg designed for the Beatles' crucial performance of "Hey Jude" symbolically captures, like the song itself, both the grandeur and camaraderie of the Beatles as icons and the celebrated four-headed monster. They would be cramped together as if on the Cavern stage in 1962 while framed by a backdrop of nattily attired classical musicians, reintroducing themselves musically and personally without psychedelic artifice, fish-eye lens camera tricks, or clever post-production techniques. Once again, the visuals would match the music, as the Beatles had already embraced a return to basics.

McCartney, wearing a burgundy jacket and a collared pink shirt, sits at an upright piano to the left of the screen. Just above him is

Lennon—light-blue tee shirt, dark vest, a red bowtie around his neck—who sits cross-legged and strumming his Gibson. Below him to the right is George Harrison, perched on his guitar amp, in a chocolate-colored ruffled shirt clutching his Fender Bass VI six-string electric bass guitar. And atop the riser is Ringo, nattily attired in a lime green suit with a matching ruffled shirt, manning his classic Ludwig drum set. Behind the band, lined up along in a pyramid, the thirty-six-piece orchestra is decked out in white tuxedos. Rounding out the staging as metaphor are some two hundred extras ranging from various generations, races, and creeds hired to appear for the grand finale. Lindsay-Hogg will direct them to engulf the band as if in a massive hug, a clear show of global unity, while everyone sings *Na . . . na . . . na . . . na na na na.*

Lindsay-Hogg recalls: "When we met to discuss ideas for the film, I told Paul, 'As captivating as the four of you are, we can't just shoot you all singing *na-na-na* for four minutes, so I told him we need 'other people.' And when he asked, 'What kind of other people?' I told him, 'The *world* . . . or as near as we can manage in London. And not just members of the Beatles' fan club, but older people, housewives, Black and Brown kids, people in turbans.' And Paul was suddenly into it, offering, 'The village postman!' So, that was it. He understood right away that we needed visual help with the chorus from 'the world.' And that is what we searched for and found."

The performance is recorded on videotape for American television and then film stock for the United Kingdom. To Lindsay-Hogg's recollection, six takes are banked. Before Take 2, television personality and media chum to the band, David Frost—whose *Frost on Sunday* is to debut the clip—works his way into the proceedings, looking to place himself at the center of the action. It is a bold move, a Frost specialty, as this was never the plan. "David Frost was *the* best-known interviewer and TV host in England," says Lindsay-Hogg. "We were sort of friends. Earlier that year he'd exec-produced a six-part comedy series I'd directed (*The Ronnie Barker Playhouse*). He assumed I knew what he was doing there, saying, 'I can do the intro whenever you want.' I asked, 'Intro for what?' 'Oh,' he said. 'I've got them for *the Frost Show*, premiering 'Hey Jude.' So, I went into the truck/control room which had been parked on a nearby sound stage, and he got on the rostrum in front of them."

The Beatles' original road manager, personal assistant, and then acting chief executive of Apple Corps, Neil Aspinall, is equally perplexed by Frost's appearance. He recounts in *Anthology*, "David Frost came down to [Twickenham] Film Studios and introduced it like it was done for his show." George Harrison sets the record straight in the same account, "It wasn't done *just* for David Frost."

Nevertheless, there he stands, centerstage, before the Fab Four. When the cameras begin rolling, Lennon careens into the pall of preperformance jitters by counting off, as in the old days when he was the undisputed leader of this unknown quartet going places. He breezily strums a jazzy version of Frost's theme song, "By George! It's the David Frost Theme," which was composed by their very own George Martin, hence the title. He is followed immediately, almost eerily, by the rest of the band. Suddenly here are the four boys together, back in Hamburg, working countless hours for no money—scared, cranked on speed, and wondering what the fuck they had gotten into. Back then when things looked grim, Johnny Boy would shout, "Where are we going, fellows?" And the other three would answer, "To the top, Johnny!" And Lennon would ask, "Where is that, fellows?" And the three voices, sometimes ragged, other times roused, would roar, "To the topper-most of the popper-most!" And Johnny Boy would shout back "Right!" Nearly a decade later, Ringo takes Johnny Boy's lead and eases into a shuffle, as George, hardly flinching or even looking up, reaches down to pluck out a solo melody. Beaming in his element, Paul punches away at the piano, perfectly accenting his partner's lead. Lennon stops for a moment, as if dramatically riding the subtle crest of what he's created, to scat playfully, *Bappity-do-dah-dah!* Paul whirs his hand across the keys in a bebop flourish. Ringo, tapping along, broadly smiles.

Frost, his back to the camera, taps his foot and exclaims like a schoolboy, "Marvelous! Wonderful!" This television veteran, a master of celebrity exploitation, finds himself without warning awkwardly stuck in this Beatles moment of immense clarity—the past, present, and future clashing up against the four lads from Liverpool. Nervous to perform, unsure they can even do it anymore, fractured from inner friction and constant ego battles, tired of the fame and the backbiting, and overwhelmed by the money and lawyers and constant haranguing from the press and fans, they escape once more into the band that had to keep the gangsters, shoremen, and angry drunks at bay in Germany; entertained the rabid hooters in Liverpool clubs; and eventually survived the whirlwind of their own desires—chased, hounded, celebrated, worshipped beyond their wildest dreams. They had once melded this cohesive unit into a singular superstar engine that had no off-button. And here they are again.

The years of twists and turns and shape-shifting and exploration with sounds, drugs, cultural ignitions are all boiled down to these thirty seconds of pure, unscripted musical joy. Frost stupidly attempts to curtail this to reclaim the spotlight. The band acquiesces reluctantly, accented by a crash from Ringo on his enormous ride cymbal. The host, decked in his finest television suit, takes this as a sign to segue gracefully. "A perfect rendition!" he says, grasping for something clever to say. He turns to the cameras—of course he does—and recovers with a snide quip, "And now you see the greatest tea-room orchestra in the world." Behind his back, John looks down embarrassingly at his guitar. George smirks sarcastically. Paul nods over at the "host" as if to say, "Who the hell is this guy?" Ever the pro, aware he is poised to make television history, Frost has wandered into the shoot as if it is his to emcee and then brazenly tries to *own* a Beatles production. But what he has actually done is interrupt this impromptu expression of pure delight.

Undeterred, Frost, in his best unassailable voice, says, "It's my pleasure to introduce now in their first live appearance for goodness knows how long, in front of an audience . . ." As the camera pushes into a close-up, it captures behind him Harrison's glare of distilled Liverpudlian disdain. Frost holds his intro for a beat, and with the serious expression of a man announcing the start of World War Three, whispers reverentially, ". . . the Beatles."

The camera is frozen on him as he turns to what he believes will be Paul McCartney politely taking his cue and launching into the Beatles' fabulous new single. Instead, there is silence. Suddenly looking disoriented about why the band isn't kicking in on his command, he fails to understand that these four men before him have *never* taken commands without some friction—strong suggestions, a few early fashion ideas, perhaps, but commands? It is no surprise that Johnny Boy makes Frost twist in the wind for a few seconds before breaking out as if a barroom drunk in a cockney rant, *It's now or never!* Choosing to caterwaul an off-key rendition of his boyhood inspiration, Elvis Presley's 1960 hit—released when the Beatles were first becoming the devastating musical unit that would soon eclipse him—says so much. By 1960, Elvis, fresh from his two-year stint in the army, would be mired in Hollywood glitz, his rebel tenacity polished over in hair-dye and spray tans manipulated by men like David Frost. Ironically, Presley would return to the live stage in what would be known as his "Comeback Special" in December, donning his leather jacket and sitting to jam with his original band and sing gospel songs with a renewed passion. Lennon's outburst is joined by another distended voice, likely his childhood pal, Paul, who also suffers no fools or TV hosts gladly, and who has always had John's back. George, happy to "take the piss" out of any situation, begins to play the chords amateurishly, upstaging Frost's clumsy tactic. According to an account in Hunter Davies' 2016 *The Beatles Book*, a tape exists somewhere of Harrison snidely asking a flustered Frost if the show will be broadcast in color as he tries another introduction. Ringo, glad to be back, bongs along mockingly. Frost is caught in no man's land and does not move; the camera unflinchingly capturing his dilemma. He shifts his weight and swallows hard. Lindsay-Hogg, knowing a slow showbiz death when he sees one, mercifully fades to black.

Don't worry, things end well for Frost. Although *Top of the Pops* tries in vain to coerce the filmmakers to get a version of the clip to them by the next day to upstage the intractable TV host, it just isn't feasible. Thus, Frost gets his premiere, if not his classic television introduction moment. Meanwhile, having left Frost in the dust, the Beatles are having a ball, running through actual live versions of "Hey Jude," all smiles and joking, taking time to interact with the audience and throwing in spontaneous versions of favorite rock-and-roll staples. "For each of the six takes we featured different audience members," remembers Lindsay-Hogg. "In between takes, the two-inch video reels would be reloaded, so there'd be a fresh tape for each performance, and the tapes had to be quality checked once they were up, so there'd be a ten to twenty-minute break. In the first break, the Beatles smoked, and we talked about how the take had gone and if there was anything we should do differently. But in the next one, they collectively realized that there were a couple of hundred people waiting around for Take 3 and the old Hamburg instinct kicked in and they began to play. They were rock and rollers and here was an audience. And after each take, they would play for the people. The go-to favorites were Tamla Motown songs, Buddy Holly, or Little Richard."

Scott Freiman: "People forget when they watch the band clearly enjoying themselves in the film of 'Hey Jude' that Ringo had quit the band for a week-and-a-half or so and returned the day before they filmed. So, there was genuine joy of having Ringo back in the fold—the Beatles, back *together* again. And I think that absolutely comes across in the video, they're clearly happy to be there."

Lindsay-Hogg recalls: "I knew the Beatles were in a stage of their evolution when, although they had stopped touring two years before, they wanted to embrace an audience they hadn't been connected to since. At least Paul did, and, I thought, John also, and once they were surrounded by all these people, they did what they knew how to do. This was the first time they'd ever played to any kind of audience in two years, and they loved it."

Of the six takes, the one readily available on YouTube is an edit of Takes 1 and 3 that is part of the 1998 *Anthology* collection. At the 2:42

mark, a really cool moment occurs. It is subtle. It is private. It is the essence of a friendship, a partnership, a professional détente between two men who'd met as teenagers, coping with the deaths of their mothers and striking out to chase an impossible dream and achieving it.

McCartney sings *Remember to let her into your heart* looking up at Lennon, who strums along above him. He keeps his eyes focused on him, as a smile creases his face. We see this from a profile shot of McCartney and catch Lennon, who must now realize he was supposed to be singing that crucial harmony . . . but did not. John glances back down at him; his eyebrows raised in recognition. McCartney keeps singing, as Lennon shakes his head as if to say, "No, wait, am I supposed to sing this?" Then, you can actually see the moment John realizes he's messed up. His eyebrows raise again, but he keeps going. Paul keeps going. Because that's what the Beatles do no matter what befalls them. It is what this cosmic kinship of John and Paul have done all along: Have a smirk, take a moment of private reflection on whatever comes, and *keep going*. Paul backs off the mic and adds a playful *Yeaaahhhh* . . . before rolling right into *So let it out and let it in* . . .

Tim Riley: "You can see the musicality between them is very intense, very intimate. It's similar to the rooftop concert that ends *Let It Be,* which for most of the movie is a rough ordeal of struggling to rehearse and record. Then they go up on stage to the rooftop, and all of a sudden, *whoa*! They get in front of an audience and become this incredible ensemble and you realize the way they play for each other is completely different than the way they play for an audience. Only *they* can hear what nobody else can hear, because they're so accustomed to playing with each other. It's like a marriage; completely unspoken. They know they're sitting on a volcano of ensemble and intimacy and talent and interplay that they have chosen not to express for the cameras but give to an audience. Provided this rare chance to perform on that roof, they flip the switch, and it's just overwhelming. This is all over the 'Hey Jude' clip; an outpour that turns into a waterfall. All of a sudden . . . here we go . . . !"

"My plan was to start on a close-up of Paul and then leisurely introduce the other band members," says Lindsay-Hogg. "It was a song you didn't want to rush. The song would dictate the camera work. Paul looked handsome and glossy in his shot, with the occasional bit of movement behind him which wasn't really a disturbance, but you couldn't quite identify. Then we got to the start of the chorus and what Paul and I talked about a week before happened. Via a close up of George, when you didn't know anything had happened, the next shot, a wide one, was *full* of people. And it worked well. The chorus became a singalong, everyone in good humor, glad to be there, part of this song, this place, this time. The Beatles too."

"The sweep of it starts very intimately, and then it ends as this great kind of global chorus, and they telegraph that on that video," says Peter Ames Carlin. "The audience is watching, and then when you get to the *na-na* part, they're all on stage, they're all together, which is visual shorthand for describing exactly what's going on in the song—it starts as a very personal intimate story, and it ends as a generational anthem."

By the final verse, Lennon is all in. Looking down at McCartney and nailing his harmony, which builds into the *Better . . . better . . . better . . . ahhhhh . . .* and suddenly the band is surrounded by the extras that come from every angle. Lennon lifts his right arm and waves to them, shouting, "Come on!"

Na . . . na . . . na . . . na na na na.

"They really go for it," says Kiley Lotz. "McCartney is hammering away at the piano at the end, screaming. It's so fun. You don't have to know English, you don't have to be a singer, you don't have to be trained instrumentalists to feel like you can express this song. *Anyone* could sing along. And you *want* to, because it's built up to this big moment."

Na . . . na . . . na . . . na na na na.

A hippie girl. A young Black kid. A Middle Eastern man in a turban. A bespectacled middle-aged white man. A woman with a beehive hairdo. A bearded beatnik. An old man with yellow and red flowers jammed into either side of his glasses, stumbling through the crowd with what looks like a pint of beer, singing madly. Michael Lindsay-Hogg's "the world" comes to life and surrounds the most famous of rock bands.

Na . . . na . . . na . . . na na na na.

Author Devin McKinney writes in his "1+—The Beatles on Video: What They Are, What They Are Not" essay for the *Critics at Large* website: "All were represented, all were equal, and for several overpowering minutes, the world as it ought to be was realized." He expounds on what he called "the greatest music video ever made" when we speak.

"It's a visualization of the world audience that the Beatles succeeded in uniting at the time, and still do in a way that no other entity in pop or rock music ever did. You look at that audience, and it's just so impossibly diverse—it's Black, white, it's Indian, it's Asian, it's old, it's young, you've got fat people and thin people and the plain girl with glasses and a hip chick and they're performing this marvelous song and you're actually getting to see Paul do his *Waaaa!* and you get to see John and Paul exchanging their looks that they do. It's a wonderful visual representation of all the Beatles achieved."

Na . . . na . . . na . . . na na na na.

Arm-in-arm, they sing, swaying, laughing, bellowing. The Beatles lead the diverse, inclusive chorale with McCartney scatting and screeching all the way. George, Ringo, John laugh and smile throughout. The band and its audience literally become one when eventually it is difficult to see the musicians swallowed by the crowd.

"When I saw it on the *Smothers Brothers Show* as a kid it left this lasting impression that the Beatles must be the coolest people in the world," says Dr. Auxier. "They had this highly diverse audience around them singing along, and for me, living in a mostly African American area of Memphis, to see this exotic gathering of people representing everyone all over the world really made a huge impression on me. And to this day, I swear Coca-Cola basically copied the international brotherhood concept of that video; *I'd like to buy the world a Coke*."

Na . . . na . . . na . . . na na na na.

"Inviting the audience up onto the bandstand to sing the refrain with them shows the self-consciousness of how *big* the song is, what the song symbolizes; a reunification of the Beatles and their audience," surmises Tim Riley. "They understood that *Magical Mystery Tour* was a botch and literally detached from the audience—it was off in the country—and reuniting with the audience is one of the goals of 'Hey Jude' and one of the key triumphs of this clip."

Na . . . na . . . na . . . na na na na.

Professor Shashko: "What I remember about that clip is you could see how much joy they found in having the fans around them, that they remember for that moment why they do this in the first place—Ringo especially, since he'd seriously contemplated leaving the group. He just looks overjoyed having all these people around him, and Paul as well. And you're reminded when you watch this unfolding that this is why the Beatles matter in the first place; this is the joy that *they* got out of it. They just look much happier once all those fans are around them, and, of course, this leads to the question; what would the Beatles have been if they continued to tour, if they had continued to interact with their fans and receive such joy out of that experience? I certainly understand why they stopped enjoying the tours, it must've been overwhelming, but you can't help but wonder what would have been different if they continued to have that experience performing on stage together and being together in that setting."

"They are absolutely having fun, and you can see they're having more and more fun as it goes along," says Rob Sheffield. "When it begins, they're professionals, they're on the job, and as they get more and more into it, George, who was very much left out of the song for a while, is having a great time, and you see how happy Ringo is to be drumming for a band, because that's what he always wanted to do and felt he wasn't getting to do, and even John, who's chewing gum in his universal, I-don't-give-a-fuck statement, is actually chewing gum very happily as it goes on. And the fact that all these people are crowding around, a very conspicuously multi-cultural crowd, allows us to see the Beatles *changed* by it as it happens. And as listeners, observers and fans of the Beatles, nothing makes us happier than to see them being happy together, doing what they're doing, which is being Beatles *together*. And that they really thrive on this, is very contagious."

Professor Stillerman: "In this way the video becomes another kind of narrative about 'what does this song mean,' whether that was the original intention of the composer or not. For the people who are experiencing it, it becomes another narrative and the visual dimension, I think, at least, psychologically reduces the distance between the performer and the audience. It's one thing to hear something on the radio, but if you see someone in front of you, and they're tangible, then you feel more connected to them, even though in fact, it's obviously a staged performance. But as a fan, you're made to feel closer to the artists and somehow you understand their message better, you are more engaged."

Professor Auxier recalls: "It looked like a party, it looked like a place I wanted to be. I wanted to be with *those* people. I wanted to hear *that* band. I wanted to sing *with* them. I wanted to be in *that* room singing *that* song."

Na . . . na . . . na . . . na na na na.

It fades slowly with the coda, the shot widening to show the room packed with revelers, framed by the orchestra, which has been an afterthought amid all these close-ups and pans, much to Paul's chagrin. The most pragmatic of the Beatles later complained that they'd wasted money on dragging them all in to pantomime to no one.

Nevertheless, the film clip, originally broadcast in black-and-white on Frost's show, precedes "Hey Jude" to the top of the British charts three days later on September 11. By the time it is seen in America five weeks hence, it has already been #1 for seventeen days and will remain so for another forty-six.

What these televised images of musical comradery and universal embrace did ultimately is temporarily replace those of war, protests, violence, assassinations, racial disharmony, and man's endless inhumanity to man. For a few minutes, seven minutes and eleven seconds to be exact, the world could exhale from the terrible news coming at them from nearly everywhere in 1968, especially on television, the medium of the age. "Psychologically we combine image with sound all the time," says professor Andrea Halpern. "Our two primary senses are first vision, we have a lot of brain devoted to our visual system, and second is auditory. Those take up way more brain real estate than any of the other senses—smell, touch, taste, and so forth. Also, very early on in neural processing, we have multimodal areas where we combine those, so it's a very natural neurological response to combine those two key senses. Again, when we look at each other to speak we combine facial expressions with auditory signal. You wear glasses, has it ever happened that you forget your glasses, and you're trying to talk to someone, and suddenly you don't understand them quite as well, because you can't see them quite as well? This is because you're combining the visual and the auditory. And normally, that works just fine because they're in sync. So, to combine the visual with the musical is completely natural for us. Again, we evolved that way back to our Neanderthal ancestors, who would have seen the people making this music as they're hearing it. That's why it's so natural in the modern era to have film scores."

Using the very tool that made them, specifically in America, the Beatles once again invade living rooms to bring their measure of musical elixir to the masses. And for a brief respite, a song *can* and *does* make all the difference. It is a fleeting moment that people, evidently, want to last, as McCartney allows his ending to go and on and on because he is having "so much fun."

"I do think the Beatles, throughout their career, were always able to project, whether it was always true or not, a genuine sincerity," says Professor Samarotto. "All the way back to, *Yeah, Yeah, Yeah.* It's what they projected as performers and that's what people heard in them early on, and what *made* their career. It's still there in 'Hey Jude.'"

"Music has expanded so much into so many genres and sub-genres and we don't all listen *together* anymore," cites Scott Freiman. "That's a key element to the impact and lasting legacy of 'Hey Jude'; it's a communal experience to sing that song, and we don't have communal songs anymore. We listen to hip-hop, or we listen to jazz, or we listen to K-pop or whatever, but we don't have a radio station that's playing all of that together. We have our own playlists on Spotify or Pandora, and we're in our little bubbles. That's why I think that you don't have a group and an album that has the same impact that some of the albums of the sixties did like a *Sgt. Pepper's*, and that's unfortunate. When we talk about the Beatles now, we talk about them as we would Beethoven or Bach, or the great jazz artists like Louis Armstrong. The Beatles are part of the discussion of lasting, seminal music for a generation and beyond. I don't think there are going to be a lot of groups now that we'll be talking about one hundred years from now, but who knows?"

Professor Werner concludes: "By the end of 1968, all different styles of music were talking to each other at that time in ways I don't think they have since. You didn't have to be part of an in-group, everyone knew who Johnny Cash was, you can recognize the voice, even country fans knew who Marvin Gaye was, they knew who Stevie Wonder was, they sure knew who Aretha [Franklin] was. I have stories from Black vets who smoked joints and listened to Doors with the surfer dudes from California in Vietnam and the kid from rural Wisconsin who listened to Sam and Dave, and the Beatles, who grew out of a crossover culture, were absolutely at the center of all that. 'Hey Jude' is trying to *make* us listen. I think that's what you've got when you say it's trying to bring us back to a sense of unity."

And so, the world, and certainly America, keeps playing "Hey Jude" and keeps singing *Na . . . na . . . na . . . na na na na,* because it indeed *is* fun. Seven minutes in the din of bad vibes and growing fear is always a good seven minutes. And because nothing lasts forever, even extended codas that seem to go on into infinity and are captured to last on record and be played over and over, must fade out eventually, as "Hey Jude" does . . . ever . . . so . . . slowly.

And soon the pages in the calendar turn. Time marches on. And the song, as with all songs, takes on new meaning.

"I've always treasured 'Hey Jude,'" says Tim Riley. "It represents the kind of leadership the Beatles had ceded in 1968; a year when the world needed a reassuring ballad *right now*. It represents the great Beatles' magic of taking in the world and synthesizing and delivering. This is a safe harbor song, and for the band, it was also definitely a comeback song."

"In terms of the time-stamp, nothing is as visceral as song," says singer/songwriter Dan Bern. "Not a book, not a painting, not a recording of a speech. That's why movies lean so heavily on music. They rely on songs to recall the feeling and the time of that age. In *Apocalypse Now*, the Doors' 'The End' opens the film and brings you immediately into that time and space. Obviously, filmmakers know how songs frame a period better than anything."

Filmmaker Lindsay-Hogg will continue to build on his work with the Beatles, directing their final film, *Let It Be*, along with many of the seminal artists of the era, culminating that year in his December production of *The Rolling Stones Rock and Roll Circus* starring the Who, Taj Mahal, a very early incarnation of Jethro Tull with Black Sabbath's Tony Iommi on guitar, and of course the Rolling Stones. The production also features the first-ever super group that includes John Lennon on guitar and vocals, the Stones' Keith Richards on bass, Mitch Mitchell of the Jimi Hendrix Experience on drums, and guitar hero Eric Clapton, formally of the power trio Cream, on lead guitar. They call it the Dirty Mac. And how things have changed in just a few months. Instead of bracing his audience for revolution or elatedly singing among a jubilant throng, Lennon furiously bellows into a microphone about being lonely and wanting to die. Having endured the remainder of the White

Album sessions in a poison fog of heroin and clinging to his new lover as if a lifeline, he would sing the tortured "Yer Blues" from the core of his being.

When all is said and done, it seems John needed "Hey Jude" as much as his son, Julian, or its composer. And as the summer echoes of *Na . . . na . . . na . . . na na na na* fade into the dark, winter chill, *The Rolling Stones Rock and Roll Circus* is shelved by Mick Jagger and not seen for another twenty-eight years. The Beatles enter their final year together under personal and professional duress. They will make great music again, but not always gleefully. There will be glimpses of the old magic when it counts, but not as naturally and not without conflicting managers, competing lawsuits, obsessive loves, and commitments to remain "Fab" looming over them. Nearly one year to the day of the release of "Hey Jude," August 20, 1969, having wrapped up work on their final opus, *Abbey Road*, John, nearly thirty years old, Paul, twenty-seven, George, twenty-six, and Ringo, having just turned thirty, will leave the studio for the last time, never to make music together again.

It's as if that long fade at the end of the "Hey Jude" film represents the last moments of the Beatles' love affair with the decade they had kick-started. And so "Hey Jude" will come to mean more as the weeks and months and years pass, at first as the Beatles disintegrate amid a deluge of lawsuits and public acrimony, and then when Lennon is brutally murdered and Harrison dies far too young from cancer. The ensuing years will be kinder to the memory of the Fab Four, for it is the good times that linger far longer than painful endings. There is even a reimagining of Lindsay-Hoggs' gloomy but brutally honest *Let It Be* film to be released by the time this book goes to press. According to reports from Ringo and Paul, and clips shared over the internet, famed director

Peter Jackson has found footage that depicts a band on the precipice of implosion as truly happy. In a way, even the memory of the Beatles has taken a sad song and made it better, echoing the simple genius of *Na . . . na . . . na . . . na na na na* that will, in time, become less pop device than timeless anthem.

CHAPTER TEN

Na . . . Na . . . Na . . . Na Na Na Na

How the Song Works

In music there's a lot of magic in what we do. There's a lot of mystery. There's stuff you just can't explain.

—PAUL MCCARTNEY, *THE LAST PLAY AT SHEA*

Over the years, Paul McCartney has repeatedly used the word "magic" to describe music—whether listening, sharing, playing, or composing it. This is significant simply because he has written more memorable songs than almost any living human. And that is not even close to hyperbole. McCartney has been writing songs since the age of fourteen and as I write this, he is seventy-eight and still at it. And people seem to really like these songs. There are thirty-two which he's composed or cowritten with the Beatles; he has also composed solo, or with and for other artists, many more songs that have gone to #1 in the United States and/or in the United Kingdom. He was named *Guinness Book of World Records'* Most Successful Songwriter of All Time in 1979—129 of his songs charting in the United Kingdom, ninety-one of which have reached the Top 10. No one else is remotely in this stratosphere. And although he's been accused over the years, and within these pages, of being a manipulative craftsman who can elicit tears, smiles, and chills with otherworldly melodies and nerve-touching lyrics, he claims to have little to no idea where any of this comes from. "Yesterday," "Eleanor Rigby," "Penny Lane," "Maybe I'm Amazed," "Band on the Run," "Hey Jude"—magic.

During my career as an author and music journalist, I have interviewed many songwriters of varying degrees of success across generations, and while some pain for weeks and months to finish songs, others crank them out like fast food. As with all of life's mysteries, the reverse sometimes also happens with these same artists—suddenly the easy becomes difficult or for those who toil, there is that one indescribable ten minutes when it all comes rushing in. Magic.

One of those songwriters is the legendary Brian Wilson, who, according to Wilson and McCartney biographer Peter Ames Carlin, wrote the music to the brilliant "God Only Knows" in eighteen minutes. "The whole thing, from Tony Asher handing him the lyric, to sitting down in the living room, and playing the piano," he says. "Asher watched him do it, and he said something like, 'At 10:01, there was nothing, at 10:19, there was 'God Only Knows,' including the harmonies and the counterparts. That is one of the epic works of the second half of the twentieth century, an absolutely beautiful song, and technically perfect on levels that I can't even describe. Brian could channel that, and so could Paul, many times over."

"McCartney has written probably sixty melodies or more in his life that if you asked, I could hum for you," says celebrated singer/songwriter, and front man for Counting Crows, Adam Duritz. "Experience provides you with reasons to write lyrics, but a melody, man, that's out of thin air. And he's made so many of them. It's the Puccini in him, writing things people are going to remember for hundreds of years. *That's* the gift."

For the rest of us, casual listeners to obsessives, there is never a formula or guideline as to how or why a song works, especially in the realm of popularity, whether timely or in perpetuity. "There are certain songs that have a very intense emotional valence for people, and it's hard to know why that is," says sociology professor Joel Stillerman. "There are, no doubt, psychologists and musicologists that consider biochemical responses that might tell us something about how a song affects us."

Professor of psychology at Bucknell University, Andrea Halpern wonders if we'll ever truly know: "There's no one answer to how songs affect us; particularly songs with lyrics, because it's difficult to separate the effect of the lyric. It's also difficult to separate from commercial interests. Not speaking as a psychologist, but an observer of society, there are certain outside forces, particularly before the era of personal listening devices, that affect the popularity of a piece of music, like when people were dependent on the radio. I have done studies on how simple instrumental tunes affect listeners. First of all, people differ. So, we can't generalize. For every song that you love, there is someone who hates it, and a bunch of people who say, 'Meh.' There's no accounting for taste, as they say. However, a study I did in 2008 with Daniel Müllensiefen [professor of psychology at Goldsmiths, University of London] looked at simple musical characteristics that enhanced memorability. We used single lines from eighties pop tunes that were unfamiliar to our listeners and did a corpus analysis to look at the particular features that seemed to relate to better recognition memory, which we found.

We then tried to model the pleasantness ratings our listeners gave, but the 'pleasantness rating' models weren't successful. We had about fifty characteristics we could measure, including first order and second order characteristics—a first order characteristic is whether it is in a major or minor key and a second order characteristic would be, 'How frequent is this feature in the song relative to other songs they heard?' We even had fancier comparisons than that, sampling the entire corpus of ten thousand pop tunes. But we never did get a paper out of the pleasantness modeling."

The difference in a song engraining itself in the public consciousness or withering away in obscurity remains a mystery, although Professor Halpern does offer this nugget on how our brains process music, which does come with a caveat that our auditory systems evolved to specifically listen to humans play music live, not in electronic form. Thanks to Thomas Edison, electronic reproduction allows us to hear the same track over and over again, which is relatively new to our vast evolutionary history while also being a boon to the pop music industry. Repeated listening is key, as we know from radio or our streaming platforms, but how do melody, rhythm, and style factor in? "We do have an auditory system that is fairly precise in encoding pitch, duration, and amplitude, so if we're talking about nonverbal songs, like instrumentals, humans are pretty good at processing that in real time and making sense of structure, which characterizes all music," notes the professor. "A simple structure is *repetition*. Even lay people who are not heavily trained know when the chorus repeats and when motifs are repeating, even if they can't name it. We learn intrinsically when the harmony is leading to either a conclusion or development. If you add words to it, it's a whole other layer. So, there are distinctions in our neural system that are more sensitive to nonverbal information like pitch and amplitude, and others that are more sensitive to words.

"But even when we don't understand the language, the brain understands that there is language there. These also can engender different reactions. If it's completely brand new, we have to use additional resources. If it's familiar, of course, we have a long-term memory operative, which allows us to predict what will come in a song, whether we realize it or not. So, it's not that we can just understand the structure, we're subconsciously predicting the next structure. The same goes for words, if we can understand them, and if it's something that is very familiar, our predictions, of course, are always fulfilled, but we're *still* predicting. *That* is active engagement in how we react to songs."

The song I have chosen to root around in happens to be a historically massive hit by the mighty Beatles—its origins, inspiration, zeitgeist, and era—and if you've gotten this far you know that this song has something special about it. It certainly helps that a special band created it. There's a little "magic" in that, right? Paul McCartney embraced the magic in what music did to heal his grief as a young man and also the magic in his love for Linda; indeed, he composed "Hey Jude" on what he called his "magic piano" and the Beatles' one-take of the song was in his estimation "magic." But, consciously or not, the Beatles effectively used melodies, keys, rhythms, and lyrics that spoke deeply to their generation. That connection may be the most magical element in the initial and lasting success of "Hey Jude."

Nevertheless, there are similar non-magical factors to what connects a tune to an audience, no matter size or scope. Keeping Professor Halpern's comments on how we psychologically process a song in mind, there is also talent, discipline, and ingenuity to consider, along with timing, collaboration, and making the best representation of the composition in its arrangement and recording, all of which we have covered already. Pondering all of this, irrespective of the art form, the visual arts, film, or literature, there is a thread that moves an audience of one to one million. This is most evident in pop music which exists to be, well . . . popular. It comes from a place that strives to seduce as many people as possible, to hook them in—the reason the word "hook" is used so often by songwriters, critics, and cigar-chomping record execs: "Does the song have a hook?" "Where's the hook?" "That is a great hook!" Despite his humble retorts, Paul McCartney possesses the secret to the magic that brings the hook. Over and over again.

This is where we can begin to dissect how "Hey Jude" moves us, over and over again.

The Natural Tunesmith

"Paul is a magician of the guileless," reasons author Devin McKinney. "And I use that word magician advisedly, a magician works a sleight of hand in what they do. And to say someone is 'a magician of the guileless' is very contradictory. Well, that's what I love about the Beatles; they're every kind of a contradiction wrapped up in a beautiful unity, and that is one of Paul's contradictions, and 'Hey Jude' might be the great example of what he does in the visible point and what he does in the invisible point, which is to look on the optimistic side, push through something as opposed to being overwhelmed by it. And yet, at a certain point in 'Hey Jude' the gates come down, and the world floods in, and it's the world that is singing this, and it's *really* overwhelming."

"That's just Paul," says prolific songwriter Dan Bern. "It's like there's Paul, and there's Elvis Costello, and there's Adam Schlesinger, there's Mike Viola, there's these world-class melodicists. It's so deceptively easy for them, we don't even think about it, it just passes through us and feels right. Dylan doesn't do that stuff. Paul McCartney does. And for most of us who write songs, the paths we take when we are writing just don't go in those directions. It's almost classical."

"One of things that I talk to my classes about is how to write melody, and not just a pop melody, but one like Beethoven would've written or a Mozart melody, because they follow much of the same principles," cites musicologist, Professor Tom Koch. "'Hey Jude' is a classical melody in the sense that it follows the classical ideas of proportion and balance. When you think about the first verse, what is it? It consists of just two phrases, and they're balanced—each one is four measures long, and together they form a period. That's exactly the same kind of phrase structure that Mozart would've given to his songs. *Hey Jude, don't make it bad / Take a sad song and make it better*, right there, next phrase, *Remember to let her into your heart / Then you can start to make it better*. So, you got these two phrases that together form a period, and, of course, we can talk about the harmony of those phrases, but within those phrases, is one heck of a melody."

Although not musically trained in the traditional sense, McCartney's preternatural grasp of melody is well documented and duly celebrated. Of course, the Beatles did their part. Lauded for their abilities to embrace and conquer several musical genres and dramatically stretch their boundaries beyond limits previously uncharted, they were, at their core, the hookiest hook that ever hooked.

"The thing that strikes me when I hear 'Hey Jude' is Paul McCartney's incredible ability to write a melody, certainly, but also the prolific nature of the Beatles that they could come out with the experimental White Album, and during its making also produce something as brilliant as 'Hey Jude,'" cites Beatles lecturer Scott Freiman. "It is a true band song, even though Paul McCartney is the lead. They're all behind him, supporting him. It's a wonderful arrangement, the production is great. It's *the* classic Beatles song."

The Beatles Factor

Adam Duritz notes with a smirk: "Typical Beatles thing is hooky-lick, hooky-verse, hooky-chorus, repeat, then *hooky*, hooky-bridge, back to the hooky-chorus. They'll do a bridge three times in a song, where the rest of us might throw it in once, because their bridges are so damn hooky! But 'Hey Jude' . . . that's *all chorus*! And then you vamp for four minutes. That's a level of melody writing that most of us can't hit. I think most artists would be thankful if they had one great melody, one great chorus, per album, and that becomes their single. Sometimes you have more than that, but the Beatles have *nothing but that*."

"What makes 'Hey Jude' work as a performance is it sounds very much like men in a room communicating," says author Rob Sheffield. "When they did the same story five years earlier with 'She Loves You,' they were boys—they were excited about the music they were playing, and now they're men working together in this song, and what you hear *sounds* impulsive and spontaneous, like pitching in. Nobody is stepping on the song, nobody's trying to steal the spotlight. The interplay between the four of them is what really drives it home—at no point does it sound like one guy by himself. This includes this empathetic Ringo thump through the song, and I think it's one of those songs, like a lot of Beatles songs, that doesn't work without Ringo keeping the pulse. Ringo always said, 'I have one rule, and that is to play with the singer,' and for whatever reason, John and Paul did their deepest confessional singing when Ringo was providing the pulse, and you can definitely hear that in the thump he provides in 'Hey Jude,' which is just an astounding drum performance that people hardly ever notice, which, by the way, is a Ringo trademark."

"What really makes it for me analytically is the layering that takes place from one verse to another and into the bridge, because although you have Paul's intimate delivery at first, eventually you have George and John come in with the vocal harmony and the acoustic guitar, and Ringo, who comes in on the second verse," says Dr. Koch. "This leads up to the outro, where you have the orchestra come in, and it is that layering which adds a dimension to the song. It's a building of the song that takes us to the outro and it actually moves me as a musicologist and as a performer; the idea of layering of texture and gradually thickening of the texture is really important."

The Beatles' famed bravado insisted that "Hey Jude" was over seven minutes in length by extending a coda that turned out to be longer than its structured part, what Rob Sheffield dubs an "extreme statement." Methodically arranged from its sparse opening, the ensuing background voices, the building of instruments leading to that searing high note, and then also during the song's rousing chorale, with its slow elevation of strings and horns, transforms "Hey Jude" into the sonic equivalent of the evolution of the 1960s—its burgeoning youth movement, new social freedoms, and expanding imagination—the Beatles turning life events into song. Yet, as the youth culture coalesced, much like the song's layering, it eventually fractured in the year it was composed, recorded, and released, and so "Hey Jude" in turn reflects this sudden schism, as the song splits into two disparate parts. It also illustrates how those parts can work in tandem—both musically and socially—simultaneously connoting a celebration of individuality *and* solidarity.

"The experience of the song is really wonderful," says author Tim Riley. "You're listening to it, and you think, 'Oh, this is really lovely,' it's a medium tempo ballad, it's got a beautiful melody, and we're kind of swelling and growing throughout the song, and then all of a sudden, it *explodes*. It turns into this waterfall of the most beautiful refrain that is intoxicating. And every time after you hear the song you're waiting for the refrain, because, you *know* there is this giant payoff, and it *never* fails. It's just an incredibly sturdy way to set up anticipation and release, and the prolonged anticipation—Oh, one more verse, it's coming, it's coming—is *really* satisfying and *always* glorious. It returns much more than it promises; this wonderful cascade of feeling, an outpouring of embrace and generosity and the glory of rock and roll and the glory of the Beatles and the glory of this moment in the Beatles' career."

"My first thought with 'Hey Jude' is that it was written by people who had perfected writing pop songs, but then I think what makes it so amazing is it sort of goes *against* all that stuff," says Eric Hutchinson, who in addition to his professional music career as an artist and producer teaches the art of songwriting. "I think that if the song was comprised of only its first half, it would have been amazing, but it's really the second half of the song that makes it *what it is*. To me, I think there's this pure boldness of saying, 'Okay, we're gonna make this song as long as we feel like.' I think that had to have been a big part of why it was just so revolutionary and well received, people had to respond; 'I can't believe they're doing this, but I like it, damnit!"

Structure

"I think 'Hey Jude' marks the difference between a typical song and a work of art," notes Dr. Koch. "A work of art finds connections and brings unity and coherence to a song when you introduce a musical notion early on, develop it, and then bring it back; there is *thought* to that. Sometimes composers do that intentionally, sometimes they do it because their genius is that they can take a thought that they introduce early on and bring it back later and develop it and 'Hey Jude' is an example of that. This is what separates the Beatles from many of their contemporaries and even beyond. Lennon and McCartney, especially Paul, could do that instinctually. And I think because of this instinctual genius, it gave license to someone like Freddie Mercury to write 'Bohemian Rhapsody.' These are songs that are extremely well-crafted with foreshadowing; a musical narrative that comes early on, and then returns us to where we began. This idea that the song takes us into a middle section that toys with our expectations of key—does it modulate or doesn't it?—and then returns to the opening idea solidly in the original key bears resemblance to what we refer to in classical music as sonata form, with an exposition, development, and recapitulation, applied to certain musical structures from the eighteenth century. It is the underlying appeal of 'Hey Jude' musically that should not be overlooked.

"In classical music, the composer has a broader timeframe in which to bring us on this journey from the exposition, the piece's prime melody, through the development, with key changes and new variations, and finally to its initial expression in recapitulation. Consequently, a pop song's stringent time constraints, even when considering a song that runs over seven minutes, forces the composer to move the listener quickly throughout its limited duration. Similarly, Paul McCartney intrigues the listener before expanding the song's scope, and then deftly brings us back home again."

"It's smart songwriting because it's so compelling," says singer/songwriter Kiley Lotz. "The song keeps you in there. First and foremost, the melody is irresistible. If the melody for the beginning of the song sucked it wouldn't matter how great the payoff was, because you wouldn't make it to the end. It *has* to be great from the start. That isolated vocal with the piano at the top is so ear-catching, because he's like, 'Here we go! I'm gonna feed you Part A, and it's good. Great. Let's get to B. Okay, now we're back at A, and the listener may think, 'But I want to know what happens next!' And Paul says, 'Not yet!' And this works so well that by the time you get to Part C, the *na-na-na* chorus, you are treated to the payoff. A is like your appetizer, and you're thinking, 'Ooh, that was good.' But then you get the entre, and you're like, 'Oh, shit, *this* is my meal. 'Hey Jude' is a three-course meal. Its structural greatness is irrefutable."

"None of the rest of what we discuss about a song matters if it does not work for you viscerally in the moment that you're hearing it," says Devin McKinney. "And the thing that grips me, the second I hear Paul's voice, is that there is a terrific gravity to what is about to happen—that you're on the precipice of something that is transformative, and you don't know where it's going to go. Even though you've heard it countless times, you *don't* know where it's going to go from this very simple beginning, this modest voice, these few piano notes. And then the other instruments enter pretty unassumingly. And then it gets a little bigger, and it gets a little bigger, and gets a little bigger to the point where the explosion and the breakout is the only thing that *could* happen, and you discover you've been climbing this mountain *without* realizing it, and there you are . . . at the top. That's how 'Hey Jude' works for me . . . from the beginning, the very first second you realize that this is something important, and all the way through you're just following a gradual, imperceptible buildup of momentum and energy. And, like I say, when the sun bursts over the mountain, you didn't even know that you were heading there, but there you are. Yeah, *that's* how it works. And all of the post-facto stuff about the sixties in memory comes later. You're listening to it and you're just feeling this stuff, *every* time you hear it, you're *feeling* it."

"Paul is always *thinking* in music as the symbol of our interior life feeling," says professor of philosophy Randall Auxier. "What it's like to hear music is what it's like to have a *life feeling,* that's what Susanne Langer says, she's my favorite philosopher of music. Langer says that when we hear music, it's like having a virtualized organization of time, an illusory semblance of our life of feeling. That's the way Paul wrote, and did so naturally."

In his book, *Metaphysical Graffiti,* Auxier delves more deeply into "virtualized organization of time": "The music sounds like what it feels like to be alive, to have a rhythmic heartbeat and a breathing pattern, to move our bodies up, down and all around, to be obliged to anticipate the next moment and join it to the last moment by means of our present sending and feeling." He continues later in the text: "The way humans become conscious of actual time is by attending to the ways that music can use actual time to suspend certain moments and contract others; the tension and release of energies in music points us to the otherwise uninterrupted continuity of our flowing experience. Consciousness itself is a virtualization of experience, and we become aware that we are conscious by way of music."

"The very structure of 'Hey Jude' as a song itself ties into *take a sad song and make it better*," observes singer/songwriter Alex Knight of yeah, sure—a power pop band. "Chop off the outro and it's a completely different piece. But when it shifts from the melancholic sincerity of its first half into Paul's rocker wail and the ensuing singalong, it takes on a whole new life that completely reframes the earlier parts. It was a bit of a sad song up until then, a great song, but a sad song nonetheless, so they went ahead and made it *better*."

Songwriter and friend Matt Sucich, who composes literate songs of pain mixed with humor, agrees: "'Hey Jude' is a slow build to an *extraordinary* and seemingly endless payoff, while the production remains so simple throughout. As a songwriter and musician both this level of production and writing is the sort of thing I always hope to achieve."

Voice

Part of the effectiveness found in the composition, production, and arrangement of "Hey Jude" is in its singer's performance. By creating his multilayered melody and selling its emotional touchstones through the connective art form of vocalizing, Paul McCartney achieves something truly remarkable. In his *Tell Me Why*, Tim Riley writes: "If the song is about self-worth and self-consolation in the face of hardship, the vocal performance itself conveys much of the journey. He begins by singing to comfort someone else, finds himself weighing his own feelings in the process, and finally, in the repeated refrains that nurture his own approbation, he comes to believe in himself. The genius lies in the way he includes the listener in his own pilgrimage."

And like any journey/pilgrimage, there are peaks and valleys, moments of danger and discovery, and, as in his life and music, McCartney wastes no time diving in. The song's vocal expedition begins with pure beseeching. "The first note is sung without accompaniment at all, McCartney's naked voice waiting for the piano to come in," notes associate professor of creative writing Katie Darby Mullins. "You can't start a song more vulnerable and genuine than that." McCartney then slowly conveys twists and turns that, as Dr. Koch cites, wander and return in kind. "One thing the Beatles and George Martin were experts at were knowing when to hold back so that the finish was even more impressive," continues Mullins. "Textured background vocals, percussive elements filter in through the second verse, and the song just keeps picking up new elements as McCartney sings each line: he seems to be letting the lyrics fall out of his mouth, as though it's second-nature to provide beauty and comfort."

McCartney vocally soothes and challenges, building to a crescendo of deeply emotional, feral wailing. The vocal *becomes* the message, beyond mere words, similar to what famed director Steven Spielberg expresses about the visual emotions in film—that one could watch it without the sound and the meaning is still effectively conveyed. Absent its compelling lyrics of endearing approbation, McCartney's vocal performance moves us.

"Lyrically, I've never *not* known what the song is about, because it was already a part of the narrative I was fed since I discovered music," says Sucich. "Regardless, it's still so simple and ambiguous that knowing the truth doesn't matter."

"And please remember the way 'Hey Jude' is mixed," adds Lotz. "The vocals are right there. There are no effects on his voice, which puts you in the song right away. You don't get lulled in like most ballads. 'Hey Jude' is a call to action; 'Hey, you're good. Get it together. Here we go, we're doing this.' And the song continues to build to an amazing payoff. So, it's the tone of his voice, the mixing, the piano, the way it's recorded that all puts you in an emotional space, as you're going for a little bit of a ride and feel like a part of it at the same time."

"Well, you know with any great pop song, the feel and tone are at the very heart of it, because some pop songs are built around melody and others are about rhythm, but the tone and the feel are always front and center and if the song has this sense of comfort and transcendence to it, it can take you to a higher place as a result," says professor Alexander Shashko. "In that way, 'Hey Jude' is comforting, but it also elevates your mood, elevates your sense of joy by the time you get to the end. I think, ultimately, that's what made the song so successful. The first half of the song is built around the melody, and I think the melody of it is fascinating as well, because I'm no musicologist, but you can hear how wide the range is in the actual notes in the melody; it is a distinctive kind of song where you're jumping from one note to the other, not easy to do, but something Paul McCartney can do, and do well, so I think it touches people because of that. He's always had that innate sense of melody, which is fantastic and then the *na, na, nas* at the end, which is lightning in a bottle. You know how many different songs have done some variation on that? But to do it in a way that could be that compelling for that many minutes is just astonishing."

Words

In my extensive discussion on "Hey Jude" with Professor Koch, when describing Tim Riley's suggestion of "journey/pilgrimage," he returned again and again to the term prosody. Normally evoked when describing rhythm and sound in poetry—how the words convey meaning and movement—the musical aspect is what intrigues Dr. Koch, who told me: "The relationship between language and music is a very important element to popular songs. I'm really getting my classes to look at prosody when analyzing *any* song that has lyrics to it."

This connection between what Koch describes as "speech accent, the rhyme, the stress and the syllable count" is the relationship between music's rhythms and pitches that the composer chooses to underline his lyrical expression. According to Professor Koch, "McCartney is a master of speech-rhythm, as in the way he sings *take a sad song*. . . . The idea of sorrow is often depicted in music with what we call nonharmonic tones," cites Koch. "These are pitches that don't really fit with the chord, instead they provide a kind of dissonance, a kind of *tension* to the chord, and so when Paul does that, we hear that chord underline the line *take a sad song*, and we can hear the shift in pitch right there."

The line, the very title of this book, marks the first time Paul raises the pitch with a measure of dissonance in the words *sad song* and draws out the notes longer than anywhere else in the phrase. It is an aural marker, making us listen intently to the song's theme to overcome distress with accepting love. The professor adds: "It is the *sound* of sorrow when taking this sentiment and accompanying it with musical dissonance, and Paul uses a suspended chord there, which adds to that dissonance; *remember to let her into your heart* or *to let her under your skin,* whichever verse you're looking at. Again, the way that it's rhythmically sung is very similar to the way it would be said; *to let her into your heart.* These are just some examples of the kind of marker in a song with effective prosody, having the language and music fit well together—because when they do so, it communicates emotion and meaning that way."

Underlining a lyric with chords that subconsciously move us in ways we cannot describe, whether a musicologist or a fan, is part of the songwriting "magic," but it is here that McCartney's developed ability to craft a song takes over. His emotive intonation is deftly executed in his internal rhyming of *pain/refrain—afraid/made—skin/begin* and, as Professor Koch points out: "His use of alliteration is very potent: *For well you know that it's a fool who plays cool / By making his world a little colder.* I love the use of *cool* into *colder* there, as well as *So let it out and let it in,* which has an equally infectious rhythmic prosody."

Method

If confronted with terms like "recapitulation" or "prosody," Paul McCartney might wince or look at you quizzically, or he might be surprised that you noticed his clever use of these devices, but although he may have started out a natural, it is important to note that when asked for comparisons to his band back in the 1960s, he likened the Beatles to Johann Sebastian Bach, not Chuck Berry. However, like both Bach and Berry, we know the magical formula found in the origins of "Hey Jude" were those echoed from childhood melodies of his choirboy days ("Te Deum") and the primacy of American sixties pop artistry in his teen years ("Save the Last Dance for Me"), which helped him to create the endearing melody of "Hey Jude," whether consciously or not.

One thing is for certain, there is plenty of evidence that McCartney, drawing from a successful method, did consciously choose to begin "Hey Jude" with the title of the song. Professor Koch cites: "If we start right with the first words, *Hey Jude,* you think about how you would say that when speaking; *Hey,* Jude—the first word is higher, then the second word is lower, and that's exactly how Paul comes in. He gives a little bit of weight to the *Hey* part of it." This, according to Dr. Koch, is McCartney's natural inclination for conversation in song, to better connect and eschew meandering wordplay. "The vocal is also a capella, so there are no obstacles," the professor continues. "There's no instrumentation to interfere with the communicative aspect of the *Hey Jude.* He is saying, 'Listen to me, I have something to tell you.' *That* is a powerful beginning."

This is something the Beatles knew well, especially Paul McCartney, who used the cold-vocal-open in one of his earliest Beatles songs, "All My Loving," which portended the Beatles wishful incantation with the opening line *Close your eyes,* and then auspiciously on the first UK #1 "From Me to You," *Da da da, da da dumb dumb da.* Most famously, the band, prodded by producer George Martin, decided to kick off one of their first #1 hits, "She Loves You," with their voices—albeit after a drum-fill—heralding the song's ebullient chorus sung with incendiary harmonies slashing out of the ether with reckless abandon. This, along with announcing the song's title, as Paul does with "Hey Jude," provided the Beatles the most effective way to announce their presence while also shrewdly ushering in the chorus *and* the blessed hook. Reinforcing its infectious structure was *Yeah, Yeah, Yeah,* a kind of joyous harbinger for *Na . . . na . . . na . . . na na na na.*

A similar technique is used to open the band's second album, *With the Beatles,* as John Lennon's cry of the title "It Won't Be Long" also features a healthy dose of call-and-response *Yeah!* The next year, "Can't Buy Me Love"—from their most famous and arguably best film *A Hard Day's Night*—bursts in with its chorus/name proclamation. Same goes with shouting the title of the 1965 follow-up film, *Help!* Voices also open the meditative "Nowhere Man" and the harmonic declaration of "Paperback Writer," both from 1966, along with a song that would shift the paradigm of popular music, "Eleanor Rigby"—again a hauntingly sung refrain that introduces a string quarter instead of an assault of guitars, bass, and drums. The most intimate example of the Beatles opening with the sound of a voice first is John's sweetly melancholic song for his mother, "Julia," which is the only track in the Beatles canon Lennon sings accompanied only by himself on guitar. Composed around the same time as "Hey Jude," it was keenly supported by Paul during its recording, the childhood bonding of grief never forgotten. All of these songs begin with a naked introduction of key words sung *before* the music. And, in many cases, the title of the song comes first.

"What's funny about 'Hey Jude' is that it doesn't necessarily have a true chorus, it's sort of an A/B section kind of thing, but if you said to someone, 'How does "Hey Jude" go?' they'd sing the very first line, *Hey Jude,*" notes Eric Hutchinson. "This is the name of the song, this is the theme of the song, this is the tempo of the song, you're going to get it all in the first five seconds."

"It definitely grabs your attention right away, and it's an immediate verse/chorus, so technically, in terms of songwriting, they are *one* and *the same*, and it happens at the top of the song structure," says Kiley Lotz. "You're hitting them in the face with the theme right away. It's very unique. I don't know if it's utilized as much in current pop music writing, but I think it's really effective in terms of grabbing people. One of the songs that I've written, 'Heaven,' which seems to have touched a lot of people, has a similar structure—you're right into it, *that's* the hook."

"I don't want to call verses throwaway melodies, but you normally try to hit your hook in a chorus," says Adam Duritz. "Ideally, you want the verse to be great too, but an average song has the big melody in the chorus, but to have nothing but hook all the way through a song? There isn't a need for a prelude in 'Hey Jude.' There it is."

Of course, the Beatles didn't invent the idea of opening songs with the title or the chorus. To name just a few meritoriously executed examples: eighteenth-century church hymnal, "Amazing Grace"; Depression era, "Happy Days are Here Again"; 1937 Disney ballad, "Someday My Prince will Come"; Rogers and Hart classic, "My Funny Valentine"; Mills Bothers, "You Always Hurt the Ones You Love"; Connie Francis staple, "Who's Sorry Now?"; and Frank Sinatra's chart-topper, "Strangers in the Night." The Beatles, however, repeatedly and effectively used this technique throughout their spectacularly successful career.

Dr. Koch: "When you talk about great songs from other eras; 'Somewhere Over the Rainbow' or 'White Christmas,' two seminal classics from the early part of the American century songbook, both have a Broadway song structure to them in which they intended the titles to act as the chorus. Normally in a Broadway song, you would have a verse that is written somewhat freely—not necessarily a clearly delineated four-plus-four phrase structure—and maybe a little more speechlike, not so lyrical. But when you get to the chorus, that's the part we all know and join along in. Yet, despite their show-tune structure, these songs happen to begin with a chorus; 'Somewhere Over the Rainbow' and 'White Christmas,' and that's really how 'Hey Jude' is approached."

Peter Blasevick is a classically trained pianist, rock performer, jazz enthusiast, and a dear friend who is my go-to for all the musical quandaries that inevitably arise when authoring books on the subject. He is also an unabashed McCartney and Beatles fan, and so when he was so effusive on the following point, it needed to be included here: "I think you'd be missing out if you did not at least somehow mention or allude to the fact that at every point in McCartney's life, he wrote songs with the Great American Songbook structure. He was sixteen years old when he wrote, 'When I'm Sixty-Four,' which is basically the same structure as 'Hey Jude' twelve years later. 'Hard Day's Night,' 'We Can Work It Out,' 'Maybe I'm Amazed,' 'Say, Say, Say,' they're all the same structure. This is how Paul McCartney wrote songs. Now, did he write wildly structured songs like 'Band on the Run'? Sure, but he is the greatest pop songwriter of all time, he knows how to do it. And although he's got a few different ways of writing tunes, and, with its extended separate ending, this is one of them, he had a formula to his songwriting and 'Hey Jude' just happens to be one of the best songs he ever wrote."

Ballad

Okay, so the song has texture and tone, taps into classical methods of composition and poetic meter, while also reflecting its narrator's empathy in a musical and lyrical undercurrent that grabs us from the start and builds from an extraordinary melody into a uniquely structured soaring chorale—all leading Beatles biographer Bob Spitz to postulate that nothing in McCartney's repertoire is "as openly tender and genuinely stirring." But how do we describe "Hey Jude"? Is it a ballad?

Professor Koch believes so, in fact, he calls its first three minutes "a classic example of a ballad." He continues: "Up to this point, our melodic contour is a series of up-and-down motions . . . we go down, *Hey Jude* . . . then we go up a little bit, *Don't make it bad* . . . then back down again; *Take a sad song* . . . and then we go back up; *And make it better* . . . back down, *Remember* . . . then we get up to the highest note so far in the song, . . . *to let her into your heart* . . . I tell my students this is a good principle of songwriting, particularly ballad songwriting. I wouldn't apply this to EDM [electronic dance music] or dance music, but in ballad writing, it is great to have a climax pitch; . . . *to let her into your heart* is that key climactic phrase. Its message is positive, and the melody is telling us this."

The song's bridge, a short interlude McCartney introduces to bring us back to the opening melody, acts as both a promise and a wry hint at *Na . . . na . . . na . . . na na na na,* not unlike what the narrator is offering to Jude, which leads to what many here refer to as its "payoff." It is in providing us a glimpse of the coming release that "Hey Jude" begins to play with our emotions, musically teasing our expectations.

This brings us back to Professor Halpern's psychological "predictions"—how we can envision where a song might go. "There are two layers of prediction," she notes. "When it's unfamiliar, your predictions may or may not be fulfilled, you have probabilities attached to them. These are, again, not conscious. But when we know it, the probabilities go to 1.00; we know what's going to happen. But that doesn't stop us from the prediction. As listeners, we still set up expectancies. It's like watching your favorite murder mystery movie and you know what's going to happen when she goes down into that basement. You still can't stop yourself saying, 'I hope she doesn't go down into that basement!' Subconsciously, we're set up to be prediction machines, to play the odds, so to speak. The odds get very favorable, when it's something we know well."

"I was going back and listening to 'Hey Jude' recently and, at one point, I asked myself at what point is Paul saying this to Julian and at what point is he saying it to himself?" mulls Professor Shashko. "There is a transitional moment in the song where he's gone from trying to convince Julian that everything is going to be okay to convincing himself that everything is going to be okay, and I think you hear that in the tone of his voice, the song grows and grows and grows, and there is almost a desperation to get to *na, na, na*."

Expectations

"There's an argument among musicians about the bridge in 'Hey Jude'; whether it actually changes key," notes Dr. Koch. "The song is in F, but then when they go to the bridge, Paul plays an F-dominant seventh so a lot of people think he goes to B-flat major there. But does he really go to B-flat major or does he stay in F major? And there's a difference, because it deals with the concept of modulation. Why do composers modulate? Because modulation adds context and interest. It's like taking a journey from a home key to a foreign key. But just like any journey, you eventually want to come back home, and eventually Paul does. If for a moment we hear him modulating to B-flat major, we want to hear him clearly return to F major and he's not there yet."

"Your ears *wait* for the results, so it's really effective in that way," adds Lotz. "You're waiting for the payoff, but he keeps coming back to *Hey, Jude . . . Don't let me down . . .* bringing it back around again and again. He uses this seventh chord to bring in what you think is the chorus, the mini *na-na-na,* and in a weird way it feels like the payoff. When a chord resolves, *that's* my favorite. And the more you can hold off and make the listener work for it, or hang in there *earning* it, eventually it feels so satisfying."

Professor Koch continues: "So it can be argued that the way that Paul arrives back to F major is through this . . . [plays on the piano what Kiley refers to as the mini-*na-na-na* part at the end of the bridge] . . . he needs to come back and he needs to play what we call a dominant seventh in F major to reinforce the shift back to F major. He *must* play the C-dominant seventh chord to reinforce it, so that's what that C-dominant seventh does, it *reinforces* the shift back to F major perfectly."

Professor Samarotto concludes: "This is a pre-taste of what's to come, but it also makes perfect sense in the song; 'Oh, we're reaching towards *something,* something's gonna happen, I don't know exactly when, but this is not finished.' And then, of course, you get to what I call the 'infinity section' and it feels then as if we've entered an infinite space."

McCartney's musical pilgrimage/journey finds its crossroads and traverses it skillfully, adding suspense and, since it was inspired by young Julian, a childlike sense of wonder. "And when we finish in F major, we're not sure where we are yet, we don't know whether we are back at home or whether we're still on this journey, so what Paul needs to do is to provide a landing," says Dr. Koch. "He needs to bring it back up to F-major to help *resolve* some of that tension, what we call tonal tension, he's built up. Could he have just gone back into . . . [plays opening 'Hey Jude' chords]? Sure, but I think the listener would be caught off-guard. When we hear this retransition, we *know* we're back home, because this has to be followed by the structure of the song that he starts out with, which provides the listener a sense of comfort. He uses these chords as a mechanism to return us safely from the journey."

"The subtle *yeah* Paul sings at the end of the second bridge sells the last half of the song right away," adds Eric Hutchinson. "I think if you just had the *Nas* come in, it doesn't do it, but Paul gets you there, he walks you right into the second half of the song."

Here is Paul, channeling the trepidations of his youth and the empathy he feels for Julian's plight in facing his parents' split, as he and John had emerged from the tragedies of their mother's deaths together, while also nodding to his partner's new love for Yoko, along with his own for Linda. You can hear in this musical journey the excitement of the unknown that comes with a new relationship but also the grieving for those disintegrating; Cynthia for John, Jane for Paul, and for the both of them, the Beatles. Confronting loss and rebuilding faith; the ballad has one foot in the past while leading us inevitably into the vast future expressed in *Na . . . na . . . na . . . na na na na.*

"Paul eases us in," says Dr. Koch. "He gives us what we can expect, but when we get to the bridge, we get this harmony with a C major chord right there, which can be interpreted as just a dominant of our tonic F. However, if you hear the bridge in the key of B-flat major, then the C major must be interpreted as a secondary chord not belonging to

B-flat. It suggests that at this point Paul could have gone in a different direction. Rather than a C chord he could have gone to E-flat (the sub-dominant of B-flat) and it would have worked. We never get an E-flat *there,* but we *do* get it in the *na, na, na* part! It's absent in the bridge but comes back in the coda."

Here again is Dr. Auxier's theory—by way of Susanne Langer, who postulates in her 1942 work, *Philosophy in a New Key*—that music can play with time as a yearning to endow meaning to the chaos of existence. This is how song can bring order and comfort to our fear of the unknown, as Dr. Koch notes: "Sometimes a composer will intentionally leave something out that you might expect to hear only to gratify you ultimately, but it's *delayed* gratification—it does eventually come, but you just have to *wait* for it, so that's my connection between the bridge and the outro—instead of something that is merely *there,* we establish that there is something there that *connects* to the outro. There is something missing that we might expect that doesn't come until then. It is an incredible release and provides us a doorway to step through to the classic ending of 'Hey Jude.'"

"As a musician, part of what catches my ear is when Paul hits a higher register in the song on lines like *And don't you know that it's just you,*" notes Dr. Auxier. "That is a conscious decision. As a songwriter, I can tell you, you don't just spontaneously change registers for no reason; sometimes that reason is driven by melodic and repetition issues, but I see that as less the case here than Paul using his uncanny ability to blur the relationship between his rich baritone and his falsetto. He is making a significant point that *it's just you . . . you'll do.* He needs you to hear this. And, for me, it's the turning point of the song."

In addition to her academic career in psychology, professor Andrea Halpern is also a choir singer, who offers this take on McCartney's ability and purpose in using the elastic range of his voice for emotional resonance. "He's effectively using his falsetto, which allows him to get to this entirely different range that is not only higher but a different timbre. Both of those together elicit attention. This is especially affecting in male voices. In Renaissance times, the male alto was so prized that some church male singers were castrated, so they could keep their range as their bodies grew. In modern times, we have men who develop their alto range with the resonance of a male body, and the results are very haunting. We call them countertenors. My favorite piece of music is the Bach B-Minor Mass, and there's an alto aria at the end that's normally done by a female alto. But the most affecting performance I ever did featured a man in his sixties with a beautiful alto voice. It was so evocative, because of the haunting nature of the male alto voice. So that device is certainly attention demanding."

The genius of Paul McCartney is that his emotional currency "pays off" on its promise—as the Beatles did for their audience, their generation, the very evolution of rock and roll. It is the musical enactment of hope in the song's lyrics telling us, *demanding* us, to hang on, to conquer our fears and look within, to accept love, to believe in ourselves, and then there will be a release, or in musical and spiritual terms, a resolution. And because he is one of the great ballad/rock singers of his generation, McCartney envelops his chords and uses this energy to eventually break through, combining his lyrical sympathies into a vocal explosion. "As good as, *better, better, better* . . . is when he hits that falsetto *ahhhhhhh* . . . it has the energy that has not been in the song yet," says Hutchinson. "It is a musical breakthrough that breaks the song in half and gets you to that section, because until that point, it's been very calm. He's also going up an octave to get up there, so the song is literally rising, and he takes us there in a visceral way."

High Note

Katie Darby Mullins notes, "It's that peak—everyone who is alive in the common era can likely replicate McCartney's more and more high-pitched screams of *better, better, better, better!* that turns the song into an imperative to become a part of the marching band that lives in your stereo."

"As much as the instrumentation has to pay off, the vocals have the payoff at the end as well," concludes Lotz. "It sounds like the joy of feeling understood, the relief of a burden can be so huge that he just wants to *scream.* And that's what Paul does. And it's not contrived. I think it's beautiful, because certain things deserve to be shouted about. And even if they're little things like a pep talk; it's so joyful and profound, it is central to human experience. And that doesn't always get shouted out about in music. It's hard to write a happy song. I am just now in my late twenties getting to a place where I feel like I can write a happy song. It's fucking hard. I don't know how to do it, and I'm actively *trying* to write happy songs. 'Hey Jude' is definitely in the happy song category for me. At the very least, it is a positive song—the confidence level, that trust in the words, the strength of the melody, and the hook from the get go is incredible. So, when we get to Paul's vocal payoff, you think, 'Yes! It's gonna be fucking okay!' It's triumphant. And that's the goal here; to get you out the door, ready to take on the thing that's getting you down, and you don't have to do it alone, which makes you immediately feel lighter."

"That scream has shaken my bones from the inside out for more than two decades," says songwriter Seán Barna. "Whatever trial or tribulations have led us to this point, we are leaving those behind. This is a stadium of people cheering us on. For what? Whatever the fuck you want. Whatever the fuck you need."

Which brings us finally to *Na . . . na . . . na . . . na na na na . . .*

Infinity

"It is like a drone," says Rob Sheffield. "Comforting but not necessarily soothing or lulling. You can't help but follow it all the way as it builds and builds."

Here the ballad *becomes* the anthem, the Beatles taking Paul McCartney's song and handing it neatly over to the world. But, according to Dr. Koch, Paul provided the musical roadmap: "Throughout the famous outro, this unexpected E-flat major chord I referenced earlier is finally there, and the melody that is sung at the same time is also something that we don't necessarily expect because it doesn't *fit* with the chord. It's a nonharmonic tone, which is an *expressive* note, the E-flat chord, accompanying the F in the melody, resolves to give us *satisfaction* in the next chord."

Upon hitting the final refrain, the music provides a conflict/resolution paradigm inherent in the best art; the realization that nothing worth having is easy. Without tension, there is no release, and as any writer will note, without conflict there can be no resolution. "The way the melody works over that E-flat chord provides that dissonance again, that tension Paul introduces that has to be *resolved*, and it ultimately is resolved in the next two chords," says Dr. Koch. "That is not something the Beatles invented, this this I-♭VII-IV-I progression. They just use it so effectively in 'Hey Jude.' It's remarkable work."

"It's interesting that Paul doesn't treat it like a chorus, where he's going to a whole new thing to launch," says Adam Duritz. "He goes back to the root of the song and launches into something new from there to take us home."

Professor Samarotto delves deeper into the musical efficacy of *Na . . . na . . . na . . . na na na na* in his University of Indiana essay "The Trope of Expectancy/Infinity in the Music of the Beatles and Others." The work cites "Hey Jude" as a starting point for a new style of songwriting that merges two disparate songs into one opus, inviting the listener to consider endless possibilities through music and imagine a universal harmony within and without. In its summation he writes, "I've always found my listening to 'Hey Jude' to be infused with the knowledge that something was going to happen, something really good, better than now, a world of possibilities, infinite possibilities."

He explained further to me: "There is the conventional song part of 'Hey Jude,' then we go to this new thing, which is the double-amen cadence that just goes on forever. And that part is not even a *real* song. Certainly, the first three minutes or so of 'Hey Jude' could be an independent song, but the other part, which I call the 'infinity part,' no matter how popular the Beatles were, they couldn't have released *that* by itself as a single. The two parts of the song *absolutely* need each other."

The professor's noting "two parts of the song *absolutely* need each other"—what Beatles author and musicologist Walter Everett cites as "an inspired deep analysis"—is what first struck me as a lasting symbol of "Hey Jude" as a unifying musical and thematic message, a sonic metaphor for the human need for connection—both emotionally and musically.

Professor Samarotto continues: "The phenomenon of 'Hey Jude' with its independent section of the song is that it doesn't relate to what came before but creates a whole new space that we're in that represents future possibilities, which always seem wonderful, like they will last *forever*. It's not a *real* space, but a space that we exalt in if we can get a little bit of it. So, the Beatles enact infinity by repeating the phrase over and over again."

"Hey Jude" has nineteen rounds of the "double amen cadence" in its long, "infinite" fadeout. And although its use as a separate musical variation is unique, its construction, in the McCartney idiom, is as traditional as songwriting gets, bringing us closer to the vast lineage of music that burrows inside us. Earlier in the song, Paul's use of modulation or hinting at changing the key in the bridge utilizes a leading tone found in blues, the bedrock of rock and roll and a common technique of changing chords in most music, and, as already noted, he also holds fast to standard ballad phrasing. The same goes for the "amen cadence," or its more technical term, plagal cadence, in his epic coda. It is the musical equivalent of a soft landing, bringing a close to a musical phrase that immediately reminds the listener of a hymn as first introduced into the public sphere in *Hymns—Ancient and Modern* in 1861, where it began to take hold in the Anglican Church. This spiritual connection, first broached to me by Professor Everett about Paul's time spent in the St. Barnabas Church as a boy and later deconstructed by organist John Deaver in our discussions about Paul's inclusion, consciously or not, of the "Te Deum" hymn for the opening notes of the song, leads us directly to the doorstep of the amen cadence.

By the mid-to-late nineteenth century, the amen cadence was *the* signature way to end hymnal music. The 1861 volume presents over four hundred hymns that *all* end with the amen or plagal cadence—a cadence, or course, being a modulation of our voices in speech patterns, a natural downward inflection denoting the end of a phrase. It is a communicative way for one person to be sure the other is finished speaking to respond in kind. In a sense, Paul is conversing with the listener—firstly, his subject, Jude in the song, and then by proxy, Beatles fans, and finally, the whole world. He provides the breath, tone, and pace of his song to share his message, something picked up by all of the songwriters I've included in the commentary here, as a universal way of bringing us along, as in telling a story that must end with *Na . . . na . . . na . . . na na na na*—the communal Beatles hymn.

"The full progression [in] the classic ending of 'Hey Jude' is F, E flat, to B flat, back to F," says Dr. Koch. "However, E-flat doesn't fit within the key of F. How do we explain this in music theory terms? One way is to say he borrows it from the Mixolydian mode to set up what progression theorists call a 'double plagal cadence.' Think of those church hymns that end with the two final chords on *Amen*. Now imagine two Amens in a row: one on E-flat to B-flat, and another on B-flat to F. In this way, the coda achieves a hymn-like quality. It *becomes* a gospel song."

"Gospel shares characteristics of religious music and pop music," says Professor Halpern. "I suspect people feel that gospel speaks very directly to them, as opposed to indirectly like some traditional Christian music based on say the psalms; they're beautiful poems, but they *are* poems, which require interpretation."

In his essay, Professor Samarotto cites the transition in "Hey Jude" from what he calls the "expectancy section" (the traditional ballad) into the "infinity section" (the plagal cadence) used in ensuing decades by artists who were inspired by the song's revolutionary arrangement to create dozens of imitations, homages, and blatant rip-offs. The paper lists some of the more classic examples artistically rendered and thus epic: "Layla" by Derek and the Dominos (1970) with its somber piano elegy grafted onto the end of an effusive guitar attack; as well as "I've Seen All Good People" and "Starship Trooper" (1971) by prog rock godfathers Yes, wherein the second part erupts into a free-form section; and from the same year the brass-added fusion pop of Chicago and their "Beginnings" (I offer the same band's "Feelin' Stronger Every Day" from 1973) that presents a singalong outro similar to "Hey Jude." Still later, the professor notes Radiohead's "Sit Down, Stand Up" (2003) in the same lineage.

Tim Riley played along when I mentioned the theory to him: "When I think of songs immediately inspired by 'Hey Jude,' I go to CSN's [Crosby, Stills and Nash] 'Suite: Judy Blue Eyes' and Derek and the Dominos' 'Layla.' In the former the late-sixties super group breaks from the main frame of the song to harmonize on *do-do-do-do* in place of *na-na-na-na*. The structure works the same," says Riley. "A song proper appended with a soaring coda that nearly upstages its setup. The Beatles' model works best, but I find these others as musical hat tips . . . they all operate on the same suspense/release tactic, so that after the first time you hear it, you do spend much of the first part of the song anticipating the withheld coda, which adds to the energy of the formal verse."

"I hear Donovan's 'Atlantis' as a direct answer to 'Hey Jude' a year later," offers singer/songwriter Dan Bern. The song's opening is a spoken word telling for about two minutes of a five-minute song that breaks into a repeated refrain, which outlasts its first part. "This is not out of the realm of possibility," adds Bern. "Donovan's a great melody writer and lyricist, and he was hanging out with the Beatles at the time in India. Yet, it doesn't have the same grit and the same peak, and it certainly hasn't lasted the same way."

"The ending of 'Hey Jude' is universal and delightfully repetitive without really becoming boring," notes Dr. Koch. "It is reflective of the late-sixties spiritual enlightenment edict, what John ends up further capturing with 'Give Peace a Chance' where the title is just sung over and over while you allow some sort of collective meditation to take place, like a musical mantra. 'Hey Jude' is intended as such, and I think it works effectively. Each pass through the *na, na, na* phrasing is unique and Paul adds a lot of interest by showing off his vocal prowess, singing all these high notes. The range of the piece is quite incredible."

"For a singalong, there's really nothing campy or forced about it, you *must* sing along to it, you don't have a choice," says songwriter, pianist, and elastic vocalist, Elizabeth Ziman of Elizabeth and the Catapult. "Mumford and Sons made singalongs on *oooohhhh,* which is very difficult for me to hang with. They become overly reverential, and therefore kind of corny. 'Hey Jude,' however, still exists in the so-to-speak golden age of singalongs, there just ain't nothing corny about *na na na nanananaaa, Hey Jude,* it's perfect."

"It's impossible, I could never do it," says Adam Duritz. "I go three times around with the *na-nas* at the end of 'A Long December' [Counting Crows 1996 hit single], that's all I can get. And I'm stretching it as it is, three times around, that's it! It's like a minute, *maybe,* it's *nothing.* And 'A Long December' was an okay hit, but not like *that.* 'Hey Jude' is one of the biggest hits *ever* and it's going on and on. But it doesn't matter, because it's so good."

Resonance

"There is no way Paul could have predicted this; but composing and arranging 'Hey Jude' the way he did couldn't have made it anymore perfect for him to perform as a solo artist decades later," notes professor Alexander Shashko. "There's even a part for him to do on top of the *na, na, na* beyond just singing along, while the rest of the audience is singing. He is, in a way, conducting it. It is kind of magical that way."

Stephen Kellogg recalls, "I sang the song at Tsongas Center, which was, at the time, the biggest venue I'd ever played, about sixty-five hundred seats up in Boston. I was opening for O.A.R. It was their biggest show at that time, too and they said, 'We need a song that's gonna destroy!' And they decided to do 'Hey Jude.' That was the first and only time I've ever actually sung that song, but I do remember that it was brought in to be a wrecking ball on an audience. And it *was* a wrecking ball."

"'Hey Jude' was the first Beatles song I ever learned on guitar," says singer/songwriter Alex Knight. "It was mostly nineties grunge and alt rock before then, taught to me by an aging hair metal guy with a beer gut and a decaying Heart poster on his wall. He perked up when I brought in a Beatles song. I noticed, and for some reason, I cared. I also noticed that the usage of those brand-new things he was calling 'seventh chords' shaped and pushed the vocal melody into a place that it never would have been otherwise, and that totally rocked my young, aspiring songwriter brain. The Beatles had just, quite literally, taken my sad songs and made them better. The depth in their simplicity and the simplicity of their depth gave me the creative guidance I needed to trust myself and get going."

"Around 1974–'75, there was a primetime special about the Beatles and they asked people what their all-time favorite Beatle song was," remembers Peter Ames Carlin. "And they were teasing out the reveal by people singing little snatches of 'Hey Jude, with *everybody* singing the tag, *na-na-na na-na-na-na*; even ten-year-old kids on Sting-Ray bikes in California. And what stayed with me was this idea that 'Hey Jude' at that time was the *ultimate* Beatles song. It had everything that you loved in the Beatles all rolled into one."

Orenda Fink, half of a unique friendship inside an intense singer/songwriter collective called Azure Ray, says: "When I think of 'Hey Jude,' I think of being in the car as a little kid, listening to the classic rock station as I'm being ferried to the Piggly Wiggly or the Kmart, some unremarkable shopping trip with my mother and two sisters. This would always be a song that *someone* turns up. You want to hear it loud because it speaks to you. It's your own personal pep talk, no matter that it's addressed to some far away person named Jude. You want Jude, and you, to take that sad song and make it better. You want Jude, and you, to not carry the weight of the world on his, *your* shoulders. And in the end, you do feel like Jude, and you, can make it *better, better, better, better, better, better AHHHH!* And the whole car sings *Na-na-na-na-na-na-na, Hey Juuuuude,* and you smile, and the wind blows through your hair, and you see your sisters are smiling too, and everything feels right in that moment."

"Hooks are what keeps a song with you, keeps you singing even when you aren't aware you're singing it," says the other half of Azure Ray, intensely personal singer/songwriter Maria Taylor. "You can have vocal hooks with the melody, but you can also have musical hooks. When you have the combination of the two, you pretty much know this song is going to follow you into the shower, on your walks, work, and even into your dreams. The Beatles mastered the art of hooks. 'Hey Jude' does everything a great song should do, effortlessly. It takes you on an emotional journey and leaves you singing it for a long, long time."

"'Hey Jude' immediately becomes a rut that's carved into your mind," concludes Adam Duritz. "We're scarred with Beatles songs! They last forever, they're not going away, it's not something that heals. You don't hear a Beatle song and forget it. 'Hey Jude' is *forever*."

In the discography section of his *Magic Circles*, Devin McKinney writes of "Hey Jude": "I used to think it was overrated; now I can't listen to it without trembling." This, of course, intrigued me, so at the end of our discussion I pressed him on it. "At a certain point in my life, once I had gotten old enough and mature enough to *really* hear it, and feel it, I realized that this unending chant is going right down to the bottom of *me*, and it's not a bottom that I had when I was twelve years old, nor was I capable of feeling this music when I was fifteen, or even twenty," says McKinney. "Eventually, you realize that you've been through enough in your life to be in touch with certain emotions that you never knew existed. And this music suddenly is speaking to *all* of that. I'm trembling now thinking about that song because it's on my phone. I listen to it in my car all the time, over and over, it never gets old for me. And yeah, when I was growing up, I'd say it was overrated, because there were plenty of other songs that I preferred to listen to. But then at a certain point, it revealed itself to me. And it's been revealing itself to me ever since."

CHAPTER ELEVEN

I Can Feel It! Can You Feel It?

Comfort & Unity

> *The enduring appeal of "Hey Jude," its lasting message, is "It's going to be cool; it's going to be all right, you're going to get through this." It's just one of those things; right song at the right time. I think people needed that message in 1968, but then people always need that message.*
>
> —Dr. William Boone

In the autumn of 2019, Paul McCartney returned to the Ed Sullivan theater to appear on *The Late Show with Stephen Colbert.* During the lengthy interview, Colbert asked him if he comprehended the expansive reach of his work. As an example, he wondered if Paul had heard of the international boy-band sensation from South Korea, BTS. Of course, he had. Always tuned into the global popular music scene, it would have been hard for him not to. The K-pop septet had sold over twenty million records in their native country before invading charts the world over. Like the Beatles, the band had also caught a critical ear with lyrics that went beyond juvenile fare to shed light on social and political issues and a universal search for loving oneself and defining individualism.

Colbert showed McCartney a clip of their *Late Show* appearance that May wherein the host mentioned to the kids that they were the first act to have three #1 albums in a single year since the Beatles. "Do you guys have favorite Beatles songs?" Colbert asked them. One member knowingly pointed to another, which prompted him to jump up and sing, *Na . . . na . . . na . . . na na na na.* The rest of the band joyfully joined in. The show band, the Roots, joined in. The crowd joined in. An insert of McCartney looking on was placed in the upper left corner. He beamed like a proud papa. Yet another phenomenon raised on his songs.

"What do you think it is about your music that transcends geographic and language barriers, so that those seven guys could jump up and start the *na-na-nas*?" Colbert asks.

Paul inhales as if embarrassed to admit it, and says, "Easy lyrics?"

The audience erupts in laughter. Colbert, impressed, as so many before him by that Liverpool wit, smiles and says, "It's true."

And it is.

But also, it isn't.

A few months before he was shot to death outside his home in New York City, forty-year-old John Lennon told journalist David Sheff that his former partner should be given due credit for his overlooked lyrical prowess. He used one song to make that point: "'Hey Jude' is a damn good set of lyrics." Lennon was recalling the irony of a song to comfort the son he was leaving behind neatly interpreted as an approbation for him to do so. "For John," Adam Duritz muses, "it was a song of absolution."

Lennon, as we know, was quite stingy when it came to doling out accolades, especially to his boyhood chum. Yet, in 1971, he told *Record Mirror* that "Hey Jude" was "Paul's best song." This must have been a pleasant shock to Paul considering Lennon's latest solo album *Imagine* featured a spiteful rebuke of his former partner called "How Do You Sleep?" It would seem, "Hey Jude" was still healing old wounds.

Lennon continued to be moved by "Hey Jude" because the moment he heard it he was convinced, like any Beatles fan, that the song was about *him*. He had sought solace in music, gurus, drugs, fame, fortune, and eventually Yoko Ono's love. "Hey Jude" encapsulated it all for him. Paul was telling him the search was over. "There's a generosity and a tenderness in the song that you can never overestimate how powerful it is," says Duritz. "There is a lot of snark from John, but you *never* hear any snark about 'Hey Jude.' It's such an act of openhearted generosity for Paul to write a song to comfort a friend's son, that there is overwhelming evidence of how much it meant to John. You want to talk about unity? *That's* unity."

"Think about when John used 'us' to defend its length to George Martin," adds author Rob Sheffield. "It would have been one thing for him to say that about his own song, but that he said it about Paul's, and using the first-person plural to talk about the Beatles at this fractious moment in their career, says a lot about 'Hey Jude' and what a unifying song it is."

McCartney biographer Peter Ames Carlin notes: "It has this extraordinary sweep; an ability to be both super intimate and super universal at the same time. And that's one of the hallmarks of a real superior piece of art."

"One thing McCartney was an expert at when it came to lyrics was finding a way to take a very personal situation and make it applicable to anyone," says University of Evansville's associate professor of creative writing Katie Darby Mullins. "His songs fit like plastic sheets on overhead projectors: no matter what the black lines of your day look like, they add the color necessary for you to see the picture more clearly and to live a more fulfilled life. In some ways, 'Hey Jude' is the ultimate test of that: it was written literally for one little boy, and it has come to be an anthem about perseverance for, so far as I know, everyone who knows it."

Similar to John's personal dilemma, the youth culture of 1968 was splintering on its own accord, breaking into warring factions rather than embracing the unity that had gotten it this far. In "Hey Jude," the movement found a voice of reconciliation. This was especially true in America, where its immense reach provided similar solace, as Beatles expert Scott Freiman notes: "The gospel side of things in the song's composition certainly appealed to Americans, even though they may not recognize it as such, it's something that *feels* very American."

"It has elements of gospel," says Duritz. "When I think about some of the piano on it, it reminds me of Aretha Franklin, and the way she plays on those early Atlantic records, but, like Aretha, if Paul was just playing gospel music that would be boring. I love gospel music, but Paul is taking things he learned from also loving gospel music and putting it into a pop song. He takes it somewhere new, like Sam Cooke or Marvin Gaye, all the artists that came from gospel and took it somewhere else. I find it to be a creative application of a genre. Artists are not supposed to be archivists. We're supposed to be originals, and Paul is an original. He's not trying to re-create gospel in 'Hey Jude,' he's taking its prime elements and distilling it into soaring pop music. In its own way, that is the gospel of Paul McCartney."

Dr. William Boone, who along with his academic background is a songwriter and guitarist with a rich history of playing gospel music, concurs: "The ending does fit with the message of the song, telling people it will get better and that gospel edict to just let it go—you've been through hard times and you're carrying all this weight around and you need to embrace that feeling of freedom. In a gospel sense, you give all your troubles over to the Lord, but here it's to a woman or a friend. In this way, 'Hey Jude' is a secular gospel song—give your burdens away. Ultimately, that's what lets it resonate beyond 1968, this sense of unburdening. *I can let go*. It is very effective."

McCartney's use of a religious musical framework ("Te Deum") and the song's pastiche of gospel style (amen cadence) works as a spiritual subtext to the comforting words he sings, but not to be ignored is the song's call to action, a self-fulfilling prophecy of chasing joy that can be achieved through the understanding and acceptance of love. The realization that enacting change for the better, having control over one's bliss, reflects the Beatles' influence over the culture—"movement" as in the act of "forward motion."

"You can't keep moving forward if the machine becomes stiff from lack of feeling," says singer/songwriter Kiley Lotz. "Part of the process of healing is breaking down. Paul writing the song to preemptively comfort this person who's about to go through something really bad and trying to reaffirm that he can make it is really sincere. I think it gets insincere when you start pushing the shame of inaction, but everybody wants to hear they have the power to overcome."

During the course of our discussions, Dr. Boone often referenced the work of African American studies scholar Ashon Crawley, specifically his book *Blackpentecostal Breath*. In it, Crawley proposes an idea he calls the Aesthetics of Possibility. Boone told me: "Crawley tells us that a lot of times we turn to art because it enacts the world that we want to live in, and in a very real sense a song creates a temporary world that we want to imagine ourselves living in and sometimes we need the song to create that for us so we can *imagine* it."

This is the thematic side of what Professor Frank Samarotto calls the "infinitely positive future of possibility" that gives "Hey Jude" its communal resonance, as McCartney quite literally fuses two songs into one, musically reflecting the fractured entities of the personal and societal coming together. Samarotto concludes: "One of the things that makes 'Hey Jude' a perfect song is the symbiotic relationship with the main ballad and its extended infinity section, which join together into a higher unity."

Lotz distills this idea down further: "The message is unrelentingly positive. *Let it out, let it in* is this idea of taking a breath, it feels like a mindfulness exercise, the inhale and the exhale—inhale on the *Hey . . . Jude* and on the walk-down bridges, and then eventually you get to the big exhale, which is slow-building, and then eventually you're *really* breathing, you're in it, your body's moving in the song and you're breathing with the song, you get release. It's a totally satisfying experience."

"There's this story about the unifying power of 'Hey Jude' that always stuck with me from a great book by my friend, Sean Howe, *Marvel Comics: The Untold Story*," recalls author Rob Sheffield. "At the Marvel 'bullpen' where all the writers and artists worked, everybody was at each other's throats with these backstage feuds, and, of course, everybody's mad at Stan Lee. And then 'Hey Jude' comes on the radio and all of them put down their pen and ink and burst into singing the *Na-na-na-na-nas* together. That is until the end of the song, when they go back to hating Stan Lee."

A sentiment proposed more than once in this book suggests that "Hey Jude" is escapist art—something to quell our minds with platitudes accentuated by a singalong chorale. "The core of its popularity, without any question in my mind, is 'Hey Jude' takes you in almost a trance-like state where you could escape anywhere you are, that's part of the genius of the song," cites Professor Alexander Shashko. "People wanted to get away from the tumult of the moment, and while I don't think it's why Paul McCartney wrote it, it certainly reached the audience in that way, because an audience will reshape a work of art once they absorb it. A song is not a literal expression of anything, so, of course, people are going to have interpretations."

Professor Joel Stillerman ponders: "Maybe because the lyrics are not obvious it lends itself to project whatever you want on them. I was talking to my daughter, a Beatles fan, about the song, and she said, 'Well, maybe they're talking about this or maybe they're referring to that.' I can see her making up themes that speak specifically to her."

"Paul has talked about not knowing what every lyric in this song really means," says singer/songwriter Seán Barna. "Of course, he knows that doesn't matter."

In this way, the "escape" proffered by the song is one of breaking the cycle of pain for a new perception, as opposed to "escaping" the grim realities found in 1968 by "dropping out" and ignoring them. "Hey Jude" confronts these realities, for the song is an *imagining* of hope—something Lennon would later put into arguably his finest song as a solo artist, "Imagine," another piano ballad that although it does not possess the audience participation of "Hey Jude" is nonetheless sung in places where people meet to promote ideas for change. The utopian vision devised in the 1960s, a romantic nostalgia of a singular rejection of the chaos and violence in the world for one of peace and love, culminates in the "Hey Jude" creed, an alternative to accepting divisiveness as the norm. The escape is not ethereal but quite physical.

In McCartney's hands, *make it better* is an attainable idea that embraces the lasting imprint of the Maharishi's words on him, "The heart always goes to the warmer place." Unlike John's "Imagine," which surmises that if we can consider the concept of wiping away borders, religion, and possessions, we can take steps toward a universal truth, Paul merely sings *Let her into your heart*... and then... *you can start to make it better*. "Paul has this amazing sense of how important time is," reasons Dr. Randall Auxier. "Just listen to his songs; 'Yesterday,' about time and regret, 'Eleanor Rigby,' how the past connects us to the future, 'The Long and Winding Road, taking stock of yourself in the middle of life with all your mistakes behind you but still the future in front of you. 'Hey Jude' gives us time to evolve. The future opens up for Paul, it always does."

"I think this song is geared towards embracing conflict as opportunity, the ability to show yourself how resilient you can be," says Lotz. "And that other people's actions aren't going to define your future, *you* get to decide your future. Its rallying cry is, 'Yes, this is hard, but you can do it on your terms, you can recover, and not only recover, but thrive! And you don't have to do it alone. That's the best part of the song for me; *Don't carry the world upon your shoulders* . . . And its theme, the biggest lyrical takeaway, is achieved sonically too. The

Beatles intentionally build it up with this warm envelope of sound. It feels like a hug."

"The song is telling us, 'You don't have to take the world on, everything you need is already there, it's your head,'" says Duritz, "that's *on your shoulders*."

McCartney would take his own advice when penning the penultimate Beatles song on the last Beatles album, *Abbey Road* (with respect to his slight "Her Majesty"), with "Carry That Weight," which offers an acceptance of the burdens of life in order to find a way to overcome them. These paeans to self-empowerment are set against Lennon's embrace of the power of suggestion in Ashon Crawley's *Blackpentecostal Breath: The Aesthetics of Possibility (Commonalities)* with his 1969 anthem, "Give Peace a Chance," which, very much like "Hey Jude," has a long outro repeating the title of the song as a mantra but chooses the "we" mantle over the primacy of "me." McCartney is providing an intimate message of finding the inspiration for greater harmony within that is also found in Gandhi's "Be the change that you wish to see in the world" or Tolstoy's "Everyone thinks of changing the world, but no one thinks of changing himself."

"When someone says, '*We* respond to the song this way or that way,' it's hard for me to relate, because I always listen to it by myself, so, to me, 'Hey Jude' is not a communal experience, it's totally *all in here*," Beatles author Devin McKinney remarked to me, pointing emphatically to his temple. "And so, I allow myself to relive that innocence *every* time. It's not like I'm looking at my friends and we're just waiting for the moment we can all sing *na-na-na*. It's always been a very private, imaginative thing for me." The author's personal experience with the song inspired him to write of all Beatles songs in *Magic Circles*:

"[T]hey survive as universalisms, expressing something (truth, passion, reality) beyond their time. That such a song speaks must be deep enough, elusive enough, substantial enough to evolve, of itself, into something else."

In the context of its communal attributes, it is hard, reasons professor Andrea Halpern, to know what may have happened when people brought the record home, put it on the turntable and listened for the first time. But during this time, a great number of them would have likely heard it in a more public setting, since radio was the primary way in which people were introduced to new music. "In that way there's a cultural, if you will, *induction* that happens when you're with other people, and this is particularly true in a concert situation, with a great many people who are prompted to sing along."

"Hey Jude" is unique in its connected tissue of comfort (ballad) and unity (chorale), replete with messages of personal enlightenment, finding and expressing love, and generational unification. These edicts, like the music, are timeless because "Hey Jude" offers more than a passive listening experience that I instinctively understood as a boy, late at night, when I needed it to overcome a nightmare. The empathetic nature of its composer, who remembers fondly the tender moments of comfort from his mom after a skinned knee ("There was a lot of sitting on laps and cuddling") combined with the Beatles' reach for higher principles ("the roar of the whole world") puts the onus on us to pay it forward.

"The Beatles had a constant message of love, which is very much needed today, but was always needed," musicologist and author Walter Everett emailed to me. "'Hey Jude' is a good example of one person looking out for another—obviously also a much-needed sentiment."

"In my humble opinion, 'Hey Jude' has the impact it has because it represents the balance that the Beatles perfected and personified," says singer/songwriter Alex Knight. "An uplifting song about divorce and a crowd-connecting catharsis built on a foundation of *na-nas.* Seasoned artists using their extensive musical chops to work together in service of a beautiful melody. And a pop masterpiece that can seemingly be a metaphor for pretty much anything in the career of the greatest band of all time, and even some of the best parts of the human experience."

Peter Ames Carlin agrees, sharing: "When my marriage broke up, about a year ago, and I moved into an apartment, I found that I was listening to the Beatles . . . all the time. That was where I was drawn. I had spent so much of the first part of my life exclusively engaged with Beatles music, but then, eventually, I branched out, but I always found myself returning to my love of the Beatles. And when I wrote a book about Paul, my mania continued, in terms of a full-body absorption into it. And then it happened again over the last year, coming at a time of real personal tumult. This was the *first* music that I loved. This was the music that accompanied me through my early childhood. Maybe that's got something to do with it, too. But also, there's something about the Beatles, a power to their four-way presence, the particular chemistry that they have that has *never* been rivaled."

When speaking to the contributors to this book, I shared my childhood memory of singing the song to calm my nerves late at night and it seemed to strike a nerve in almost everyone.

"I think music in general is one of the most powerful hooks that can get into your brain when you're a child," Devin McKinney told me. "It might be a Walt Disney record or something outstandingly trivial, but we remember the music that we absorbed when we were a kid, and if it's music of a power and a variety and the subtlety and the layered-ness that the Beatles have, that music continues to grow as you grow with it. And so, it becomes only *more* powerful as you age and the memories that you're creating around that music and your experience with it today is interacting with memories that you have from when you were six. The fear and the wonder, and the darkness and the nighttime, all those associations make no sense on their own, but all of them come together to make an atmosphere. It's not the comprehensible link that you can make between them, it's just the fact that they were all there and they came together. Music has an inherent power to implant itself that way. That accounts for a lot of why, I think, 'Hey Jude' continues to work for so many of us."

"When you're young, all music is an invitation into a different place—before you understand that you're supposed to clap on the two and the four, before you can separate the harmonies and melodies, the bass and guitar—it's all magic," says Associate Professor Mullins. "No part of the Beatles' catalogue explores alchemical processes more than 'Hey Jude': even as an adult, I often find myself floating away a bit on McCartney's vocals into a better world than the one outside my window."

"It's interesting that you found the second part soothing, because it's a primal scream of dealing with *it all*," says Eric Hutchinson. "Where it makes sense, as a songwriter, I can see that it's written very much for a child. It is as soothing as a lullaby, and its repetition is reassuring."

"When you've heard *na-na-na-na-na* seventy-five times you think that you'd get tired of it," says Professor Auxier. "But kids don't. Kids *love* repetition."

"I would point to the repetition as being its most salient characteristic, it's a very simple structure," cites Professor Halpern.

"'Hey Jude,' in particular, beautifully translates the universal forever struggle of always adapting to new things that make us feel inadequate, or new things that feel challenging, whether it be queerness, in my case, or just trying to come to terms with all these things that feel so impossible," says Lotz. "But then you hear it at the *right time*, all of a sudden *anything* seems possible."

There is a key scene in John Hughes' classic eighties teen film, *Sixteen Candles* in which the main character, Samantha, played with great empathy by Molly Ringwald, is despondent at a school dance in which she cannot connect with a boy she has a crush on, while being constantly annoyed by a younger geeky kid named Ted, played for broad laughs by Anthony Michael Hall. When Samantha reveals to him that her parents have forgotten her sixteenth birthday, he attempts to curry favor with her by singing the Beatles' "Birthday," which she antagonistically dismisses. There is a moment of uncomfortable silence in which you can feel Ted's humiliation mixed with youthful camaraderie. He begins singing *Hey Jude* . . . Samantha predictably cuts him off, but this kid, who was born after the Beatles had broken up, chooses a song he thinks will quell her angst and against all odds capture her heart.

"It's a moment of pure transcendence, sounding a note of hope in a film that's about to take a turn toward the despairing," writes Noel Murray and Matt Singer in a 2013 *Dissolve* piece on the soundtracking of "Hey Jude" by celebrated director Wes Anderson in his brilliant 2001 film, *The Royal Tenenbaums*. Specifically referencing an instrumental of "Hey Jude" by the Mutato Muzika Orchestra (composer, Mark Mothersbaugh) underscoring Anderson's use of voiceover and images of the dysfunctional Tenenbaum family history, this stirring interpretation soars into the coda with the image of a troubled Tenenbaum son letting his pet falcon Mordecai fly into the air above the stress and turmoil of his life. No more "on the money" visual metaphor for the song's message of hope (escape?) can be imagined.

Delving more deeply into this message is how McCartney chooses to convey it—a second-person narrative to speak directly to the mythical Jude, presuming his audience already knows whom he is actually addressing. This had been established by the Beatles long before the summer of 1968. McCartney told Beatles historian Mark Lewisohn in 1988: "We wrote for our market. We knew if we wrote a song called 'Thank You Girl' that a lot of the girls who wrote us fan letters would take it as a genuine 'thank you.' So, a lot of our songs—'From Me to You' is another—were directly addressed to the fans. So, 'From Me to *You*,' 'Please Please *Me*,' '*She* Loves *You*,' personal pronouns. We always used to do that. '*I* Want to Hold *Your* Hand.' It was always something personal. 'Love *Me* Do,' 'Please Please *Me*.'"

"I had an old mentor named Carter, who always told me that pronouns and/or proper nouns were the way to communicate in song, because you could latch onto something you're already familiar with," says Eric Hutchinson. "The Beatles were the kings of using pronouns and proper nouns, so starting off 'Hey Jude,' a name the audience can connect to, is something you can get your head around easier than say, 'Tomorrow Never Knows.'"

"It's interesting to note that when John and Paul first started writing songs, 'Please Please Me," "P.S. I Love You,' 'Love Me Do' were all in the first-person," notes Beatles lecturer Scott Freiman. "And I recall their commenting on when they wrote 'She Loves You' how the big lightbulb went off. This was now a 'someone else telling someone else' narrative. It's not me, no . . . *she* loves *you*, and if you don't take care of her, then I'm going to come in.' So, this idea of writing in the second person goes back all the way to 'She Loves You,' where they decide that it's enough with the "me" songs, let's write to other people. It is hard to write in the second person, definitely, but they were already adept at it by the time they get to 'Hey Jude.'"

"I've always thought that 'Hey Jude' was modeled on 'She Loves You,'" agrees author Tim Riley. "The best friend is giving advice on a love affair; 'Hey, I just talked with her, she's crazy about you, you blew it, but she'll take you back, she's waiting for you, go to her!' The Lennon subtext of that angle is 'If you don't go for it I'm gonna totally swoop in here because she's really fab.' In 'Hey Jude,' it's a triangle, but it's the best friend giving advice, 'This relationship has not worked out, but don't carry the world on your shoulders. We are gonna get through it.'"

"It's narratively similar and very much a sequel to 'She Loves You,' which was also the Beatles' biggest selling single until 'Hey Jude,'" says Rob Sheffield. "It's very much the same conversation, to the same guy, about the same situation, and it's really funny that the only times that Paul McCartney is ever interested in having a conversation with a man is when he's telling him that he should do right by a woman."

Eric Hutchinson adds: "It's very hard to not come off preachy when you're writing a song in the second person, you end up sounding like you know everything and the listener doesn't. It's a complicated one, but again, at this point Paul McCartney had earned the right for the listeners to pay attention to what he was saying and so in 1968 when all the world was breaking apart and Paul McCartney comes in and says to everybody, 'Hey, it's gonna be fine, we'll *take a sad song and make it better*' the world believes him."

"He is definitely taking the position of the superior over the person he's advising," agrees Dr. Auxier. "But it's not pushy advice. It's not like Polonius giving his advice to Laertes, 'Neither a borrower nor a lender be.' It isn't Shakespeare's windbag telling him, 'Above all things to thine own self be true' where you just feel like saying, 'Shut the fuck up, dude.'"

Walter Everett concurs: "It doesn't sound preachy because of the gentle tempo, diatonic simplicity, and the lyrics' sympathetic attitude all the way through. Obviously, encouraging words such as 'you'll do' are supportive. The rhyme scheme for every verse, wherein the end rhyme always alternates with internal rhyme, keeps the lyric from any sense of rigidity—it sounds loose and free."

"I feel one of my roles as an artist is to share what I've learned and share it in a way that's not too heavy-handed, but more, 'Hey, here's what I found,'" says singer/songwriter Stephen Kellogg, who is also a published author. "And I think the Beatles were very aware that they had an audience that was going to consider what they were saying. It is as if a song like 'Hey Jude' is making a point that needed to be made. I like a song like that when it's well done."

"It's not like hyping or gassing somebody up in a way that's insincere or machismo or polemic," adds Lotz. "It's a sincere petition, 'You can do this. You don't have to play it cool, just be true to yourself. This is gonna suck, but you can do it and it's all gonna work out fine.' And that's a very kind gift to offer to a friend. 'I'm not gonna tell you everything's gonna be okay, but I think *you* have the capability to handle it.' It's pretty baseline human stuff that everybody wants to hear; that they're handling something to the best of their ability. It might not be perfect, and it's okay to *not* be perfect. Let yourself be broken down. Then once you do, it's so much easier to get back up."

Professor Auxier: "If you think about it, we take ownership as observers of this advice precisely because it *isn't* addressed to us. In other words, it's safe. 'Hey Jude' is written in the second person, but not to you, right? And so, it's a form of direct address, but we're overhearing the advice and so that gives us a certain amount of distance on it. Yes, I do feel like he's talking to me, but since he doesn't intend to, I'm safe."

"I would imagine it takes time and experience to write a song that comes from a place of comforting another," says Lotz. "When I was a teenager or in my early twenties, I was always coming from a place of yearning, dissatisfaction or shame. And now as I'm getting older, I'm writing songs that have a bit more contentment, gestures of feeling some resolve and hopefulness. Understanding that it can and *will* get better. When you're younger, and you have your first heartbreak, you think it's never going to get better. My world is over. But you get older and you have more experiences, and you can offer comfort to yourself and others."

"I do not believe Paul is saying pull yourself up by your bootstraps and be like me," adds Kellogg. "If anything, 'Hey Jude' says, 'If you're going to learn about what went wrong, the only way that that serves any purpose, is if you actually *learn* from it,' if it just provides you an excuse for explaining to others why you're not where you want to be in life, then that's not really a useful thing. But if you go, 'Okay, I'm wired this way and I'm prone to these things, so this is what I need to watch out for. This way when I slide into that next time, maybe I'll better understand that this really doesn't serve me and the greater good of humanity, and I'm going to try to be braver about this.' It doesn't guarantee everybody all the same outcomes or anything, and nobody's going to reset life for you and make it the way you imagine it should be. You've got to find some peace wherever your ball is sitting."

"It's a very friendly pep talk," says Sheffield. "I don't think the word 'should' is anywhere in this song."

Dan Bern cites: "There are a lot of second-person narrative songs; 'When You Wish Upon a Star,' 'You Are So Beautiful' and Bob Dylan songs, where he sings, *You got a* [*lotta*] *nerve to say you are my friend . . .* ('Positively 4th Street') and [*Because*] *something is happening here / But you don't know what it is / Do you, Mister Jones* ['Ballad of a Thin Man']. Dylan even called his protest songs 'finger-pointing songs.' Talk about second person narrative! But 'Hey Jude' isn't finger-pointing. It's a hand on a shoulder."

Scott Freiman: "What I love about the lyrics is that you could read them on so many levels. You can absolutely read it as Paul talking to Julian, and saying, 'Hey, I know your parents are going through this divorce but it's going to be okay.' You can look at it as him writing it to Lennon, and writing to himself, saying, 'Look, I know we got all this change going on, it's gonna be okay.' Then you can look at it as a song to the world. So, you've got these multiple levels and that's why songs like that are timeless because they have a message that isn't confined to a specific place and time and it's not confined to specific people. Anyone can sing it to anyone else and when you say *take a sad song and make it better* it reverberates."

Professor Shashko: "It's both really perfect and kind of ironic that Paul is the one who wrote and is singing 'Hey Jude,' this comforting, soothing song, at least as it is heard by everyone, because in it he's the one confronting all of the problems and drama that are going on around him and around the band and it also has got to be partly about him too, because he's also decided not to get married to Jane and [to] pursue Linda. It seems to me he is the narrator *and* the audience."

Katie Darby Mullins concludes: "Lyrically, McCartney keeps it simple by focusing on emotions, and then comfort: . . . *take a sad song / and make it better, so any time you feel the pain / Hey Jude, refrain / Don't carry the world upon your shoulders.* There is almost no hard time that wouldn't be improved by listening to that."

"How does a song touch and continue to communicate to us?" posits Dr. Koch, bringing to mind, once again, the power of music to inform, assuage, and inspire. "In the end, 'Hey Jude' touches us because it's a positive song in a negative time; you have to understand in 1968 the Beatles were falling apart, the world was falling apart in war, but here is a song of hope, a song of resolution. Everything about this song, both musically and lyrically, *cries* resolution. There is a lot of tension presented in the chording and phrasing of the song with its nonharmonic tones, with some of the chords that Paul uses, but apart from all that, both the lyrics and the ultimate harmonic progression bring about resolution, and I think connecting it to the time period, or *any* time period, it works. The verses all end with *begin to make it better* or *start to make it better,* it's not like you've arrived there, it's not like one of those Pollyannaish messages where we've solved it. It's always about the start, and to keep going, keep striving to make it better. I think that reaches people. I think that's a great message that people *want* to hear."

And, of course, not to be forgotten, "Hey Jude" is a love song to its core. Through Jude, it entreats us to leave ourselves open for love, to accept it unconditionally, to be brave against the instinct to put up social barricades that we tell ourselves keep us from being hurt but instead prevent us from taking a chance on love. It tells us to remain open to happiness.

"When I was eight, the image that caught me was *let her under your skin*," says Dr. Auxier. "I had heard the phrase 'someone is getting under your skin' before, and it was always negative. 'Hey Jude' was the first time I ever heard it like, 'Oh, you mean I *should* do that?' And I began to realize, even at eight years old, that there's more than one way that a person could be getting under your skin. So, Paul took this negative connotation and turned it on its head and said, 'No, you *should* do this, rather than try to keep it from happening.' And of course, *let her into your heart* is the other one, but he also says *under your skin* because it's a condition for getting through your exterior *into* your heart. It may start as an irritation, but it's a potentially good irritation. You've got to learn how to enjoy when somebody's getting under your skin. We've never seen this as a positive thing before 'Hey Jude.' I'm supposed to let her under my skin, how do you even do that? And, of course, Paul's point is how do you stop it? So, *let it out and let it in* might be the answer."

It was queried by several voices in this book that perhaps it was McCartney's other late-period piano epic, "Let It Be," that spoke more directly to the band's comforting message in *times of trouble*. However, "Let It Be," with its rather conciliatory tone and lyrics, was officially released *after* the Beatles were already finished. It didn't help that the dreary portrayals of dissolution in the film of the same name debuted when the band was no more. In that context, the passivity of "Let It Be" appears more of a requiem, an acceptance of plight, rather than railing against the dying of the light. "Hey Jude," and its message of embracing a new day with self-empowerment, is forward-thinking; it speaks of the infinite positive future envisioned by Professor Samarotto. The resigned complacency of "Let It Be" is absent in "Hey Jude," which expresses the spirit and purpose of a viable band at the height of its powers—same composer, same anthemic ballad structure, far different thematic results.

Beatles author Rob Sheffield notes, "When people have complaints about 'Hey Jude,' I think they're thinking of a song like 'Let It Be,' which is the homily that 'Hey Jude' *could* have been but wasn't."

In the end, "Hey Jude" speaks to us because it comes from an authentic place of origin—from his past and his present, his triumphs and travails, his place in the biggest band in the world and as a man madly in love, perhaps for the first time—Paul McCartney pointedly put into song his revelations as to the power of music in the wake of childhood tragedy, in his search for the woman who would eventually complete him, in his genuine yearning to keep the Beatles alive, and in his acceptance of the importance of his art in the world. Paul concluded to Barry Miles: "Looking back on all the Beatles' work, I'm very glad that most of it was positive and has been a positive force. I always find it very fortunate that most of our songs were to do with peace and love, and encourage people to do better and to have a better life. When you come to do these songs in places like the stadium in Santiago where all the dissidents were rounded up, I'm very glad to have these songs because they're such symbols of optimism and hopefulness."

"In terms of, can a song save the world? That's always the question, that's what every new song is *trying* to do," Dan Bern told me before we parted ways. "I don't know for sure, but a song has as good a chance as anything else of at least turning people's minds and hearts around, so I ask myself that all the time: Can a song save the world? I think that's what Paul is asking with 'Hey Jude.' In it, I hear what I tell myself all the time; I'm not going to run for office, I'm not going to write policy, I do what I do. And I'll just keep doing it and keep my fingers crossed."

"I will always love 'Hey Jude' for its invitation to reflect," singer/songwriter Seán Barna concludes. "It is an invitation to keep your chin up, to feel joy, if not peace."

Professor Tom Koch left me with this: "'Hey Jude' was always a song that moved me, and it moves every generation, no matter how old you are, there is something timeless about this song. It could be simply because it's a message to us all. Paul is not talking just to Julian; he's talking to *everyone*. There's this hopefulness about it that we always need to hear no matter what political situation we find ourselves in. Ironically, as we speak, we are all dealing with a global pandemic and times are hard and scary, and it speaks to us now. Because of that, I would consider this to be in the pantheon of great songs musically and lyrically."

Dr. Auxier observes with a wink and smile: "I always thought Paul was singing; . . . *and don't you know that it's just you . . . Hey, Jude, you, too*. I like that better than *you'll do* because if he is saying *you, too* then I'm thinking there's a third person in the room; maybe it's John, but it also could mean that it's all of us. Jude's need for love and acceptance and strength of spirit is just like you and me. I think John was right, after all, I think it *is* about him. I also think Paul's right. It's about *him* too. They're all of us."

Rob Sheffield recalled a personal connection to "Hey Jude" at the end of our discussion: "It was a special song for my dad and I when I was a little kid. So much so, this one time we decided to stretch out the *Na-na-na-na-nas* to an entire side of a forty-five-minute tape. We spent an entire day on this. I still have the tape now, and every few years I listen to it and think how wild it was for my dad to spend a Saturday afternoon doing this silly project with his son—stop, rewind *na-na-na*, repeat—just the two of us. And every time I hear it, that tape tells me something that I didn't know then about how lucky I was to have that kind of relationship with my dad. He was such a good sport about it, *really* enthusiastic. It connects the warmth that's in 'Hey Jude,' inspired by Paul singing it to his friend's kid, but mostly the empathy built into every moment of that song."

"I teach an honors class on popular music, and in it we examine music's three-pronged relationship to culture," says Professor Boone. "At any given time, pop music *reflects* culture, we can say that it *is* culture, and we can say that it *shapes* culture: Reflect, Is, and Shapes. And sometimes a great song, for its times, can do all three. Of course, the shaping part is much harder to see in the moment. At the time it's happening we look at it as merely part of pop culture; it's just the Beatles with another #1 song, big deal, it's not shaping culture. But then you look back twenty, thirty years or more and you realize it definitely did. And it still does. When you consider its timing, and its impact, and the band that made it, 'Hey Jude' answers yes to all three questions."

Na . . . na . . . na . . . na na na na.

Seven notes comprising a single musical phrase.

I'll let my friend Pete have the last word here, because, I think, after all this discussion, history, and analyzation, he hits the mark. "At the end of the day, Paul McCartney had a great ear and heard a million songs and wrote a million songs. And he probably had no idea why he was doing that, he just did it. And it sounds fucking awesome."

If I may add an understatement, the Beatles were a great band, perhaps the most influential and successful of the rock-and-roll era, and for what it's worth—this *is* my book—I think "Hey Jude" is their finest work. Or, to put a finer, final point on it, it is my favorite Beatles song. It was the last song I heard just before my father died, only a few months prior to my work on this book. *Na . . . na . . . na . . . na na na na* comforted me as it did a half century earlier, and it still sounds fucking awesome.

ACKNOWLEDGMENTS

This book could not have been conceived, begun, or certainly completed in one year without the support and love of my girls. My wife Erin and my daughter Scarlet took my pledge to work on the project during the time we were quarantined from April of 2020 until the end of March 2021 and summarily came along for the ride, providing me time, space, quiet, and an enviable amount of leeway to pace and moan without murdering me. We were all in this together—Erin teaching yoga and Scarlet in virtual school days—toughing out the long months of isolation in our own tight-knit hub. I am the luckiest of men. I get to be a loner, writer crank, obsessed with minutia and fast-approaching deadlines, engulfed in research (books and such strewn everywhere) while simultaneously feeling loved or, at the very least, tolerated. I love them so much and need every reader to know what you hold in your hands would not exist without their emotional sustenance, patience, and fortitude.

A true champion in the making of this book is John Cerullo, senior executive editor at Rowman & Littlefield, who got my idea right away and prompted me to pursue it. When I wrote him as the pandemic hit to tell him I was diving in, he was extremely supportive and an excellent guiding light throughout. John was the voice from outside the hub that kept me grounded in some kind of reality.

Carol Flannery, senior acquisitions editor at Backbeat Books, was a kind and reassuring voice in the readying of my manuscript.

Laurel Myers, editorial assistant at Rowman & Littlefield, is my hero. Sorry you had to deal with a crazy writer. You did so with grace and determination, always making me believe this book was your baby too.

Naomi Minkoff, associate production editor, in London for R&L, did a masterful job chaperoning the editing of this book with my intrepid copyeditor Jocquan Mooney, who kept the thing from going off many cliffs. The same goes for Chris Chappell, who jumped in at the eleventh hour to see this project to its conclusion. I thoroughly enjoyed even our most contentious discussions. Look forward to working with him in the near future.

Many thanks to the professors who gave their time to this crazy idea, all of whom I had never met previously. They provided gravity to my research and depth in our many discussions on the musicology, history, sociology, psychology, philosophy of song, and "Hey Jude" in particular. Author, composer, musician, and philosophy professor, Dr. Randall Auxier of Southern Illinois University; Dr. William Boone, popular music lecturer at North Carolina State University; adjunct assistant professor of keyboard studies, at University of Cincinnati College–Conservatory of Music, John Deaver, who is also the director of music at Trinity Episcopal Church, Covington, Kentucky; professor of psychology at Bucknell University, Andrea Halpern, who is also an accomplished vocalist; recording engineer veteran, and lecturer at NC State University, Aaron Keane; musicologist and musician Dr. Tom Koch of North Carolina State University; associate professor of music theory at Indiana University, Frank Samarotto; associate professor of writing at the University of Evansville, Katie Darby Mullins; professor of Afro-American studies at the University of Wisconsin–Madison, Alexander Shashko; sociology professor Joel Stillerman, at Grand Valley State University; and professor emeritus at the University of Wisconsin–Madison, Craig Werner. The entire foundation of this endeavor rests on their dedication and expertise.

My journey to meeting these learned minds began before I even started writing, when I reached out to professor of history at Rutgers, Jennifer Mittelstadt. Despite rejecting my request for an interview on the grounds that she thought her academic discipline might be "boring," she politely thanked me for honoring her and introduced me to one professor that led to another and then another. She started all this. Blame her. A second woman/culprit in all this, who was instrumental in expanding my professorial scope, is my beloved cousin Lynn Ruggiero. She sprang into action when I informed her of my project in the spring of 2020 while taking in a morning constitutional with her and my mom in Apex, North Carolina. Turns out she conveniently had a neighbor who's a musicologist. After interrupting Dr. Koch as he mowed his lawn with the out-of-the-blue summation of my idea, I was on my way.

Perhaps my favorite part of any research is picking the brains of fellow authors who have trod the paths I find myself traversing, and not one of these gentlemen disappointed. Gratitude goes out to them all for not only adding texture and humanity to these pages but for being crucial sounding boards and rooting me on, assuring me that I was finding new ground on a well-worn subject and to keep plugging no matter what. McCartney biographers Peter Ames Carlin and Howard Sounes; essayist and archivist Devin McKinney; *Rolling Stone* contributing editor, Rob Sheffield; and the deans of Beatles musical deconstruction, professor of music theory at Michigan University, Walter Everett; and Tim Riley, associate professor and graduate program director at Emerson College. The fluidity in these authors' thinking and our lively discussions went beyond mere interviews. They were a primary part of the narrative and the creative process. Special thanks to Professor Riley, who enthusiastically prompted me to read McKinney's and Sheffield's books, both of which are my favorite summations of the Beatles phenomenon. He then vouched for me with both these guys, and man, this book is better for it.

I would also like to thank the legendary music journalist, author, and my hero, Greil Marcus, whose correspondence and kind words on my work were an incredible boon to my spirits throughout. This is likewise true of the encouragement I received from leading Beatles historian Mark Lewisohn, along with his quick email responses to my goofy questions, which sustained my momentum.

I truly appreciate the time and enthusiasm Beatles lecturer and founder of the "Deconstructing the Beatles" seminar, Scott Freiman, lends to this book. The same goes for one of the most important visual artists of the golden age of rock and roll, Michael Lindsay-Hogg. His generous correspondence and uncanny memory for detail on working with the Beatles and his planning and directing one of the most influential promo films in pop music is nothing short of a literary blessing.

Last, but certainly not least, are the contributions, interviews, chats, phone calls, emails, and general insights from my songwriting heroes and friends from nearly every generation of the pop/rock craft. I could not have gotten to the core of "Hey Jude" without Seán Barna, Dan Bern, Adam Duritz, Jesse Epstein, Orenda Fink, Eric Hutchinson, Stephen Kellogg, Alex Knight, Kiley Lotz, Jackie McLean, Matt Sucich, Maria Taylor, and Elizabeth Ziman.

All the interviews herein were duly transcribed by my two hearty assistants Leslie Acuna (the former) and Jessica Marshall (the current). They are the stalwarts behind this project. Jess was also a huge help in tracking down some leads.

Special thanks to a creative partner who always raises my game, Roberto Tatis, for coming in and designing the cover to this book when we were all at a loss. He continues to astound after these many years.

As always, I cannot complete a music book without the stamp of approval and much-needed analysis from my dear and talented friend Peter Blasevick.

Finally, my work stands on the shoulders of the love and support of my entire family. I have found their joy in Paul McCartney's song of comfort, unity, encouragement, and hope, and thus, in the words that fill this book. To my mom, Phyllis Mary Campion, who had to endure the grief of losing her husband of fifty-eight years, my dad, James V. Campion, throughout the time I spent on this project. Our nightly FaceTime chats were a cherished part of this experience. My brother Phillip John Campion, who could not care less about any of this but will always be my lb (little brother) and inspires me to be a better dad and person. My sisters and brothers-in-law, who never fail to breathe new life into this aging and ornery author, Lauren and Don Brown,

Shannon and Tom Carlson, and my beloved nieces and nephews, Alex and Matthew Campion; Claudia and Ava Brown; Claire, Sydney, and Ty Carlson. My dear cuz (sis) Michelle, her husband Gene, and their lovely daughters, Nicole and Gianna. Love all you guys.

And thank you, Paul for your song.

And the Beatles, for all the songs.

SOURCES

Author Interviews

Dr. Randall Auxier—2/2/21
Seán Barna—1/8/21
Dan Bern—4/20/20
Peter Blasevick—1/18/21
Dr. William Boone—5/19/20
Peter Ames Carlin—10/14/20
Adjunct Assistant Professor John Deaver—10/1/20
Adam Duritz—2/15/21
Jesse Epstein—6/11/20
Professor Walter Everett—7/10/20
Orenda Fink—2/8/21
Scott Freiman—6/5/20
Professor Andrea Halpern—3/13/21
Eric Hutchinson—4/29/20
Professor Aaron Keane—5/14/20
Stephen Kellogg—4/29/20

Alex Knight—1/22/21
Dr. Tom Koch—5/7/20
Michael Lindsay-Hogg—12/9, 12/11/20
Kiley Lotz—5/6/20
Devin McKinney—12/9/20
Jackie McLean—11/17/20
Associate Professor Katie Darby Mullins—12/22/20
Tim Riley—10/1/20
Professor Frank Samarotto—9/29/20
Professor Alexander Shashko—4/13/20
Rob Sheffield—1/12/21
Howard Sounes—9/23/20
Professor Joel Stillerman—1/29/21
Matt Sucich—11/12/20
Maria Taylor—3/5/21
Professor Craig Werner—4/27/20
Elizabeth Ziman—1/14/21

Selected Bibliography

Auxier, Randall E. *Metaphysical Graffiti: Deep Cuts in the Philosophy of Rock* (Open Court, 2017).

The Beatles. *Anthology* (Chronicle, 2002).

The Beatles. *The Beatles (The White Album)*, 50th anniversary super deluxe edition (Capitol, 2018).

Brown, Peter, and Steven Gaines. *The Love You Make: An Insider's Story of The Beatles* (New American Library, 1983).

Carlin, Peter Ames. *Paul McCartney: A Life* (Touchstone, 2009).

Du Noyer, Paul. *Conversations with Paul McCartney* (Harry N. Abrams, 2017).

Emerick, Geoff. *Here, There and Everywhere: My Life Recording the Music of the Beatles* (Avery, 2006).

Everett, Walter, and Tim Riley. *What Goes On: The Beatles, Their Music, and Their Time* (Oxford University Press, 2019).

Gitlin, Todd. *The Sixties: Years of Hope, Days of Rage* (Bantam, 1987).

Gould, Jonathan. *Can't Buy Me Love: The Beatles, Britain, and America* (Crown, 2008).

Hammack, Jerry. *The Beatles Recording Reference Manual*, volume 4 (Jerry Hammack/Gearfab, 2020).

Howe, Sean. *Marvel Comics: The Untold Story* (Harper Perennial, 2013).

Kennedy, Robert F. "Statement on Assassination of Martin Luther King, Jr., Indianapolis, Indiana, April 4, 1968." John F. Kennedy Presidential Library and Museum. https://www.jfklibrary.org/learn/about-jfk/the-kennedy-family/robert-f-kennedy/robert-f-kennedy-speeches/statement-on-assassination-of-martin-luther-king-jr-indianapolis-indiana-april-4-1968.

Langer, Susanne. *Philosophy in a New Key* (Harvard University Press, 1942).

Lennon, Cynthia. *A Twist of Lennon* (Avon, 1980).

Lewisohn, Mark. *The Complete Beatles Recording Sessions:* "The Paul McCartney Interview" (Harmony, 1989).

MacDonald, Ian. *Revolution in the Head: The Beatles' Records and the Sixties*, 3rd revised edition (Vintage, 2008).

Marcus, Griel. "The Beatles," *The Rolling Stone Illustrated History of Rock & Roll* (Random House/Rolling Stone, 1976), 181.

Martin, George, and Jeremy Hornsby. *All You Need Is Ears* (St. Martin's, 1979), 211.

McKinney, Devin. *Magic Circles: The Beatles in Dream and History* (Harvard University Press, 2004).

Miles, Barry. *Paul McCartney Many Years from Now* (Secker & Warburg, 1997).

Norman, Philip. *Paul McCartney: The Life* (Little, Brown, 2016).

———. *Shout!: The Beatles in Their Generation* (MJF, 1981).

Oldham, Andrew Loog. *Stoned: A Memoir of London in the 1960s* (St. Martin's, 2001).

Quantick, David. *Revolution: The Making of the Beatles' White Album* (Chicago Review, 2002), 27.

Riley, Tim. *Tell Me Why—The Beatles: Album by Album, Song by Song, The Sixties and After* (Knopf, 1988).

Robertson, John, and Patrick Humphries. *The Beatles: The Complete Guide to Their Music* (Omnibus, 2004), 91.

Sanchez, Tony. *Up and Down with the Rolling Stones* (William Morrow, 1979), 88.

Sheff, David. *The Playboy Interviews with John Lennon and Yoko Ono* (Playboy, 1981).

Sheffield, Norman. *Life on Two Legs* (Trident, 2013).

Sounes, Howard. *Fab: An Intimate Life of Paul McCartney* (De Capo, 2010).

Spitz, Bob. *The Beatles: The Biography* (Back Bay, 2006).

Wenner, Jann. *Lennon Remembers: The Rolling Stone Interviews* (Fawcett, 1972).

Suggested Reading

Cleaver, Eldridge. *Soul on Ice* (Dell/Random House, 1999).

Cottrell, Robert C., and Blaine T. Crown. *1968: The Rise and Fall of the New American Revolution* (Rowman & Littlefield, 2018).

Crawley, Ashon T. *Blackpentecostal Breath: The Aesthetics of Possibility* (Fordham University Press, 2017).

Didion, Joan. *Slouching towards Bethlehem: Essays* (Farrar, Straus and Giroux, 2008).

Kurlanksy, Mark. *1968: The Year that Rocked the World* (Vintage, 2005).

Lindsay-Hogg, Michael. *Luck and Circumstance: A Coming of Age in Hollywood, New York, and Points Beyond* (Knopf, 2011).

Mailer, Norman. *Armies of the Night: History as a Novel, the Novel as History* (Plume, 1995).

Santoli, Al. *Everything We Had: An Oral History of the Vietnam War* (Ballantine, 1985).

Sheffield, Robert. *Dreaming the Beatles: The Love Story of One Band and the Whole World* (Dey Street, 2017).

Turner, Steve. *A Hard Day's Write: The Stories Behind Every Beatles Song* (HarperCollins, 2005).

Magazines/Newspapers

Billboard

Dissolve (Noel Murray and Matt Singer, "Five Non-Beatles Movies that Make Great Use of Beatles Songs," *Dissolve*, February 3, 2013.)

London Telegraph

Mojo (Chris Hunt, "The Story of Hey Jude," *Mojo*, February 2002.)

New Left Review

New York Times ("Tet Offensive: Turning Point in Vietnam War," *New York Times*, January 31, 1988, https://www.nytimes.com/1988/01/31/world/tet-offensive-turning-point-in-vietnam-war.html.)

Ramparts

Record Mirror

Rolling Stone

Variety (Kenneth Womack, "How Beatles Producer George Martin Recorded 'Hey Jude' to Be 'Hypnotic' (Exclusive Excerpt)," *Variety*, July 12, 2018.)

Television/Radio

Later with Bob Costas, NBC, November 5–7, 1991.

The Nation's Favourite Beatles Number One, special broadcast program on British channel ITV, November 11, 2011.

"Paul McCartney: 'Still Prancing'," *David Frost Interview*, Al Jazeera, November 20, 2012.

Internet

Breihan, Tom. "The Number Ones," *Stereogum*, November 13, 2018. https://www.stereogum.com/2022558/the-number-ones-the-beatles-hey-jude/columns/the-number-ones/.

Hyden, Steven. "The Best Beatles Songs, Ranked," *Uproxx*, September 14, 2020. https://uproxx.com/indie/best-beatles-songs-ranked/.

McKinney, Devin. "1+—The Beatles on Video: What They Are, What They Are Not," *Critics at Large*, November 21, 2015. https://www.criticsatlarge.ca/2015/11/1-beatles-on-video-what-they-are-what.html.

The Paul McCartney Project. https://www.the-paulMcCartney-project.com/.

Papers

McKinney, Devin. "Weeps Happiness—The Dysfunctional Drama of the White Album," paper delivered at The Beatles' White Album: An International Symposium, Monmouth University, West Long Branch, New Jersey, November 11, 2018.

Samarotto, Frank. "The Trope of Expectancy/Infinity in the Music of the Beatles and Others," paper, Indiana University Bloomington, Jacobs School of Music, 2012.

Institutions

Amusement & Music Operators Association

National Academy of Recording Arts and Sciences, Grammy Hall of Fame

INDEX

Photos in the photo insert are indicated by *"p1, p2, p3,* etc."

ABOUT THE AUTHOR

James Campion is a freelance journalist and essayist, as well as a columnist and contributing editor for the *Aquarian Weekly*. He cohosts a music podcast, *Underwater Sunshine*, with Counting Crows front man Adam Duritz, as well as a music interview show, *Sunshine Spotlight*. He lives in the New Jersey woods with his wife, daughter, three cats, and one lizard. This is his eighth book.